Tempting the Bride

SHERRY THOMAS

BERKLEY SENSATION, NEW YORK

THE BERKLEY PUBLISHING GROUP
Published by the Penguin Group
Penguin Group (USA) Inc.
375 Hudson Street, New York, New York 10014, USA

Penguin Group (Canada), 90 Eglinton Avenue East, Suite 700, Toronto, Ontario M4P 2Y3, Canada
(a division of Pearson Penguin Canada Inc.) • Penguin Books Ltd., 80 Strand, London WC2R 0RL,
England • Penguin Group Ireland, 25 St. Stephen's Green, Dublin 2, Ireland (a division of Penguin
Books Ltd.) • Penguin Group (Australia), 250 Camberwell Road, Camberwell, Victoria 3124, Australia
(a division of Pearson Australia Group Pty. Ltd.) • Penguin Books India Pvt. Ltd., 11 Community
Centre, Panchsheel Park, New Delhi—110 017, India • Penguin Group (NZ), 67 Apollo Drive,
Rosedale, Auckland 0632, New Zealand (a division of Pearson New Zealand Ltd.) • Penguin Books
(South Africa) (Pty.) Ltd., 24 Sturdee Avenue, Rosebank, Johannesburg 2196, South Africa

Penguin Books Ltd., Registered Offices: 80 Strand, London WC2R 0RL, England

This is a work of fiction. Names, characters, places, and incidents either are the product of the author's
imagination or are used fictitiously, and any resemblance to actual persons, living or dead, business
establishments, events, or locales is entirely coincidental. The publisher does not have any control over
and does not assume any responsibility for author or third-party websites or their content.

TEMPTING THE BRIDE

A Berkley Sensation Book / published by arrangement with the author

PUBLISHING HISTORY
Berkley Sensation mass-market edition / October 2012

Copyright © 2012 by Sherry Thomas.
Excerpt from *Beguiling the Beauty* by Sherry Thomas copyright © 2012 by Sherry Thomas.
Cover art by Gregg Gulbronson. Hand lettering by Ron Zinn.
Cover design by George Long.
Interior text design by Laura K. Corless.

ISBN: 978-0-425-25102-7

BERKLEY SENSATION®
Berkley Sensation Books are published by The Berkley Publishing Group,
a division of Penguin Group (USA) Inc.,
375 Hudson Street, New York, New York 10014.
BERKLEY SENSATION® is a registered trademark of Penguin Group (USA) Inc.
The "B" design is a trademark of Penguin Group (USA) Inc.

PRINTED IN THE UNITED STATES OF AMERICA

10 9 8 7 6 5 4 3 2 1

To Ivy Adams,
for your limitless generosity and awesomeness

ACKNOWLEDGMENTS

Wendy McCurdy, for her patience and insight.

Katherine Pelz, for making everything easier.

Kristin Nelson and everyone at the Nelson Literary Agency, for their unparalleled dedication and competence.

Janine Ballard, for boldly going where all great critique partners do—right to the crux of the problem.

Shellee Roberts, for her concurring opinion that kicked my ass back into gear.

Tiffany Yates Martin of FoxPrint Editorial, for always helping me out when I really need it.

Margaret Toscano, for generously sharing her knowledge of Latin and the classics.

My family, especially my husband, for shouldering nearly the entirety of our move while I was hunched over my laptop, desperately trying to figure out what to do, and my mother, for all the food, which is nothing but love.

And as always, if you are reading this, thank you from the bottom of my heart.

PROLOGUE

January 1896

*D*avid Hillsborough, Viscount Hastings, had never been in love. And he had most certainly never been in *unrequited* love. Why, his was a heart buoyantly and blissfully unattached, while he devoted himself to sampling all the charms life had to offer a young, wealthy, and handsome bachelor.

This was, in any case, his official position.

He suspected that several of those closest to him had guessed the truth—possibly a long time ago, as his particular instance of unrequited love had lasted nearly half of his life. But he took comfort in the fact that *she* hadn't the slightest idea. And, God willing, she never would.

For he would be in hell if she ever learned.

Not that he was very far from it at the moment, watching the girl of his dreams, Miss Helena Fitzhugh, gazing at another man with adoration. Her elder sister was the

1

acknowledged Great Beauty of their time, but it was always Miss Fitzhugh from whom he couldn't look away. Her flame-bright hair, her luminous skin, her clever, wicked eyes.

He did not begrudge her falling in love with another. After all, if he refused to participate in the contest, he could not complain when someone else won the prize. But he did mind, very much, that this man on whom she lavished her attention did not deserve it in the least.

Years ago, Andrew Martin had had the opportunity to marry her. But his mother had expected him to marry someone else in order to unite two adjacent properties. Lacking the courage to defy the elder Mrs. Martin, he'd married that someone else.

Even in a land full of cold, formal marriages, Mr. Martin's marriage stood out for its coldness and formality. Husband and wife dined at different times, moved in different circles, and communicated almost entirely via written notices.

None of it mattered. Happy or otherwise, a married man was a married man, and a respectable young lady ought to search elsewhere for fulfillment.

Miss Fitzhugh was a rule breaker. Until now, however, those she'd trampled had not been so much rules as recommendations. When she became the only one of her siblings to pursue a university education, it was looked upon as an eccentricity. And when, upon coming into her small inheritance, she'd used the funds as capital for a publishing firm that she ran herself, the venture was dismissed as simply another idiosyncrasy in the family—after all, her brother, Earl Fitzhugh, managed the tinneries his heiress wife had inherited.

But indulging in a close friendship with a married man pushed the boundaries of acceptable behavior. She needed not commit any actual sins; the *appearance* of impropriety would be quite enough to wound her.

The drawing room at Lord Wrenworth's country estate was awash in laughter and good cheer. Mrs. Denbigh, Miss Fitzhugh's married friend who was her chaperone at the Wrenworth house party, was all too busy amusing herself. Hastings waited for a natural pause in the conversation in which he'd been taking part, excused himself, and crossed the room to where Miss Fitzhugh and Martin sat on a chaise longue, their bodies turned toward each other, effectively blocking anyone else from joining their tête-à-tête.

"Mr. Martin, what are you still doing here?" Hastings asked. "Haven't you your new great tome to write?"

Miss Fitzhugh answered for Martin. "But he *is* working. He is conferring with his publisher."

"And he has been conferring with his publisher since morning, if I'm not mistaken. A cook can confer with the mistress of the house all day long, but that doesn't put dinner on the table. Mr. Martin would quite deprive his readers of his next excellent volume of history were he to spend all his hours talking about it and none setting the actual words to paper."

Martin reddened. "You have a point, Lord Hastings."

"I always have a point. I understand that you are here to work and that you've asked Lord Wrenworth to put a nice, quiet room at your disposal. You haven't put that room to use, have you?"

Martin reddened further. "Ah—"

"I personally cannot wait for the next appearance of Offa of Mercia."

"You've read the book?"

"Of course. Why do you look so surprised? Did I not display a ferocious intelligence and a wide-ranging curiosity when I was at university?"

"Well, yes."

"Then consider yourself honored to count me among your readership. Now off you go. Write deep into the night. And stop monopolizing Miss Fitzhugh. You are a married man, remember?"

Martin chuckled uneasily and rose. Miss Fitzhugh shot Hastings an icy look. He ignored it, shooed Martin away, and took the spot on the chaise the latter had vacated.

"I don't believe you read Mr. Martin's book."

Hastings read every book she published from cover to cover, even the ones she took on purely for financial gain. "First page and last page—and did I not sound impressive discussing it?"

Her gaze brimmed with disdain. "You sounded pompous and overbearing, Hastings. And to dismiss my friend from my presence? Truly, I expected better, even of you."

He leaned back against the armrest of the chaise. "Let us spend no more words on Mr. Martin, who is surely beneath your notice. I'd much prefer to speak of how delicious you look tonight, my dear Miss Fitzhugh."

He was not subtle about where his gaze dropped: directly into her décolletage. He'd loved her since before she'd sprouted breasts, and felt no compunction in enjoying the sight of them anytime her neckline allowed.

In reaction she snapped open her fan and neatly blocked his view of her bosom. "Don't let me keep you, Hastings. Mrs. Ponsonby is trying to get your attention, if I'm not mistaken."

"You are not mistaken," he murmured. "They are all trying to get my attention, all the women I've ever met."

"I know how this goes. You want me to protest that I've never wanted your attention. Then you'd counter that I've only ever pretended to ignore you, and that all along my indifference was my pitiful attempt to pique your curiosity."

She sounded half-bored. He used to be able to anger her to a greater intensity, and for longer duration. More than even her scorn he feared her apathy—the opposite of love was not hate, but indifference: to exist in such proximity to her, yet make no impression upon her awareness, upon her soul.

He tsked. "Miss Fitzhugh, I am never that unoriginal. Of course you want my attention, but it is only so you can toss it back into my face. You take great pleasure in thwarting me, my dear."

A spark flashed in her eyes—gone almost before he'd perceived it. He lived for those moments—moments when she was forced to look at him as who he was, instead of who she believed him to be.

The worst thing about falling in love with her so early in life was that he'd been an absolute snot at fourteen, at once arrogant and self-pitying. Almost as bad was the fact that he'd been nearly half a foot shorter than she at their first meeting—she'd been five foot nine, and he barely five foot four. Though she was only a few weeks older than he was, she'd looked upon him as a child—while he broiled with the heat and anguish of first love.

When nothing else garnered him her attention, he turned horrid. She was disgusted by this midget who tried to trick her into broom closets to steal kisses, and he was at once miserable and thrilled. Disgust was better than indifference; anything was better than indifference.

By the time his height at last exceeded hers—six foot two to her five foot eleven—and his baby fat melted away to reveal cheekbones sharp enough to cut diamonds, her opinion was firmly set against him. And he, no longer self-pitying but prouder than ever, refused to humble himself and ask for a fresh chance.

Not that he didn't want to. Every time he came across her, with her perfect assurance, her winsome face, her lithe, sylphlike figure, he meant to repent aloud of all his past stupidity.

Yet all he ever did was further his record of obnoxious-ness. *A women's college, is that what they call a hotbed of lesbianism these days? Becoming a publisher—so you think there still aren't enough bad books to be had? That is a ravishing dress, my dear, dear Miss Fitzhugh; a shame you can't fill it out with a few more curves—or any, for that matter.*

Her ripostes always set his heart aflame. *I knew I chose a women's college for all the right reasons, but a hotbed of lesbianism—my goodness—that is like discovering a vein of gold on the land you've just bought, isn't it? Of course, you would find the vast majority of books taxing, given your trouble with basic literacy—rest assured I will publish a few picture books just for you.*

And his favorite, in response to his slur against her fig-ure: *My dear Lord Hastings, I'm afraid I didn't quite hear you. You are mumbling. Is your mouth full of—why, it is!—indeed, a whole cluster of sour grapes.* With the tip of her index finger, she'd drawn a line from her chin to just beneath the top of her neckline, cast him a look of pure derision, and swept off. And he'd never been more hopelessly in love.

"You are staring at me, Hastings," said the present-day Miss Fitzhugh, an edge to her voice.

"Yes, I know, grieving over your soon-to-come deterioration—of course, you are still comely, but age will inexorably catch up with you. You really aren't getting any younger, Miss Fitzhugh."

She fluttered her fan. "And do you know what they say of women of a certain age, what they want above all?"

Desire simmered in him at her not-quite smile. "Do tell."

"To be rid of you, Hastings. So that they don't have to waste what remains of their precious few years suffering your lecherous looks."

"If I stopped looking at you lecherously, you'd miss it."

"Why don't we test that hypothesis? You stop and I'll tell you after ten years or so whether I miss it."

He gazed at her a little longer. He could watch her all night—in fact, he *would* watch her all night, from wherever he was in Lord Wrenworth's drawing room—but the time had come for him to depart her chaise before she forcibly evicted him.

He rose and bowed slightly. "You wouldn't last two weeks, Miss Fitzhugh."

*T*he ladies retired by half past ten. The gentlemen smoked a few cigars, played a few hands of cards and a few games of snooker. At half past twelve, Hastings was the last person to head up.

Except he didn't go directly to his room. Instead he took himself to an alcove that allowed him a limited view of her room—unrequited love meant staring at closed doors, imagining otherwise. A faint light still shone under her door; she was probably reading in bed.

Just a few more pages.

Hampton House, her childhood home, had been of a modest size. When he'd visited, he'd had a room three doors down from hers. Every night, her governess would come around and urge her to turn off her lamp. Invariably she would answer, *Just a few more pages.*

And when the governess had left, he would slip out of his own room and peer at her door until her light was extinguished at last, before he returned to bed to stew anew in lust and yearning.

A habit that he'd kept to this day, whenever they happened to be under the same roof.

Her light turned off. He sighed. How long would he keep at this? Soon he would be twenty-seven. Did he still plan to stand in a dark passage in the middle of the night and gaze upon her door when he was thirty-seven? Forty-seven? Ninety-seven?

He ran his hand through his hair. Time for his lonely bed, which he could have filled with women, but for his reluctance to sleep with anyone else when Miss Fitzhugh was in the vicinity. Perhaps it was some hidden wellspring of gentlemanliness protesting this act of hypocrisy, or perhaps it was merely him being superstitious, afraid that such an infraction would destroy what slender hope he still had.

Her door opened.

He sucked in a breath. Had she sensed him? He pressed his back into the curved inside of the alcove. It was too dark to see well, but she seemed to be poised on the threshold. Was she searching for him?

The door closed softly. He let out the breath he held— she must have returned to her room.

Suddenly she was before him, a disturbance in the air. His heart leaped to the roof of his mouth; endless disastrous possibilities flashed across his mind, all his years of careful pretenses stripped bare at once. She would lift one fine brow and laugh at the futility of his desires.

She walked past him. He blinked, disoriented by the abrupt evaporation of what had promised to be an eventful confrontation. She hadn't come for him; she was going for a snack, perhaps, or another book. But she did not even have a hand candle to illuminate her way. It was as if she didn't want anyone to see her—or where she was going.

He might not have been able to follow her had it been summer—she'd have heard his footsteps on the echoing floor. But it was winter and a thick carpet had been laid down. He walked soundlessly, keeping to the walls.

She approached the stairs. If she were headed for the warming kitchen or the library, she would go down the steps. She didn't: She climbed up. Most of the guests had been placed on the same floor, the unmarried ladies and gentlemen put into separate wings. Above, in this wing, at least, were only the guests who'd arrived late—and Mr. Andrew Martin.

An airless sensation overtook him. He could not possibly be correct in his suspicions. She was far too clear-thinking a woman to visit the room of any man, let alone a married man, at this hour of the night.

On the next floor there was only one door with light still underneath. And when she approached, the door opened from inside. In the gap stood Andrew Martin, smiling.

She slipped in. The door closed. Hastings remained numbly in place.

She wasn't just Martin's friend and publisher. She was his lover.

$\mathcal{H}$e found himself seated on the floor—his elbows on his knees, his head in his hands. She stayed in Martin's room for two hours, leaving as quietly as she'd arrived, slipping down the stairs like a phantom of the night. Hastings did not return to his own room until almost dawn.

She had no obligation to care for his sentiments, but did she not care about her own future? What she had done was utter madness. Had she slipped into the room of a bachelor, Hastings would be no less annihilated, but at least then her lover could marry her, should the worst happen.

With Andrew Martin there was no such last resort.

Late the next morning he came across the two of them in the library, reading in two adjacent chairs. She radiated satisfaction. He turned around and walked out.

That night she visited Martin again. Hastings stood guard near the stairs, trying, unsuccessfully, to not imagine what might be taking place inside Martin's room.

He spent his second sleepless night.

The following night, he sat on the carpeted steps, his head resting against the cold banister. He had to leave in the morning—he never remained away from his daughter for longer than three days. On his way home, should he stop by Fitz's estate and gently break the news of Miss Fitzhugh's misbehavior? He might be nothing and no one to Helena Fitzhugh, but her twin brother, Fitz, was his best friend.

Would she ever forgive him if he did?

He sat up straight. A pair of giggling guests were coming up the stairs. He recognized their whispering voices: a man and a woman, married, but not to each other.

They sounded more than a little drunk.

His heart pounding, he coughed loudly. The would-be adulterers fell silent. After a few seconds there came a hushed exchange. They turned around and descended.

It was several minutes before he could unclench his fingers from around the banister.

Not that those two were certain to have tried Martin's door. Not that Martin's door wouldn't have already been securely locked, with a chair wedged beneath the door handle as an additional bulwark against intruders. But if this continued, someday, somewhere, someone would open a door that hadn't been properly secured.

He slowly rose to his feet, leaning on the balustrade. He knew her. It was easier to pull a lion's teeth than to change her mind. She would barrel down this path, refusing to be diverted, until she crashed into the limit of society's tolerance.

And he, as much as even now he still wanted to, could not always protect her.

A lover's embrace made one look favorably upon the entirety of the universe. As Helena Fitzhugh returned to her empty, unlit bedroom, she sighed in contentment.

Or rather, as much contentment as possible, given that her particular lover's embrace had happened through her chemise and his nightshirt—Andrew was adamant that they not risk a pregnancy. But still, how new and thrilling it was to kiss and touch in the comfort and privacy of a bed, almost enough to pretend that the past five years never happened and that the only thing that separated them was two layers of thin, soft merino wool.

"Hullo, Miss Fitzhugh," came a man's voice out of the darkness.

Her heart stopped. Hastings was her brother Fitz's best friend—but not exactly a friend to her.

"Mistook my room for one of your paramours'?" She was proud of herself. Her voice sounded even, almost blasé.

"Then I would have greeted you by one of their names, wouldn't I?" His voice was just as nonchalant as hers.

A match flared, illuminating a pair of stern eyes. It always surprised her that he could look somber—intimidating—at times, when he was so frivolous a person.

He lit a hand candle. The light cast his features into sharp relief; the ends of his hair gleamed bronze. "Where were you, Miss Fitzhugh?"

"I was hungry. I went to the butler's pantry and found myself a slice of pear cake."

He blew out the match and tossed it in the grate. "And came back directly?"

"Not that it is any of your concern, but yes."

"So if I were to kiss you now, you would taste of pear cake?"

Trust Hastings to always drag any discussion into the gutter. "Absolutely. But as your lips will never touch mine, that is a moot point, my lord Hastings."

He looked at her askance. "You are aware, are you not, that I am one of your brother's most trusted friends?"

A friendship she'd never quite understood. "And?"

"And as such, when I become aware of gross misconduct on your part, it behooves me to inform your brother without delay."

She lifted her chin. "Gross misconduct? Is that what one calls a little foray to the butler's pantry these days?"

"A little foray to the butler's pantry, is that how one refers to the territory inside Mr. Martin's underlinens these days?"

"I don't know what you mean."

"Should I use the scientific names?"

And wouldn't he enjoy doing that. But as it was her policy to never let him enjoy himself at her expense, she declared, "Mr. Martin and I are friends of long standing and nothing more."

"You and I are friends of long standing and—"

"You and I are *acquaintances* of long standing, Hastings."

"Fine. Your sister and I are friends of long standing and yet she has never come to spend hours in my room. Alone. After midnight."

"I went for a slice of cake."

He cocked his head. "I saw you go into Mr. Martin's room at forty minutes past midnight, Miss Fitzhugh. You were still there when I left twenty minutes ago. By the way, I also witnessed the same thing happening for the past two nights. You can accuse me of many things—and you do—but you cannot charge me with drawing conclusions on insufficient evidence. Not in this case, at least."

She stiffened. She'd underestimated him, it would seem. He'd been his usual flighty, superficial self; she wouldn't have guessed he had the faintest inkling of her nighttime forays.

"What do you want, Hastings?"

"I want you to mend your ways, my dear Miss Fitzhugh. I understand very well that Mr. Martin should have been yours in an ideal world. I also understand that his wife has been praying for him to take a lover so she could do the same. But none of it will matter should you be found out. So you see, it is my moral obligation to leave at first light and inform your siblings, my dear, dear friends, that their beloved sister is throwing away her life."

She rolled her eyes. "What do you *want*, Hastings?"

He sighed dramatically. "It wounds me, Miss Fitzhugh. Why do you always suspect me of ulterior motives?"

"Because you always have one. What do I have to do now for your silence?"

"That will not happen."

"I refuse to think you cannot be bought, Hastings."

"My, such adamant faith in my corruptibility. I almost hate to disappoint you."

"Then don't disappoint me. Name your price."

His title was quite new—he was only the second Viscount Hastings after his uncle. The family coffer was full to the brim. His price would not be anything denominated in pounds sterling.

"If I say nothing," he mused, "Fitz will be quite put out with me."

"If you say nothing, my brother will not know anything."

"Fitz is a clever man—except when it comes to his wife, perhaps. He will learn sooner or later, somehow."

"But you are a man who lives in the present, aren't you?"

He lifted a brow. "That wouldn't be your way of saying

that I am empty-headed and incapable of thinking of the future, would it?"

She didn't bother with an answer to that question. "It is getting late—not too long now before someone comes to lay a new fire. I don't want you to be seen in my room."

"At least I can marry you to salvage your reputation should that happen. Mr. Martin is in no position to do so."

"That is quite beside the point. Tell me what you want and begone."

He smiled, a crooked smile full of suggestions. "You know what I want."

"Please don't tell me you are still trying to kiss me. Have I not made my lack of interest abundantly clear on this matter?"

"I don't want to kiss you. However, *you* will need to kiss *me*."

She, kiss him?

"Ah, I see you were hoping to stand quiescent and think of Christian martyrs mauled by the lions of the Colosseum. But as you always tell me, I am a man of unseemly tastes. So you must be the lion, and I the martyr. I shall expect exceptional aggression, Miss Fitzhugh."

"If I were a lion, I'd find you a piece of rotten fish, not at all to my taste and hardly edible, whereas I've just dined on the finest gazelle in the entire savanna. You will excuse me if I fail to summon any enthusiasm to fall upon you."

"Quite the contrary. I cannot excuse such failure. Not in the least. You will somehow summon the enthusiasm or I shall be on the earliest train headed south."

"And if I do manufacture enough false zeal to satisfy you?"

15

"Then I shall say nothing to anyone of Mr. Martin."

"Your word?"

"*Your* word that the kiss will be more debauched than any you've pressed upon Mr. Martin."

"You are a pervert, Hastings."

He smiled again. "And you are just the sort of woman to appreciate one, Miss Fitzhugh, whether you realize it or not. Now, here is what I want you to do. You will seize me by the shoulders, push me against the wall, reach your hand under my jacket—"

"I feel my bile rising."

"Then you are ready. Onward. I await your assault."

She grimaced. "How I hate to spoil a perfect record of repelling you."

"Nothing lasts forever, my dear Miss Fitzhugh. And remember, kiss me passionately. Or you'll have to do it again."

She might as well get it over with.

She closed the space that separated them in two big strides and gripped him by the sleeves of his dressing gown. Instead of pushing him backward as he'd instructed—as if she'd allow him to dictate the specifics of her ordeal—she yanked him toward her, fastened her mouth to his, and imagined herself a shark with hundreds of razor-sharp teeth.

Or perhaps she was a minion of the underworld, her mouth a welter of burning acid and sulfur fumes, devouring his soul, savoring all the idle immoralities he'd committed in his lifetime as a palate cleanser between courses of more substantial sins.

Or a Venus flytrap, full of delicious nectar, but woe was he who thought he could dip a proboscis inside and sample her charms. Instead, she would digest him in place, stupid sod.

Vaguely she sensed something hard and smooth against her shoulder blades. They'd been in the middle of her room; why was she being pressed into a wall? And why, all of a sudden, was *she* the one being devoured?

The muscles of his arms were tight and hard beneath her hands. His person was as tall and solid as a castle gate. His mouth, instead of tasting like a furnace of greedy lust, was cool and delicious, as if he'd just downed a long draft of well water.

She shoved him away and wiped her lips. She was panting. She didn't know why she ought to be.

"My," he murmured. "As ferocious as anything I've ever imagined. I was right. You do want me."

She ignored him. "Your word."

"I will say nothing of Andrew Martin to anyone. You may depend on that."

"Leave."

"Gladly, now that I have what I came for." He smirked. "Good night, my dear. You were well worth the wait."

CHAPTER 1

Six months later

*H*traffic logjam had convened on Fleet Street, and
Hastings's brougham was caught in the midst.
The assembly of vehicles advanced at a ponderous pace that
would not have won races against his daughter's pet tortoise.
Enterprising men and boys went from carriage to carriage,
hawking ginger beer and hot buns to a captive crowd.

Had the logjam happened on a different street, Hastings
would have alighted and walked. But he'd chosen this particular route for a reason: a window that differed little from
the two dozen others that looked out from the same build-
ing. His eyes, however, were always unerringly drawn to
those particular panes of glass—their luster quite dulled
this hour by the shadows of an approaching storm.

If he could rise some fifteen, twenty feet in the air, he'd
be able to see Helena Fitzhugh, sitting with her back to the
window. She would be wearing a white blouse tucked into

a dark skirt, her flaming hair caught up in an elegant chignon at her nape. A pot of tea was likely to be found on her desk, brought in by her conscientious secretary in the morning, and largely ignored the rest of the day.

Much could happen in six months—and much had. Hastings had done what he'd promised to do, keeping Andrew Martin's name out of any discussions. But he had not kept her actions a secret. In fact, the morning after their confrontation, he'd left at first light, traveled to her brother's estate, and informed her family that she'd been out and about at night when she ought not to be.

Her family had immediately understood the implications. She was half coaxed, half ordered across the ocean to America, under the pretext of an article that needed writing concerning the ladies of Radcliffe College, a women's college associated with Harvard University.

The events that took place on the campus of Harvard University had led to one of the more intriguing scandals of the current London Season, a scandal that involved Miss Fitzhugh's elder sister and the Duke of Lexington, resulting in an unexpected wedding.

On the heels of that, her twin brother, Fitz, at last realized that he was—and had been for years—in love with his heiress wife, a woman he'd married under the most trying of circumstances and never believed could become the love of his life.

For Hastings, however, little had changed, other than that his beloved disfavored him more than ever. Their lives went on, occasionally intersecting in a burst of sparks. But like images produced by a magic lantern, the drama and movement were but illusions going round and round. Nothing of substance happened. They'd dealt with each other thus since they were children, and he was no closer to her heart than that pot of tea at her elbow, a fixture in her life yet utterly inconsequential.

And so he stared at her window in the light of the day, as he'd stared at her door in the dark of the night.

The window opened. She stood before it, looking out.

He knew she could not see him—could not, thanks to the carriage immediately adjacent, even make out the crest on his carriage. All the same his breath quickened, his heart constricting.

Then, after the quake of nerves, a familiar dejection. She did not even look down, but only gazed distantly toward the direction of Andrew Martin's town residence.

Despite Hastings's keeping to the letter—if not the spirit—of his promise, members of her family discovered on their own the identity of Miss Fitzhugh's partner in crime. Hastings subsequently received a perhaps well-deserved punch to the face from Fitz for not having told the whole truth. Andrew Martin did not receive a just-as-well-deserved (if not more so) punch to the face, but Fitz made it clear that Martin was never to contact Miss Fitzhugh again.

She missed him. Hastings was but a shadow in the crowd, but Martin was her air, her sky.

He watched her until she closed the window and disappeared from sight. Then he got out of the brougham, instructed his coachman to head home as the logjam allowed, and walked away.

*T*he window must not have latched properly, for Helena could once again hear the din of the impasse below.

She pressed a palm to the side of her head, the fingers of her other hand tapping restlessly against Andrew's last letter to her. She'd gone over it countless times, but, inveterate reader that she was, she could not help scanning the words that had been set down before her.

My Dearest,

I am relieved to learn that you have returned safe and sound from America. I have missed you desperately during the long weeks of your absence. I need not tell you how delighted I am to receive your note requesting a meeting, and I need not tell you how dearly I'd like to see you.

But I've been giving the matter much thought. As wondrously euphoric as I've been of late, and as honored as I am by the bestowal of your affections, I cannot forget that every moment of our stolen joy comes at terrifying peril to you.

It is my fault, of course. I should never have allowed myself to be swayed by the idea of my own happiness. It was the utmost selfishness on my part to not understand sooner that I am keeping you from pursuing your own life, a life that can be lived in the open, that need never cower for fear of discovery.

It had taken her ages to gradually convince Andrew that her desires were worth something. That if she wished to lie with him in a state of near intimacy, she was old enough to make that choice with full understanding of the possible consequences.

But with one quick reminder from Fitz, Andrew's

thinking had tipped back the other way. He'd dutifully stopped seeing her, even in her capacity as his publisher. And his letters, too, had ceased altogether. Except for one chance encounter at a rail station some time ago, she had not seen him since before she left for America in January.

Such useless conventions society clung to, valuing a marriage that was essentially a transaction of property above the truths of the heart, and judging her on her possession of a hymen rather than her actions and character. Even her own family—her brother and sister, who'd let her make her own choices most of her life—had proved unyielding on this particular point.

But it is still not too late for you. You are kind, charming, and beautiful. I wish you all the blessings my heart can carry, and I shall remain

Your faithful and devoted friend

It *was* too late for her; couldn't he see? It had been too late since the very first. And it wasn't as if she hadn't taken a good, hard look at the gentlemen available to her. But she'd yet to meet one with whom the thought of spending the rest of her life was remotely tolerable.

She would not accept that this was the end. Taking advantage of a moment of privacy—even if they were standing on a rail platform full of travelers—she'd made an impassioned plea that reputation was not the only thing that mattered. That her happiness, too, counted for something. And that he, of all people, ought to have a care for her happiness.

His resolution had seemed to waver at the end of her entreaty. It was possible that ever since then he'd been reconsidering his decision. If only she could know the thoughts that coursed through his mind this very moment.

A stiff breeze blew and nearly made off with Andrew's letter. She caught it, stowed it in the locked drawer where she kept all his letters, tossed out the pot of tea Miss Boyle insisted on making for her every day, and went to the window. The crowd below still hadn't eased, hundreds of carriages crawling along like a parade of snails. The sky had become even darker. The coachmen were shrugging into their mackintoshes; the pedestrians, heads bowed, picked up their pace.

One particular pedestrian caught her eye. The angle of his hat, the width of his shoulders, the cadence of his gait . . . She must be imagining things. Hastings would not walk about Fleet Street at this hour of the day; he was far more likely to be mid-tryst with his lady du jour.

An all too vivid image came to mind: Hastings pressing an anonymous woman against a wall, one hand on her hip, the other at her nape, kissing her—no, devouring her with his lips and tongue. The woman was no less indecent in her lust, her fingers clutching his hair, her body writhing, whimpers and moans of all descriptions escaping her throat.

Helena slammed the window shut, jarring her arms.

Though he was her brother's best friend, Helena had paid him little mind: Hastings was the wasp at a picnic, or the occasional fly that fell into one's soup—irksome when he was around, but hardly a preoccupation when he wasn't.

Until, that was, six months ago, when he'd demanded the kiss in exchange for his fraudulent silence. She still managed to mostly not think of him, but when she did, her thoughts flew in unruly directions.

She returned to her desk and opened the bottom drawer again, intending to read a few more of Andrew's old letters to drown out the part of her mind that persisted in imagining Hastings at his illicit rendezvous. Instead, from the same drawer she pulled out quite something else: a manuscript that Hastings had sent her not long ago.

An *erotic* manuscript titled *The Bride of Larkspear*, in which the titular bride existed in a state of literal bondage, trussed to her husband's bed.

The raspberries have been picked only hours earlier. They are tiny yet plump, a lovely deep red. I rub one against her lips.

"What is this?"

"Something delicious and succulent." I speak easier when I do not need to look into her eyes, when the blindfold replaces the scorn in them with a strip of black silk. "Like you."

She opens her mouth and takes the raspberry. I watch her as she chews, then swallows. A tiny smear of raspberry juice remains on her lower lip. I lick it, tasting the tart sweetness.

"Would you like another?"

"Why such tenderness?" she demands archly. "I am already naked, fettered, and blindfolded. Go ahead. Have your way with me."

How I would love to descend upon her like a pack of wolves. My body is certainly primed, my cock hot and hard, my muscles straining against my own urges.

"No," I reply. "I am going to play with you a little longer."

There was an illustration of the naked bride at the bottom of the page. The view was from the side. Her face was obscured by one of the thick bedposts, but her breasts were taut, her legs endless. Helena's gaze, however, was drawn to her feet, one arched and flexed, the toes of the other pressing hard into the sheets, as if in silent arousal.

Her own toes were digging into the soles of her boots. The moment she realized it, she picked up the manuscript, jammed it back into the drawer, and turned the key in the lock.

She really ought to burn it. Or, failing that, read the whole thing and send him a politely snide letter of rejection. But she could no more consign the pages to the fireplace than she could read more than a few paragraphs at a time.

That, perhaps, was the true reason she was angry at him: He'd broken through a formerly invisible barrier and forced this awareness upon her—this awareness of him as a man.

And she did not want it. She wanted him relegated back to the periphery of her existence, there to stay for the remainder of his natural life. To never again be a cause of irregular heartbeats and agitated breathing.

It was a while before she could resume working.

Hastings did not head home directly, but stopped by his club. The Season was drawing to a close, and the club was sparsely attended. Soon Society would repair to the seashore or to the country. He might see some more of Helena when Fitz and his wife held their annual shooting party in August. But after that, there was a long stretch until Christmas during which there would be no doors of hers for him to stare at.

"My lord, a telegram for you," said one of the club's footmen. "Your staff thought you'd like to have it."

"Thank you," he said, taking the cable.

It was from Millie, Fitz's wife, informing him that she and her husband would be taking a short holiday in the Lake District. The news pleased Hastings: Fitz and Millie had had such a long road to happiness and deserved to wallow in their newfound joy.

He almost missed the postscript at the very bottom of the cable.

Upon reflection, dear Hastings, I realize I should have disclosed my true sentiments years ago. And, if I may be so forward, so should have you.

He should have, of course. A more rational, less proud man would consider the prize at the end, swallow his humiliation, and proceed apace to woo his beloved. Hastings was not that man. In every other regard he was quite reasonable, but when it came to Helena Fitzhugh, so futile was his approach he might as well have built a temple to the rain god in the middle of the Sahara Desert.

He certainly prayed a good deal for her to miraculously change her mind, to wake up one day, look at him with completely different eyes, and see him as he wished to be seen.

"Something the matter?"

He looked up. The speaker was Bernard Monteth, a thin man with prematurely grey hair. They'd belonged to the same clubs for years, but it was only in the past six months that Hastings had cultivated a greater acquaintance with Monteth: Monteth's wife was Mrs. Andrew Martin's sister.

Hastings raised a brow. "Speaking to me, good sir?"

"You seem to be brooding."

"Brooding? Me? I was but imagining the pleasures that await me tonight. Must make hay while the sun yet shines, you see, before it is off to the country to rusticate."

Monteth sighed. "You have my envy, Hastings—make hay while the sun yet shines indeed. Don't marry too soon like the lot of us."

"I'll make sure not to mention our conversation to Mrs. Monteth," Hastings said lightly. "How is the missus, by the way?"

"Always up to something, that woman," grumbled Monteth.

"I hope she isn't conspiring against you?"

"Not me, thankfully—not yet, at least. But the wife is always conspiring against *somebody*."

It was not an exaggeration. Mrs. Monteth was not so much a gossip as a self-appointed guardian of virtue and righteousness. She spied on the servants, opened random doors at country house parties—for which reason she was seldom invited anywhere these days—and did just about everything in her power to expose and punish the private moral failings of those around her.

"So whom is the missus going after this week?"

"Don't know," grumbled Monteth. "But she's been spending an awful lot of time with her sister."

Hastings felt an odd tingle in his spine. "Could she have something on Mr. Martin?"

Monteth shook his head. "That man sits in a room with his books and his typewriter and never comes out. The missus wouldn't waste her time on him."

If Monteth only knew.

"No," continued Monteth. "Martin doesn't have the stones to overstep the bounds."

Martin had done it once. He could most certainly do it again, his promise to Fitz notwithstanding.

"Well," said Hastings. "Keep me abreast of the missus's intrigues, will you? Nothing I love more than a good old-fashioned scandal."

CHAPTER 2

$\mathcal{W}$ ork had become Helena's refuge, solid stretches of time during which she could forget that she'd become a prisoner in her own life. A particular source of solace of late had been *Tales from Old Toad Pond*, a collection of children's books, the rights to which she'd acquired earlier in the year.

The books depicted the escapades of a pair of ducklings and their friends around a seemingly placid pond that nevertheless offered all the adventures any young heart could desire—or handle, as foxes came sniffing in spring, crocodiles arrived to escape the heat of Egypt in summer, and silly little bunnies sometimes set their houses on fire while toasting carrots during the equinox celebrations.

Helena planned to publish one story a month for twelve months, beginning in September, and then a handsome boxed collection for the following Christmas, to be followed by a single volume containing all the previously published stories, plus a pair of new ones to make for a lucky fourteen in total.

She'd never met Miss Evangeline South, the author of the tales, but found the woman easy to work with. The tales hadn't originally been intended to be a round-the-year series, and Helena had asked for a number of modifications. The changes completed thus far had been made quickly, and very much to Helena's satisfaction.

She toyed with the idea of hiring a calligrapher to render the text of the books, which would increase her initial cost of production, but which—

A knock came at her door.

"Yes?"

Miss Boyle, her secretary, poked in her head. "Miss, Lord Hastings to see you."

Helena's chair scraped rather audibly.

Hastings occasionally came to fetch her at Fitz's behest, but Fitz and Millie were not in London—they were on their way to the Lake District, in fact.

"You may show him in, but warn him I have only a few minutes to spare."

"Yes, miss."

Helena took a quick look at herself in the small mirror on the wall. She was in her usual white shirtwaist, an antique cameo brooch at her throat. Her sister, Venetia, two years older than she, was the Great Beauty of their generation. Helena was often grateful that she hadn't been burdened with Venetia's stunning looks, which made most men and quite a number of women incapable of seeing Venetia beyond her face.

Today, however, she wished she were as staggeringly

beautiful as Venetia. She would have enjoyed flaunting all that gorgeousness before Hastings, and rendering him agape at what he could not have.

Hastings walked in with the smile of the Cheshire cat and the gait of a Siberian tiger, a big man who moved surely but lightly, always on the prowl.

Helena gritted her teeth—she could swear she'd never noticed his gait before the beginning of this year.

He sat down. "Miss Fitzhugh, how glad I am that you can spare five minutes to see me."

"I'd offer you a seat, but I see you've already taken one," she said by way of greeting.

"Shall I bring some tea?" Miss Boyle asked eagerly.

"Lord Hastings is busier than you and I combined, Miss Boyle. I'm sure he won't stay long enough for water to boil."

"Indeed, I shall stay only long enough for Miss Fitzhugh's blood to boil." Hastings smirked. "But thank you for the lovely offer, Miss Boyle."

"Of course, my lord," answered Miss Boyle, flushing with pleasure.

"Don't do that," Helena said sharply, once Miss Boyle had closed the door behind her.

"Do what?"

"Flirt with my secretary."

"Why not? She enjoys it, as do I."

"And what happens when she falls in love with you?"

He smiled. "My dear Miss Fitzhugh, you attribute such powers to me. I can only imagine you must find me difficult to resist."

"And yet my resistance remains intact, after all these years."

"A mere husk—the faintest gust will blow it away.

But truly, you need not fear for Miss Boyle. She has a promising young man who works in the city and waits for her outside each afternoon to walk her to her lodging. They have even met twice on Sundays to picnic in the country."

"I've never heard of such a thing."

"And why should she mention such distractions to her employer? Do you speak to her of your love affairs?"

"Then why should she tell you?"

"I take an interest. She does find my attention flattering, but she is quite sensible, that young lady, and not about to let my lovely plumage turn her head."

Lovely plumage. "You flatter yourself a great deal."

"I learned the trick from Lord Vere. It makes my listener's blood boil faster."

He had a good voice—his words emerged like notes on an arpeggio. Had she never noticed it before?

She was beginning to be thoroughly annoyed with herself. Leaning back in her chair, she made her voice cold and impatient. "Why are you here?"

"Because I am a good and loyal friend and I am worried about you."

She snickered. "I am touched, Hastings. Tell me, is the way I'm not filling out my bodice bothering you again? And are my Amazonian footprints cracking London's streets?"

"It's about Mr. Martin."

"I've already heard a number of warnings from you on that front, Hastings," she said dismissively.

"But you have not heeded any of them."

"Which is no one's fault but your own."

He looked down a moment before raising his eyes

34

again—had he always had eyes that particular depth of blue? "Would you take me more seriously if I promise never to try for another kiss from you?"

She rolled her eyes. "Your promise not to kiss me will translate into attempts to grope me instead, from what I know of the caliber of your promises."

"What if I promise never again to come within three feet of you?"

Something in the timbre of his voice gave her pause. Was this what sincerity on Hastings's part sounded like? She dismissed the thought out of hand. "Then no doubt you will demand that I disrobe and tie myself to a bedpost—as you've described in your smutty novel—while you watch from three feet away and do whatever disgusting things men do in such situations."

"You do put such ideas in my head," he murmured.

Now, this mocking tone was far more familiar. Not that she fared much better against it—inside her stockings, her toes clenched again. "You manufacture such ideas by the gross without any help from me."

He sighed exaggeratedly. "I see it is futile for me to offer any promises."

"Utterly pointless."

He rose. "Sometimes you must disregard the messenger and consider only the message—or have you forgotten that I was exactly right about Billy Carstairs? Mrs. Monteth is on the loose, and you will be foolish to ignore the lengths to which she is willing to go to unmask what she considers wrongdoing."

Mrs. Monteth was Andrew's wife's sister, a guardian of virtue in her own eyes. Her idea of virtue consisted largely—one might say entirely—of chastity. She lived to expose maids who had granted too much liberty to their fellows, or young ladies who might have been indiscreet with someone who was not an approved suitor.

"I am perfectly capable of disregarding the messenger when the message is worth my time." But his reminder about Billy Carstairs did give her pause. She'd disregarded everything Hastings had said about that erstwhile favorite cousin, but time had proved her good opinion of Billy sadly deluded. "Go to my window and have a look."

"Fleet Street? I know what it looks like."

"Humor me. Look across the street to your right, second lamppost."

He crossed to the window. "There is a man reading a newspaper," said Hastings.

"He is there to make sure I do not climb down the exterior wall—before the crowd on the street, mind you—and escape to indulge in unsuitable shenanigans. And you know very well that my maid sits out by the other exit of this room to prevent me from walking off. On days I walk to work, she follows two steps behind. On days I take the carriage, the coachmen are instructed to never let me off anywhere except directly at work, where she is already waiting. And when I am dragged about various parlors and ballrooms, either my sister or my sister-in-law stands within three feet, even for my trips to the water closet."

Contrary to what she'd expected, her enumeration of the close watch under which she'd been placed failed to make an impression on him. "Is that all?"

"Is that *all*? How will Mrs. Monteth catch me at any scandalous action when I can't even sneeze without it being duly reported?"

"I have more faith in you, Miss Fitzhugh. You haven't

broken free of this surveillance yet, but it's only a matter of time before you spot an opportunity." He paused and gazed at her for a moment. She was disconcerted by something that flickered in his eyes—something suspiciously close to true concern. "When that time comes, and an opportunity presents itself, I beg you to exercise wisdom and restraint and remember that not all opportunities are created equal. Some are nothing but steps leading down toward catastrophe."

And with that, he bowed and took his leave.

Helena tried to reimmerse herself in *Tales from Old Toad Pond*. Miss Evangeline South was an accomplished illustrator with a deft, yet whimsical touch. The pond was a perfect shade of springlike green, the cottages laden with ivy and blooming window boxes, the large log that was the summer boat of the turtles—seasonal visitors from warmer climates—charmingly festooned with enormous bouquets of bulrush.

But whereas earlier the drawings had made her smile, now she frowned at them. Surely . . . surely she could not possibly think that there were any similarities to be found between the cheerful innocence of Miss South's illustrations and the blatant obscenity of Hastings's.

She took out Hastings's manuscript again, flipping the pages, each pornographic image reassuring her that indeed, her mind had been playing tricks on her: There was not the slightest likeness between the artwork of *Old Toad Pond* and the filthy scribbles in *The Bride of Larkspear*.

A few pages from the end of the manuscript, however, she came across an illustration that could not be termed indecent. This time the bride of Larkspear was clothed—properly clothed, in a dress that buttoned to her chin. She lay in a field of grass, the brim of her hat covering most of her face. Only her mouth showed, curved in a teasing—or perhaps mocking—smile.

Without the distraction and discomfiture of the woman's nakedness, the likeness in the artists' styles leaped off the page and punched Helena in the lungs. She had not been imagining things after all: There was a marked resemblance in the use of color, the curvature of the lines, the weight and solidity of the shapes.

Before she could quite take her thoughts to their logical conclusion, a knock came at her door. She hastily locked the manuscript away. "Come in."

Miss Boyle entered. "Another cable for you, miss."

"Thank you, Miss Boyle."

Fitz had sent a cable not long ago. Did he remember something else to tell her?

But this telegram did not have the name or the address of the sender. The text was short and impersonal. *Next Monday. The Savoy Hotel. Four o'clock in the afternoon. Ask for the Quaids' room.*

Her breath suspended. Andrew. At long last. She pressed the cable against her heart, her mind running away with the imagined pleasure of this longed-for reunion. A few minutes passed before she let go of her elation and began contemplating the realities of arranging for such a rendezvous on her part, with all the surveillance that had been placed upon her.

Well, if the Count of Monte Cristo could escape the Château d'If, it ought not be impossible for her to shake free of her watchdogs.

Hastings's words unexpectedly came to mind, echoing with an ominous, almost prophetic ring in her head. *I beg you to exercise wisdom and restraint and remember that not all opportunities are created equal. Some are nothing but steps leading down toward catastrophe.*

She wavered for several minutes before she realized what she was doing.

No one would stop her from seeing Andrew, least of all Hastings.

CHAPTER 3

$\mathcal{H}$ elena stumbled upon a piece of luck the next morning. Her maid Susie, hired to keep a close eye on her, resigned: A former employer's housekeeper had died after a sudden illness, and Susie had been approached to become the new housekeeper—immediately. Helena was all too happy to let her go with extra wages and a glowing letter of character.

To her sister, Venetia, the Duchess of Lexington, with whom she was staying, Helena recommended that since Fitz and Millie had gone off on a quick holiday in the Lake District without servants attending, Venetia could ask Millie's maid, Bridget, to be the one sitting outside Helena's office for a few days, until a satisfactory replacement for Susie was located.

It certainly did not escape Helena's attention that Fitz and Millie would return on Monday afternoon. Bridget would be eager to get back to her mistress, and Helena just might exploit that time gap to her advantage.

In the meantime, Helena smuggled out a set of livery from the Lexington household and contacted a company that leased carriages.

The board was set, the pieces moving. She awaited only the arrival of Monday afternoon to see whether her strategy would procure a victory on the field.

Saturday evening the Lexingtons gave a dinner at their house. As was usually the case when one of her siblings played host, Hastings was invited to the gathering. He was, however, not seated anywhere near Helena, who'd long ago requested that he never be put next to her at dinner, so as not to diminish her enjoyment.

But after dinner, once the gentlemen had finished with their port and cigars, they rejoined the ladies in the drawing room, and at such times there was no escaping Hastings. As inevitable as the day's descent into night, he appeared at her side, sleek and smug, like a predator freshly returned from a bout of hearty slaughter.

She wondered, not for the first time, whom he'd been bedding before he arrived at the Lexington house—and exactly what he'd been doing with her.

"Miss Fitzhugh," he murmured. "My dear, I don't wish to impugn your toilette, but you look lonely and deprived."

"The recommended cure for which is no doubt a few hours in your bed, my lord?"

"My dear girl of little faith, no one leaves my bed after only a few hours. Ladies clear their schedule for at least a week before they leap in."

When he lowered it just so, his voice practically purred,

uncomfortably attractive. She had to tamp down an involuntary flutter in her stomach. "What do you want, Hastings?"

He slanted a look at her. His eyes seemed to have shifted in color, a blue-grey tonight.

"I've found a ring for you among my mother's jewels, my dear, an emerald ring to match your eyes."

She arched a brow. "And since when do I take jewelry from gentlemen to whom I am not related?"

"Oh, I believe we shall be related very soon, the way you are going. I can see it in your eyes: the machination, the impatience. You are scheming hard, Miss Fitzhugh, against everyone else's better judgment."

He might be a bastard, but he was a clever bastard.

"I have been leaning on Mr. Monteth for news concerning his wife," he continued. "Daily she calls on her sister, the wife of your beloved, and comes home excited and agitated. Mr. Monteth is convinced she is up to something. If I were you, I'd do nothing as long as Mrs. Monteth might be paying the slightest attention to her brother-in-law."

But if Helena didn't take this opportunity, when would she have another one?

"You are not listening, Miss Fitzhugh." Hastings's voice dropped even lower, a dark, smooth mellifluousness. "Think of wearing my ring and what *that* would entail. Does it not stop you cold that I may be the one to rescue you from a disaster of your own making? And remember, I already told you that I don't want to be your husband. But if I must, out of duty, I will exact my price and make demands you've never even dreamed of."

She'd read snippets of his erotic novel—she had a very

good idea of the sort of degrading lewdness he'd stipulate. It vexed her that she wasn't as revolted as she ought to be. "That I am not concerned about a possible future chained to your bedpost—shouldn't you take it as a sign that all my scheming is but a figment of your imagination?"

"But you *are* concerned. Just now your voice caught and your shoulders recoiled." He looked directly into her eyes. "And unless I am very much mistaken, your pupils are dilated."

"That is just how I react to finding a worm in my apple, my lord."

"Then think about how you'd feel finding such a worm— indeed, half a worm—in every apple you'll ever henceforth bite into. Be careful, Miss Fitzhugh. More pieces are moving on this board than you think, and you may yet find yourself outmaneuvered."

Sunday afternoons Hastings and his daughter painted the wall of her tearoom at Easton Grange, his estate in Kent. Or rather, Hastings painted and Bea watched.

The mural was almost complete. The sky, the trees, and a number of cottages along the edge of the pond had been painted. The pond itself, done the previous week, had dried to a glossy, sunlit green.

"See?" He showed the palette to Bea. "I take some red and some yellow, and when I mix them I get orange."

Bea watched intently, but without comment.

"Would you like to put in a few orange flowers among the red ones?" he asked. The window box he was adding to the cottage in the foreground was a riot of nasturtiums.

Bea bit her lower lip. He could sense her desire to participate. Silently he encouraged her to say yes.

She shook her head. He sighed inwardly—at least it was taking her longer and longer to decline.

"Maybe another time, then. It's quite fun, painting. You take a blob of color, you put it on a brush, and soon you have a picture."

He would have liked for her to join him. For a girl who spoke very little, and reluctantly at that, color and images could have become useful substitutes for words. But he didn't start this mural to lure her to paint, just as he didn't devote all the hours and days to the mural in his town house to impress Helena Fitzhugh.

Painting had become a form of prayer. When he lurched between hope and despair, a brush in one hand and a palette in the other was one of the ways he dealt with sentiments too raw to be discussed and too big to shove away. And this mural was his prayer for Bea: that she would grow up strong, happy, and unafraid.

He took up a new brush. "Now I am going to paint some leaves. You like watching me mix yellow and blue to make green, don't you, Bea? Would you like to try your hand at it?"

He waited the usual few seconds for her to say no. To his shock, she nodded and reached out for the brush in his hand. But then she didn't move. He realized, after a while, that she meant for him to hold her hand and guide her.

After what had happened when she was younger, he never felt quite worthy of her trust. But for some miraculous reason, she did trust him wholeheartedly.

He wrapped his hand around hers, kissed her on the top of her head, and showed her what to do.

* * *

*A*t half past three Monday afternoon, a coachman dressed in the Lexington livery came for Helena at her office.

"Well, there is my carriage," she said to Bridget. "I know you must be anxious to get back and prepare for your mistress's return. Take a hansom. Mrs. Wilson has already been instructed to add the cost of your transportation to your wages."

"Thank you, miss, I might then. I want to make sure everything is ready—Lady Fitzhugh won't have much time to change out of her traveling dress before she is to head to the duchess's for tea."

"Indeed she won't."

And neither, after so much trouble, would Helena enjoy much more than half an hour with Andrew—she, too, was expected at the five o'clock tea. And she had better arrive before Millie, to avoid questions about why she'd taken so much time en route.

She hopped into the brougham, directed the coachman to a nearby post office, and made a telephone call to the Lexington town house, letting the staff know she'd be coming home on her own, accompanied by Millie's maid; no need to send the carriage.

Now to the hotel—and Andrew.

Inside the carriage with all its shades drawn, she fiddled with the drawstring of her reticule. She thought she'd done enough, but what if she'd underprepared? Granted, her presence at the Savoy would raise no eyebrows—the hotel's terrace was a popular place for a cup of afternoon tea. But would it not have been even better had she disguised herself as a man with a big beard—or something of the sort?

Damn Hastings and his incessant warnings of disaster. She ought to be exhilarated at the prospect of seeing Andrew again so soon, not fretting about everything that could go wrong.

Enough with the troubling thoughts. She'd worked hard for this morsel of stolen time. She would clear her mind and relish her triumph.

Or at least, she would do her utmost.

*H*astings did not expect to see Andrew Martin at the club. After Fitz had spoken to him earlier in the Season, Martin had avoided locales where he might run into any of the Fitzhugh siblings. But with Fitz away, Martin probably thought the club a safe venue for whiling away a few hours.

Except he wasn't exactly *whiling* away the hours. He seemed distracted and jumpy, getting up from his chair every few minutes to pace about the periphery of the room. At some point during each circle, he'd pull out a piece of paper from the pocket of his day coat, read it, stuff it back into his pocket, sit down, chew his lips for some time, and then repeat the procedure all over again.

As his restlessness grew, so did Hastings's. Why the hell was Martin so agitated? And why did he keep looking at that piece of paper?

The next time Martin crossed the room, Hastings rose and bumped into him.

He steadied Martin. "Sorry, there, old fellow."

"My fault," said Martin meekly.

Many children talked of running away with the Gypsies; Hastings had actually done so—more than once. His pickpocketing skills were rusty, but Martin was a spectacularly easy target.

Standing before a bookcase, his back to the room, Hastings looked down at the loot in his hand. It was a telegram. *Next Monday. The Savoy Hotel. Four o'clock in the afternoon. Ask for the Quaids' room.*

He looked at the date on the telegram. Today was the Monday that had been specified—and soon it would strike four on the clock. Had Helena Fitzhugh sent the cable despite all his warnings to the contrary?

Martin sucked in a loud breath. Hastings turned around to the sight of him frantically feeling his pockets. The telegram tucked inside his sleeve, Hastings meandered to Martin's chair and dropped the telegram on the floor.

"Something the matter?" he asked.

Martin turned around and exhaled in relief at the sight of the telegram next to Hastings's shoes. "Nothing. I dropped a cable—that's all."

Hastings picked it up and held it out facedown toward Martin. "This one?"

"Yes, thank you, sir."

Martin pocketed the telegram. But this time, instead of returning to his seat, he bade Hastings good day and walked out of the room.

The bastard was going to the Savoy Hotel.

There was no inherent malice to Martin. But he was born without a spine of his own and always yielded to whichever person exerted the greatest influence on him. On the matter of his marriage, he'd deferred to his mother. Earlier in the Season, he'd obeyed Fitz. And now he'd let himself be once again persuaded by the forceful Helena Fitzhugh.

Hastings didn't know whom he wanted to punch more, Martin or himself. Why did he still care? Why did he persist in manning his temple in the Sahara, praying for rain, when all about him the evidence of his failure stretched as far as the eyes could see?

On their own, his feet carried him toward the door. If he was going to drown his sorrows in whiskey, he preferred to do it at home, in the privacy of his own chambers, where his heartache would be visible to no one but himself.

Someone pulled him aside.

"You could be right after all, Hastings," Monteth whispered. "I ran into Martin outside just now and tried to bring him in here, but he gave me all sorts of shifty reasons why he couldn't have a drink with me."

"A man not wanting to have a drink with you, Monteth, is not exactly reason for suspicion."

"You don't understand." Monteth looked about the largely empty room and lowered his voice even more. "This morning I saw a letter the missus was writing. It said, 'I will catch him in the act very soon.' And guess to whom it was addressed? 'My dear Alexandra'!"

Alexandra was Mrs. Martin's Christian name.

"My goodness," Hastings heard himself respond, sounding calm, almost detached. Or perhaps he was merely in shock, although a sharp cold was beginning to spread between his shoulder blades.

"Precisely. I tried to bring Martin back in here, where he can't get into much trouble. But as I told you, he wanted none of it."

"Right-ho," Hastings managed. "Keep me abreast of

any interesting developments, will you? I must be off now. My lady awaits."

He strolled toward the door, when it was all he could do not to sprint.

"Your lady?" called Monteth behind him. "But you haven't a wife."

Nor did Hastings want one who preferred another man. But should things go ill, his bachelor days would be numbered.

*M*artin was no longer outside the club. Hastings hopped into a hansom cab and asked for the Savoy Hotel and great haste. It did not escape his attention that he might again stand guard while she trysted with Martin—but today he'd almost volunteer for the odious duty, if only he could thwart Mrs. Monteth.

As the hansom cab approached its destination, he saw Martin enter the hotel, looking left and right as he went, radiating quite the aura of a man who knew he was up to no good. Hastings wasted no time in alighting from the hansom. He crossed the lobby to the clerk's station. "The Quaids' room."

"Room five on the top floor, sir."

"I was told there would be a key waiting for me," he fibbed.

"I'm sorry, sir. My instruction was that only the first person to ask for the room would be given a key."

"And was the first person to ask for a key the gentleman of a minute ago?"

"No, sir. I gave the key to the lady who came a few minutes before him."

Martin had not instigated this tryst, judging by the cable he'd received. Yet if Miss Fitzhugh had been the one to arrange for this meeting, she would not have needed to ask for a key. She would have been the one who'd issued the instruction to give the key to Martin.

The possibility that a third party was pulling the strings had just shot up to near certainty.

"How many keys do you have to the room?"

"Three, sir."

"Where are the other two?"

"One is with the guest under whose name the room is registered. The other key we hold."

And if Helena Fitzhugh had taken the third key, then she was definitely not the one under whose name the room was registered.

Hastings reached inside his day coat and slid across a one-pound note. "Give me the third key and say nothing of me to anyone."

The clerk looked at the note for a long moment—then quickly pocketed it. "Here you go, sir."

The key was heavy and cold in Hastings's hand as he walked toward the lift. It had seemed imperative that he should have a key. But now that he did, he didn't know what to do with it. He couldn't very well interrupt a lovers' rendezvous without clear and present danger.

A moment later, clear and present danger arrived in the form of Mrs. Monteth, approaching the clerk's station.

His heart seized. Not the lift then, with its unpredictable speed. He walked to the stairs as fast as he dared without attracting undue attention, glancing at Mrs. Monteth every two seconds. The moment he was out of her sight, he sprinted up the steps, praying the lift would require a long wait and then stop at every floor along the way.

His lungs burned. He ran faster.

*T*he Savoy was not as tall as the hotel Helena had stayed at in New York City, but still, from the top floor it was a long drop to the ground. Helena stood just inside the balcony, waiting.

Sometimes it still seemed only last week that she and Andrew first met, and the world was glorious with the promise of happiness. Sometimes it seemed a lifetime ago, and she'd always had this crux of desolation in her heart.

A scratch came at the door. She rushed to open it. Andrew stood before her, his face at once glowing and apologetic. "Sorry I'm late. Monteth wanted to drag me back inside the club for a drink—and I always underestimate how long it takes to get anywhere in London nowadays."

It didn't matter why he was late; it mattered only that he was here. She pulled him in, shut the door, and threw her arms about him. "Andrew, Andrew, Andrew."

How well she remembered the first time she'd hugged him, impulsively, after he'd told her he didn't see why she wouldn't make a terrific publisher. They'd been on the banks of her brother's trout stream, having known each other all of a week. But what a glorious week, spending every waking minute together. She'd gone to sleep each night with an enormous smile on her face.

The present-day Andrew nuzzled her hair. "I've missed you terribly, Helena."

The sound of pounding feet reverberated in the

passage—a vibration she felt in her own shins. Her chest tightened. Surely it couldn't be Mrs. Monteth making such an uncivilized racket.

"I shouldn't be here at all," Andrew went on. "But ever since we ran into each other at the rail station the other day, your question of whether a promise to your brother was more important than a promise to you has agonized me. I did promise to be always at your side, didn't I?"

She barely heard him. But she heard all too clearly the sound of a key turning in the lock. She sprang back from him as if he'd suddenly developed the pox.

But it was only Hastings, clutching onto the doorjamb, breathing hard.

"What are *you* doing here?" she cried, flabbergasted, relieved, and outraged. Her action might carry risks, but he had no right to interfere in such a crude manner.

"It's not what it looks like," blurted Andrew at the same time.

"I know what it is and I don't care." Hastings pushed the door shut behind them. "Mrs. Monteth is on her way up here. She also has a key."

Helena was cold all over. "I don't believe you."

But there was no force in her words, only fear.

"Did you send the cable to Mr. Martin?" demanded Hastings.

"No, of course not. He sent the cable to me."

"I didn't," Andrew protested. "I received one from you."

She couldn't speak at all.

"Mrs. Monteth must have been the one to send cables to you both," said Hastings forcefully, "arranging for this meeting so she could catch you in the act."

He opened the door a crack and looked out. "She's

coming out of the lift as we speak. And—dear God—the senior Mrs. Martin is with her."

"My mother?" Andrew's voice quavered.

The elder Mrs. Martin set strenuous standards for her sons—Andrew had ever feared her. If she learned that he had compromised a young lady of otherwise fine standing, she'd hold him in contempt for the rest of her days. It would crush him.

Hastings closed the door and peered at the locking mechanism. "Someone has tampered with the door. It cannot be secured from inside."

"What are we to do?" Andrew gazed at Helena beseechingly. "What are we to do?"

"Mrs. Monteth went to the clerk's station after me," said Hastings, holding the door shut with his person. "If the clerk kept quiet about me, as I'd asked, all she has learned is that a man and a woman had asked for the key. What do you want to do?"

The question was addressed to Helena.

She was surprised she heard Hastings so clearly—there seemed to be someone screaming inside her head. She swallowed. "Andrew, my dear, go into the bath and lock the door. If you love me, you will not make a single sound no matter what you hear."

"But, Helena—"

"There is no time. Do as I say."

Andrew still hesitated. She grabbed him by the elbow and shoved him into the bath. "Not a sound—or I'll never forgive you."

She shut the door of the bath in Andrew's face and prayed she'd conveyed her point with enough authority.

When she turned around, Hastings was already stripping off his jacket and waistcoat.

He raised a brow. "You don't mind, I hope?"

Without waiting for an answer, he pushed her onto the divan in the center of the room. His hand behind her skull was warm and strong. His other hand opened her jacket as he bent his head to her neck.

Her hair tumbled loose. His teeth grazed her neck, sending a hot jolt to her middle. His fingers worked the buttons of her blouse and pushed both the jacket and the blouse from her shoulders.

Their eyes met. Without hesitation he kissed her. His weight was solid. His hair—she didn't know when her fingers had plunged into his hair—was cool and soft. And the hunger in his kiss . . . contrary to everything she knew, he made her feel as if he'd never kissed anyone before and never wanted to kiss anyone else.

Without ever making a conscious decision about it, she kissed him back.

The door burst open.

"Now I've caught you in delicto flagrante!" shouted Mrs. Monteth. "How do you explain yourself, Mr. Martin?"

Hastings swore, pulled away, and rose. "That is in flagrante delicto, you gorgon. And what is the meaning of this? Get out before I throw you out, the both of you."

Helena barely remembered to squeal and clumsily right her clothes.

Mrs. Monteth was stunned. "Lord Hastings, but—but—"

"Leave, Mrs. Monteth. And you, too, Mrs. Martin. Can't a man celebrate his elopement in peace?"

"Elopement?" Mrs. Martin, a bird of a woman, gasped.

Elopement? Helena felt as if she'd been electrocuted. She hastily lowered her head.

"Yes, elopement," said Hastings. "Surely you don't think I would consign my best friend's sister to this sort of situation, where apparently any nosy woman could interrupt us, without marrying her first."

Butter wouldn't melt in his mouth.

Helena clamped her right hand over her left. She was only trying to restrain herself from saying anything foolish or compromising before Mrs. Martin and Mrs. Monteth. But with this show of seemingly hand-wringing mortification, no one could see that she was not wearing a wedding band.

Mrs. Martin squared her shoulders. "Our apologies, Lord Hastings, Lady Hastings. We wish you much happiness in your union."

Mrs. Monteth still sputtered. "But—but—"

Mrs. Martin took her by the arm and yanked her out. Hastings closed the door and leaned his weight against it.

Helena counted to ten, to give the women time to walk down the passage, out of hearing. Then she counted to another ten.

Eight. Nine. Ten.

"Eloped?" she erupted, barely managing to keep her voice to a reasonable volume. "*Eloped?* What in the world caused you to say that? Have you lost your mind?"

He looked incredulous—and none too pleased. "You wanted me to tell them that we were having an affair of our own?"

"Yes!"

His expression turned sober, then blank. "The result

would have been exactly the same: I'd have to marry you. So I decided to spare us the scandal."

He did not *have* to marry her. Or rather, she would not have married him under any circumstances. "You can't make such decisions for me."

"I've been telling you ever since you came back from America not to put me in this kind of situation."

"Nobody put you in anything." Her voice rose with her exasperation. "You inserted yourself into the situation."

"And where would you and Mr. Martin be if I hadn't come along?"

She shivered. "The worst would have happened—I will admit that. But that doesn't mean the two matters are related. To save Mr. Martin, we had to create an illusion that you, not he, were my lover. That was it—nothing more."

"To save *Mr. Martin*? What do I care about—" He stopped. "And what then? What do I tell Fitz?"

"The truth, of course. Tell him Mr. Martin and I were ambushed by Mrs. Monteth, and to shield him we chose to make it look as if the two of *us* were meeting illicitly."

"And you think that would be the end of the matter? That Fitz would allow such a state of things to stand, for Society to believe his best friend and his sister are sleeping together, without doing something about it? He would have compelled me to offer for you."

"And I'd have gratefully declined your offer. *I* will deal with Fitz. *I* will deal with the consequences of my own actions. I do not need any man to save me and I particularly do not need you."

His voice hardened. "So you will become a fallen woman? As you so often like to remind everyone, there isn't just reputation to consider; there is also happiness. Do you not realize that you would not only tarnish your family's reputation, but forever taint your brother's and sister's happiness? It doesn't matter whether you stay in London and keep running your firm or repair to the country to rusticate; they could never be seen with you in public again, never talk about you, never let you see their future children except in utmost secrecy. And they would worry about you every hour of the day and pull their hair out over your obstinacy for the remainder of their natural lives. You would subject them to that?"

The trap was closing about her. Her family was her Achilles' heel. She did not fear consequences for herself, but she could not bear to hurt her loved ones.

She thought she'd steeled herself for this moment—still she had to put a hand against the wall to keep herself upright. She wanted to rail against the unfairness of life: that he, with his debauchery and his illegitimate child living under his roof, was still accepted everywhere, but she, unless she accepted his suit, would suffer the harshest punishments for this one small overreach.

But there was no point blaming the rules of the game when she'd known them all along.

A timid knock came from the door of the bath. "May I come out now?"

Andrew. She'd forgotten him. "Yes, do come out."

He opened the door and slunk into the parlor, his hand clutched around his hat. Her heart gave an awful throb at his red, disconsolate face. Her poor darling, he must think it was all his fault.

"It's quite all right, Andrew," she said encouragingly.

"No, it's not." His voice shook. "It's all gone wrong—like your brother said it would."

She took hold of his hands, the brim of his hat hard in her palm. "Listen to me. This is not your fault."

Behind her Hastings rolled his eyes—no doubt he meant for her to see it in the mirror opposite. She clenched her jaw and repeated herself. "None of this is your fault."

Hastings shrugged into his waistcoat. "Stay here for now, Martin. Let me make sure it's safe; then I'll smuggle you out through a service door."

"Thank you," Andrew said, his voice barely audible. "Most kind of you."

"And, Lady Hastings, I trust you will conduct yourself with some decorum." Hastings shot her a look that was almost hostile in its intensity. She stared back, but had to break his gaze when her heart started to thump unpleasantly. "When I return, we'll speak to your family, my love."

CHAPTER 4

$\mathcal{H}$astings's soon-to-be wife looked out the window of the hansom cab, her back straight, her jaw set, her hands clasped tight in her lap, as if she were Napoleon arriving upon the stark shores of Saint Helena, understanding deep in her bones that this time there would be no escape.

The interior of the hansom cab was narrow. They sat shoulder to shoulder, the expanse of her skirt brushing against his knee. In the seconds before the scandalmongers had burst in on them, she had been anything but frigid. He could still taste their kiss upon his tongue, still feel the heat of her slender body pressed into his. But now she might as well have been on the far side of Siberia, as cold and remote as the Bering Sea.

He had not meant to force her into marriage: It simply had not occurred to him that there were any other possible explanations for him to be seen making love to her. Apparently she thought him the sort of man who entertained himself by ruining unmarried young ladies from good families.

And she'd rather become a pariah than his wife.

It did not console him that he was largely to blame for her antagonistic views. She was blind, this girl, as blind as Justice, except her set of scales had broken years ago, and all she weighed in her hand were her prejudices.

He looked down at his own hand, at his index finger poised atop his walking stick, applying the merest pressure to keep it upright, as if he hadn't a care in the world beyond the balancing of this gentlemanly accessory.

"It's unfortunate that maid of yours left," he heard himself say, in a tone as insubstantial as his hold on the walking stick. "She would have tied you to the bedpost without blinking an eye."

Her skirts twitched. She said nothing.

"No matter," he continued. "I'm sure I'll find someone for the task. Perhaps I can teach you a few knots myself. You are a clever girl. There's no reason you can't truss yourself in a most satisfactory manner."

Her voice was a low growl. "The man I love is beyond my reach. I must marry a man who holds no appeal for me whatsoever. Have some decency, Hastings. Save your gloating until after the wedding."

There, he'd successfully provoked her again, out of habit—out of pure reflex, almost. And his satisfaction was emptier than ever, his heart all but losing its beat.

He'd gone too far. Well before he opened his mouth, he'd known he'd go too far. Yet he hadn't been able to help himself, the way a man who'd lost his footing on a steep hill only gathered speed as he stumbled toward a precipice.

"I never do anything for as silly a reason as decency. I will, however, grant you a reprieve of silence, but that is only because now I shall expect even greater gratitude from you, once we are married."

His words were met with silence. For a stretch of several minutes, he looked out the window on his side of the hansom cab, dumbly noting their progress. Then he glanced back toward her.

For the first time in their long acquaintance, he witnessed her with her shoulders slumped. And then a shocking realization: She was crying. He could not see it or hear it—her face was turned completely away from him and she made not the slightest of noises—but her despair was palpable, leaden, a thing that choked the air from his lungs.

He looked away from her, back to the window, to the street outside overflowing with carriages and pedestrians. His own eyes were quite dry, but that was only because he'd long grown accustomed to despair, that old companion of his.

S'd like to speak to my family alone, if you don't mind," said Helena, as the hansom cab turned onto the street where the Duke of Lexington's town house stood.

Her tears had dried; her voice was even enough. Her turmoil she would keep to herself: If this was the bed of nails she'd made, then she would lie on it with all the dignity and impassivity she could muster.

Hastings cast her an inscrutable glance. "I'll wait outside for some time, but no more than ten minutes. And I trust you will sing my praises properly—I am the hero of the day, after all."

He would be heralded as such, wouldn't he? And Andrew, who was guilty of nothing more than the desire to see her, cast as the dastardly villain.

"You will be acknowledged as you deserve," she answered.

As she stood before the door of the town house, she couldn't quite feel the granite beneath her feet or the bell-pull in her hand. Her whole person was numb, except for a dull burning in her heart.

"Right on time, Helena," said Venetia, when Helena was shown into the drawing room, where Venetia had been chatting with Fitz and Millie.

Her raven-haired, blue-eyed, and ineffably beautiful sister was, if possible, even more dazzling than usual. Fitz, though he was Helena's twin, shared Venetia's coloring and bone structure, and had always been considered by Helena's friends as swoon-inducingly gorgeous. As for his wife, Helena vaguely remembered thinking Millie somewhat mousy when they'd first met, but now she couldn't remember why she'd ever thought so, for Millie, petite and fine featured, was extraordinarily lovely in her own way.

"Fitz and Millie were just telling me all about the Lake District." Venetia winked at Helena.

They were all thrilled that Fitz and Millie, who'd known some heartbreaking years, had finally found the happiness they deserved. Without waiting for Helena to respond, Venetia waved her to a chair. "Sit down, my love. I've been bursting to share the news all day. Now that we are at last together in the same place—"

"I—" Helena began.

"The duke and I will be parents soon."

Helena's jaw dropped, as did Millie's. It had long been thought that Venetia was barren. No wonder she had glowed so beatifically of late.

"Congratulations," Helena, Fitz, and Millie shouted in near unison.

But Helena was the first one out of her seat to embrace Venetia. "I'm so happy for you I can scarcely stand it."

A round of hugs and kisses followed, then another round, amidst laughter and squeals of delight.

"Where is Lexington?" asked Fitz. "He ought to be congratulated, too."

"He has decided to arrive a few minutes later, in case there are questions you'd rather not ask in front of him."

Fitz cocked his head. "Such as when the baby is due?"

Venetia blushed slightly. "Yes, that one."

Millie raised a brow. "So, when *is* the baby due?"

"End of the year."

"End of the year? But you've been married only—" Millie covered her mouth. "The duke's mysterious lover during his crossing on the *Rhodesia*—you were *her*!"

"And when you fainted and we had to call in Miss Redmayne, you weren't suffering from some mysterious illness. You were with child!" exclaimed Helena.

"He never knew who I was while we were on the *Rhodesia*. And I never told him until after I found out that I was in a delicate condition."

Helena bit her lip. "My goodness, he must have been furious."

"He was, but we have patched things up rather nicely since then, and we couldn't be more thrilled about the baby."

The duke walked in, a coolly handsome man—and a celebrated naturalist who shared a love of fossils with his wife. "Is it safe for me to join the conversation?"

"Yes, my dear, quite safe."

Fitz offered his hand. "Congratulations, Lexington. Shall we drink to an heir?"

"And to the possibility of a girl as generous and capable as my wife," said Lexington.

Helena's eyes misted. It was a lovely thing to say to a woman who had struggled at times with the possibility that perhaps she was nothing more than a beautiful face. Venetia had chosen well after all.

"Shall I send for champagne—and some champagne cider for Lord Fitzhugh?" asked Lexington.

Fitz abstained entirely from intoxicating beverages and usually contented himself with champagne cider at celebratory occasions.

But before anyone could answer, a footman announced, "Viscount Hastings."

In swept the realities of Helena's life; all the gladness drained from her heart. "Perhaps not just yet," she muttered under her breath. "The champagne, that is."

*F*itz and Lexington both shook hands with Hastings, with Fitz looking openly puzzled.

"I didn't expect to see you until later this evening, David. But I'm glad to see you now."

Hastings glanced at Helena, then at the gathering, perhaps noticing for the first time the general good cheer. "What did I miss?"

"The duke and I will soon be parents," a still giddy-looking Venetia told him.

"My goodness, this is the best news I've heard all day. I shall spoil the child rotten." He kissed Venetia on her cheek and shook hands again with the duke. "Well done, old fellow."

"My pride is nearly infinite," said the duke dryly.

Venetia motioned the gentlemen to sit. "Tomorrow the news will be all over town—ladies Avery and Somersby will do the trumpeting. But we wanted all of you to know first."

"I take it that in the face of your marvelous news, nothing else has been discussed?" asked Hastings.

Helena's stomach tightened. "No."

Hastings glanced at her. "I see that I have arrived too soon."

Fitz, always perceptive, frowned. "What do you mean, David?"

"Do you wish to tell them, Miss Fitzhugh?" asked Hastings, his expression a wall of amiability. "Or shall I?"

The point of no return—they'd come to it all too soon. The dull burn in her heart was now replaced by the sheer void of inevitability. "I assume it will be no surprise to anyone in this room that Mr. Andrew Martin and I have been seeing each other in a manner that would not receive widespread approval."

There was a collective intake of breath. Instantly, the atmosphere turned tense.

"But don't fret. I am still a lily-white virgin."

They'd been surprised by her admission of the affair, but *this* shocked them—especially Hastings, it would seem. Why, did he think she'd be so stupid as to risk a pregnancy? Or that Andrew was so lacking in honor and responsibility?

"But I did something unwise today. I agreed to meet Mr. Martin at the Savoy, not realizing it was a plot by Mrs. Monteth to expose us. I wish to stress that my mobility was not due to negligence on the part of either Bridget or the gentleman who has had the unenviable duty to stand watch beneath Fitzhugh and Company. I played a trick to get free—and walked into Mrs. Monteth's trap."

Millie gripped Fitz's arm. Venetia gripped the armrests. Lexington rounded behind his wife's chair and placed a hand on her shoulder. Only Hastings, now that he'd recovered from his earlier astonishment, seemed entirely unaffected. He sat sprawled in his bergère chair, for all intents and purposes twiddling his thumbs as he waited for her to continue.

"Lord Hastings arrived in the nick of time. To save Mr. Martin, we hid him out of view. To save me, Lord Hastings told Mrs. Monteth and the senior Mrs. Martin that we have eloped."

"Good gracious," mumbled Venetia.

Millie and Fitz exchanged a look.

"It was quick thinking on Lord Hastings's part and I am indebted to him."

The words were grateful enough, but she could not make her voice sound anything other than lifeless, as if she were reading her own obituary aloud.

Hastings crossed his legs at the ankles. "We will, of course, marry as soon as possible. In the meanwhile, it is advisable for Miss Fitzhugh to be addressed as Lady Hastings—and for her to remove to my house today, to keep up the appearance of having eloped. The news of our 'elopement' will spread with the speed of a wildfire; we do not want anyone to question its veracity."

Remove to his house *today*? The possibility had not even occurred to Helena. She'd counted on a few days of privacy, at least, to come to terms with what was to become the rest of her life.

"We will, of course," added Hastings, "conduct ourselves with the utmost decorum."

There was nothing objectionable in his reassurance to her family. All the same, Helena shivered.

Fitz sighed. "Are you sure about this, Helena?"

It dawned on her that he was offering her a choice, letting her know that she did not need to force herself into marriage if it made her unhappy. Tears welled in her eyes. Before they could fall, she blinked and set her face to a blank nonchalance. "By tomorrow morning the news will be all over town—there is nothing to be unsure about anymore. Lord Hastings and I have known each other a long time. We will deal favorably together."

Perhaps her nonchalance wasn't quite nonchalant enough, for a heaviness settled over the room, which only made her angrier with herself for having ruined what should have been a buoyant celebration.

She turned to Venetia. "Enough about Hastings and me. Let's talk more about the baby. And do tell me why ladies Avery and Somersby knew about your condition before we did. I smell something juicy."

CHAPTER 5

*U*nfortunately, the topic of conversation was not so easily changed. Venetia's baby would not need any special consideration until it was born, but Helena's "elopement" was very much a problem that had to be dealt with here and now.

Venetia sent an announcement to the papers right away. Millie and Fitz, who happened to have scheduled a dinner for the following evening, decided they would use the occasion to fete the "newlyweds." Lexington, who'd originally intended to hold only a small house party in August, said he would now open the invitation list and throw in a country ball to mark Hastings's entry into the family.

Their kindness made Helena feel twice as wretched. She'd not only betrayed their trust, she'd done so in the most incompetent manner possible. But they did not censure her; instead, they were throwing their combined influence behind her, so that no one would dare question her actions or her place.

None of it would have been necessary if only she'd—and this was the worst realization of all—if only she'd listened to Hastings's repeated warnings.

When her siblings were at last satisfied that they had a workable strategy, Helena was allowed to leave with Hastings in the duke's best town coach, a large portmanteau of her belongings having already been sent ahead on a lesser vehicle.

"You will need to do better at my house," said Hastings as the carriage rolled away from the curb. "My staff, unlike your family, do not know you have been carrying on with someone else. They will expect far more enthusiasm from a pair of eloped lovers."

He sounded bored, as if the novelty of having her for a wife had already begun to fade. It struck her: In three months' time he'd grow entirely weary of her.

The thought should have brought her relief, yet it filled her with something akin to horror. "I will give every impression of being happy," she said through gritted teeth.

"See that you do. I have a reputation to uphold: I am never seen with reluctant women."

"No, those you save for fiction."

"And closed doors, perhaps," he murmured. "But you won't be reluctant. You'll like it too much, if anything."

Not for the first time did the memories of their kiss resurface in her mind. She had not wanted to acknowledge it then—or ever—but her body had liked his, had enjoyed their contact most mindlessly.

She was afraid of that mindlessness, her own hidden

sybaritic nature that would allow her to be enthralled with the intimate touches of a man whom she disdained intensely.

"Oh, I'm sure I shall enjoy myself well enough by pretending you are someone else." She made her tone cutting.

He flicked away an invisible mote of dust from his shoulder. "Maybe I'll take you only under strong light and with your eyes wide-open."

He raked her with a slow, heavy-lidded glance. A point of infinite heat flared low in her abdomen—while chills spread everywhere else.

*H*elena had stepped into Hastings's town house several times before—he hosted a dinner every Season and her siblings always dragged her along. It was a good house at a fine address, eminently respectable, well proportioned, and it gave an impression of comfort and durability rather than magnificent wealth, even though he did possess a great fortune. Or rather, he'd inherited one; he could have squandered it in the years since, for all she knew.

She entered the house on Hastings's arm. His staff, lined up to congratulate and welcome her, was half bewildered and wholly curious. She acquitted herself with nods and a few half smiles, leaning into him the entire time—and becoming increasingly and uncomfortably aware of his body. Beneath her hand, his arm was hard as granite. From time to time, he placed his hand over hers with a possessive familiarity, the heat of his touch penetrating her glove. And worse, whenever he had something to say, he did so with his lips almost touching her ear, the caress of his breath broiling her nerve endings.

The housekeeper, Mrs. McCormick, informed her that her portmanteau awaited her in her rooms. She seized upon the opportunity to let go of Hastings. "You will excuse me, my dear, won't you? I must see to the placement of my wardrobe."

He lifted her hand and pressed a kiss to her wrist, a very slightly moist kiss that shot a sensation that was almost pain into her arm socket. "Of course, my dear. Do get yourself settled in your new house. I will have supper sent up for us."

She escaped, knowing her reprieve would be brief—that henceforth her reprieves would always be brief. With Mrs. McCormick in front of her, and two upper maids trailing behind, Helena made her way upstairs, her face frozen in an expression of counterfeit pleasure. But as she stepped into her bedroom, that counterfeit pleasure swiftly gave away to a groundswell of genuine delight.

Above the wainscoting, the walls of the room were not papered, but painted. For a disorienting moment, she felt as if she stood upon the rampart of a high castle, surveying her own private kingdom. Green, terraced hillsides sloped away from her, vineyards and orchards in full cultivation. Streams and rivulets tumbled toward a blue, distant lake. Drays piled high with wine barrels and bales of hay wended their way along meandering roads.

On one wall, golden and glowing, the sun peeked just slightly above the horizon. The color of the sky, just like that of dawn—or dusk, for that matter—changed as one's gaze marched across the ceiling, to a twilit blue on the opposite wall, upon which a few faint stars twinkled.

"My goodness," she murmured. "Who painted this?"

"The master, my lady," said Mrs. McCormick.

Helena's pleasure wilted instantly. Not him.

"Very nice," she said stiffly. Then, realizing she sounded insufficiently enamored, she added more truthfully, "Breathtaking."

She spent the next hour with Mrs. McCormick and a pair of upper maids, directing them in the arrangements of the various dresses, blouses, and skirts that had arrived in the portmanteau that Venetia's maid had packed for her—when there was nothing she cared for less now than the whereabouts of her clothes. But she kept at the task doggedly: It was one of those overwhelmingly feminine flurries that kept away any masculine presence.

After there was nothing more to be done for her wardrobe, she bathed and emerged to find her supper. To her surprise, it had not come with Hastings's company. She didn't know whether she was further relieved or insulted.

The food she barely tasted, but the mural she could not help study with a scowling concentration. She supposed she ought not be so surprised. Hastings drew well. No reason he couldn't have also studied oil painting. But the sheer scale of the work, the grandeur and fineness of it, spoke of a dedication she found difficult to ascribe to him.

A sense of déjà vu stole upon her. She was certain she'd never set foot inside this room before. Yet with her initial astonishment fading, the murals began to feel like dear old friends whom she had not seen for quite some years.

The panorama was that of Tuscany, made familiar by Renaissance masters who substituted the vistas of their native country for those of the Holy Land. It wasn't, however, a generic sweep of hills and cypresses. The ocher-colored house with those green-framed windows, where had she seen it before? The same was true of the line of pristine washing, and the small roadside shrine with bouquets of marigolds laid at the Virgin's feet.

A maid entered and took away Helena's plate. Helena repaired to the vanity and ran a brush through her hair. On the vanity was a framed photograph the size of her palm of a small, fair-haired girl in profile. She puzzled over it for a moment before she realized the girl must be Hastings's daughter.

It was, she supposed, commendable enough of him to see to the child's welfare. But at the same time, it infuriated her that he could have so many sins under his belt—the fathering of an illegitimate child with a Cyprian included—and still be accepted in every drawing room in the land. Whereas she had to marry the first man who would have her, or be sundered forever from the bosom of her family.

"Lovely sight," came Hastings's voice.

She glanced sharply at the connecting door. He stood in the doorway in a black dressing gown, one shoulder leaning against the doorjamb.

"It has been a long time since I last saw you with unbound hair."

"You speak of the occasion when I found you loitering outside my window and pushed you off?"

"You were murderous. I could have fallen to my death."

"Instead you lived to enjoy the rosebushes' thorny embrace."

"I must have a yen for thorny embraces—I daresay there is no embrace thornier than yours." He pushed off from the door and stalked toward her. "Let me brush your hair for you."

Her grip tightened on the hairbrush. "No, thank you."

She'd gladly whack him if he dared to take the hairbrush from her hand. But he only walked about her, unsubtly inspecting her from all angles.

She took a deep breath. "Is there something you wish to say to me?"

"Why speak when I can look?"

The slow drawl of his words, the light in his eyes, the closeness of his person . . . Her throat constricted.

He settled a hip on the vanity table. "Actually, let me contradict myself. I do have something to say. What do you mean, you are a virgin?"

She rose and marched to the window to put some distance between them. "What any woman means when she says she is a virgin."

He snorted. "What then were you doing all those nights you spent with Martin?"

"Pleasurable activities that did not impact my virginity."

His brow rose. "Did those pleasurable activities include buggery?"

Another woman might have flushed. She was only further offended. "No."

"I find it inconceivable that Martin has that sort of self-control. How could he have you in his bed and not profit from it?"

"We remained clothed, both of us."

"At your insistence or his?"

"His, but how does it matter?"

"You would have taken them off?"

"Yes, I would have gladly disrobed for the man I love."

He said nothing, but picked up her jar of toilette cream, unscrewed the cap, and dipped a finger inside. She couldn't say why, but the gesture made her face burn.

He rubbed the unguent between his fingers. "Nice. I can probably find some use for it later."

Behind her, her hands gripped the windowsill.

He glanced at her, a heavy-lidded look she felt all the way to her soles. "And you, my dear, will learn to love the idea of disrobing for me."

She was still, her gaze focused somewhere behind him.

Redheads were often characterized as passionate and temperamental. He didn't doubt that she was passionate, but Helena Fitzhugh had always been cool, a woman who liked being firmly in control.

Presently her coolness was almost glacial, sharply contrasted against all that Titian hair spilling down her shoulders and back in soft, gleaming waves. Words usually came easily to him, a versatile, malleable medium to be layered and blended like paint on a palette. Yet when it came to her hair, his mind could not conjure anything more imaginative than *fire* and its various synonyms.

Flame. Blaze. A conflagration to swallow him whole.

Her body, leaning against the windowsill, was elegantly elongated. He used to call her a giraffe to her face, which she'd always taken as an insult. But a giraffe in person was an impossibly beautiful creature, a testament to the Creator's skill and imagination.

78

And just a few hours ago, that body had pressed into his, her fingers plunging into his hair.

"Why?" she asked, snapping him out of his reverie.

He almost couldn't recall what they'd been talking about. "Why learn to love the idea of disrobing for me?"

"No. Why are you involved at all? Were you a more gallant man, I might have understood your action. But you possess not an ounce of chivalry. How does this profit you?"

Everything he did, he did because he loved her. Her entire family knew it, but she was determined to perpetuate her ignorance.

He thought of Millie's advice. She and her husband had been the most affectionate of friends for years, and still she'd hesitated to make her true feelings known. What if she and Fitz had locked horns at every turn? Would she have ever taken her own advice?

"Were your bosom more bountiful, there might have been something in it for me." He shrugged. "Oh well, I trust eventually I will come to enjoy straddling your bony person."

She pulled her lips taut. "For someone with so little interest in my person, you've certainly spent a good deal of time attempting a measure of intimacy."

"It's the nature of man. No one really *wants* to go to the South Pole or cross the Sahara; they just want to see whether it can be done."

"Whether it can be done," she repeated slowly.

"Indeed. Shall we proceed?"

"You will wait until we are, in fact, married," she said coldly.

"Mr. Martin didn't have to wait."

"Mr. Martin didn't actually get to *sleep* with me."

He grinned. "Do to me what you did to him—I should be more than happy enough."

She took a deep breath. "You are a disgusting pig, Hastings."

She'd compared him to far baser entities over the years, but something in her tone struck him. He'd always been a game to her, a somewhat unsavory game, but one she played with finesse and nonchalance. Now, however, she could no longer rap him on the hand and saunter away; now he was her present and her future.

Her dismay was a sharp twist in his heart, a feeling of utter futility. As ever, when he felt trampled, he turned to ever greater frivolity and callousness, those false friends who led him only deeper into despair, but who, at least on the surface, imbued him with an appearance of flippant nonchalance.

"The slings and arrows I suffer for my honesty," he said, barely feeling the words sliding past his lips. "Very well then, I'll settle for a *description* of what you did."

"That is none of your concern."

"It very much is—I have to do those exact same things, don't you see, to wipe away his fingerprints from your body, so to speak."

She smiled, an expression of arctic certainty. "You needn't even try. His fingerprints will always be on my body."

He walked slowly toward her, his height and breadth somehow multiplying with each step, as did his menace. She realized, for the first time in their long acquaintance, that she'd never encountered his anger—hadn't even known it was an emotion he ever encountered in his glib existence.

His voice, however, was utterly velvety—if an upholstered wrecking ball could be called velvety. "I won't need to *try*, my dear. My touch will burn away his."

She couldn't breathe.

"You were always quiet in his bed," he went on, "but you won't be in mine. You will scream with pleasure—and you will do it again and again."

If she gripped the windowsill any harder, she'd break off a piece of it. "If you are quite finished with your theatrics, I am weary and would like to rest—in private."

He loomed over her, his gaze harsh. For a moment she thought he'd flick aside her request and shove her against a wall. But the next moment he shrugged, very much back to being his normal self—the breaking of the tension oddly vacuumlike inside her chest.

"Of course. I wish you a pleasant night's rest. I'm sure one of the maids will be eager to entertain me for a couple of hours in your stead."

Suddenly it was she who was closing in on him, her finger stabbing into his chest. "I can't stop you from pursuing affairs, but I will not tolerate any carrying-on with the staff."

"That is terrible—such a convenient source of gratification, the maids. Why, one doesn't even need to leave the house!"

"You will keep your hands off the maids."

"Fine. What about my housekeeper?"

Mrs. McCormick was rather youngish, only in her late thirties. Helena grimaced. "Not Mrs. McCormick, either."

Hastings sighed, as if his patience were being tested by

an unreasonable toddler. "Can't we make a bargain? You can have a go at my grooms while I dally with the maids— provided I get to watch, of course."

She hoped he was jesting. But Hastings was such a swine, it was quite possible that he indeed hoped for such a debauched tableau.

"No. Nor with your footmen, your coachmen, your gardeners, nor anyone else in or out of your employ."

"My God, you are turning into Mrs. Monteth."

"Don't compare me to that harpy—I am not interested in exposing you. But I will protect the staff from your predation."

She'd not quite realized it, but she'd been advancing against him and he'd been moving backward, and now they were both back where they'd started, at the vanity table, where she was greeted with the image of his daughter, looking small and meek in her photograph.

The poor girl, growing up in such a salacious household.

"When do I meet Miss Hillsborough?"

He looked nonplussed at the sudden change of topic— and, for once, genuinely surprised. "My daughter, you mean? You wish to meet her?"

"Of course I wish to meet her. Henceforth I am responsible for her upbringing."

"You've never asked about her before."

"Your illegitimate child is not a subject considered suitable for an unmarried woman to broach. But that is not her fault, only yours. She is approaching an age when she will be in dire need of good guidance—or at least of being spared the sight of you copulating with her nanny."

"I don't copulate with Bea's nanny—not in front of her,

82

in any case. It bores her terribly and rather spoils my mood when she keeps asking when I'll be finished."

His shallowness and frivolity were fully back to the fore. She didn't know whether to be relieved or confused. "When do I meet her?"

"We can leave London as soon as your brother's dinner takes place—in any case, it will look odd should we continue to remain in town."

"That will be satisfactory enough. Good night, Lord Hastings."

He nodded. "Lady Hastings."

But at the connecting door he turned back. "An experienced virgin, my dear—you are a dream come true. I shall think of you all night long."

You never sleep in your own bed anymore," Millie teased Fitz.

Her lovely face and sweet eyes—he could not get enough of looking at her. He lifted a strand of her hair and brought it to his lips. "What a shame. And I like my own bed so well, too."

She waggled an eyebrow. "I have an idea: From time to time we can both sleep in your bed."

He brushed the tip of her nose with the ends of her own hair and lifted a brow back at her. "Does that mean you will actually come into my chamber at night, undress me, and demand satisfaction?"

She trailed a finger down the center of his torso. "I thought I already did that—twice—when we were on holiday."

"That there will be a third time still astonishes me—for

almost eight years you said nothing about how fervently you wished to seduce me."

"All the more reason for me to do it as often and as brazenly as possible."

He laughed softly. "Shall I tell you again how complete my happiness is?"

She rubbed the inside of her wrist against the beginning of his stubble. "Even with Helena almost ruined today?"

"You are not still blaming yourself, are you?"

"Let me assure you, lover dearest, that having gone to America and back, and dragged Helena all over town this Season just so she was never left alone, I don't feel as guilty as I probably ought. My mother used to say, 'There is no stopping a determined mischief maker.'"

"And your mother, bless her memory, was always right."

"But I am worried. Helena will want to ignore Hastings to the best of her ability. And Hastings . . . he'd rather be buried alive than be ignored."

Fitz shook his head. "Those two. I'll have a word with him tomorrow."

"I already had a word with him in the last telegram I sent—I don't suppose he took my advice to heart."

"You would no more have followed the same advice had he given it to you a few weeks ago."

"True, but I've changed. Now I will openly admit my true feelings, which are that"—she cleared her throat playfully—"I am resolutely committed to being the joy and the light at the center of your existence."

He couldn't help smiling: How fortunate he was, how privileged, to have her tonight and always. "Come here, Joy-and-Light," he murmured. "Let me hold you with both arms."

* * *

*H*astings very much wished to bang his head on a bedpost. Another time he might have done so, but Helena was in the next room. Should she hear any suspicious sounds coming from his direction, she'd immediately assume that he'd defied her edict and was rutting with a housemaid in a deliberately noisy fashion. He was almost tempted to make his bed squeak, just to see whether she'd kick down his door in anger.

This was not at all how he'd imagined it would be when he finally had her in the mistress's room. At this point in the night, after having exhausted themselves making love, they should have been snuggled under the covers, whispering and giggling like children, telling each other naughty jokes, describing slightly impossible sexual feats they planned to try as soon as they'd regained their breath.

That future was not supposed to feel more distant than ever.

CHAPTER 6

$\mathcal{H}$astings had instructed his staff not to trouble their new mistress until eight o'clock in the morning. But she was awake at the crack of dawn, moving about in her room—so close, yet so inaccessible.

He bathed, dressed, and entered her room after a quick knock. She wasn't in the bedroom, but in her sitting room, standing before a shelf of books in a visiting gown, examining the titles on the spines. Each title had been chosen either because she'd expressed a preference for it, or because he'd inferred, based on what he knew of her tastes, that it would meet with her approval.

Indeed, when she turned around at the sound of his approach, she wore a small frown of disorientation. "Who put these books here?"

He shrugged. "Who knows? The study probably became

too crammed and the staff used the shelf to house the overflow."

"I see." She set back the book of Sappho's poems that had been in her hand. "And what are you doing here?"

"I thought it would not be amiss to exchange a cordial greeting the morning after our wedding night—and to sacrifice a few drops of my blood to the sheets to preserve your reputation."

"I already did that."

"Did you?"

"Go look for yourself."

He reentered her bedroom, lifted the covers, and grimaced at the drops of blood smeared onto the sheets. "It would look like this only if your hymen had been broken with a knife."

She appeared in the doorway. "What do you mean?"

"When a hymen is disposed of by a cock, as it usually is, there is never just blood on the sheets."

"There is nothing I can do about that."

"I suppose I must do something about it, contribute my share to the stains."

The corners of her lips turned down in distaste. "Suit yourself. I am going out."

"Where are you going at this early hour?"

"To call on my family. They would like to know that married life has not disagreed too terribly with me—and I will lie accordingly."

Something in her demeanor made him ask, "And then?"

She barely glanced at him, speaking to the doorjamb. "And then I plan to meet with Mr. Martin. At the offices of Fitzhugh and Company, preferably. At his home, if necessary."

He felt as if he'd been slapped. "To finish what you didn't have time for yesterday?"

"Mr. Martin will be worried about me. He will be blaming himself. I'd like to assure him that I am fine, public marriage notwithstanding."

"He *ought* to blame himself. If he'd kept to his word, you would not be in your current predicament."

"And if he did not, it was only because I convinced him otherwise."

"Why do you keep taking responsibility for his actions?"

"I care about him and will therefore do my utmost to ensure his happiness, a concept I am sure is entirely alien to you."

"One that is no less alien to Mr. Martin. What has he ever done for your happiness? And think carefully before you answer. His acquiescence to your wishes—and he acquiesces to everyone's wishes—does not constitute effort on his part."

He was glad to see a flicker of doubt in her eyes, but when she spoke again, her tone was as firm as ever. "I will decide whether Mr. Martin has done enough for me."

"And I will decide," he heard himself say, "whether a woman who arranges to see the man who compromised her isn't too stupid and morally adrift to meet my daughter, let alone be an influence in her life."

*H*astings sat slumped in Fitz's study, his hand over his eyes.

Fitz, thank goodness, drank his coffee and left Hastings alone.

For about a quarter hour or so.

"All right, David, enough moping," said Fitz, setting down his coffee cup.

Reluctantly, Hastings removed his hand from his face and sat up straighter. "I haven't formally congratulated you, have I, Fitz, on making the right choice in your marriage and being blessedly happy as a result?"

Fitz smiled. "Thank you. Although, looking back, it wasn't just one choice, but the accumulation of many choices."

Hastings sighed. "I'm afraid the same can be said about Helena and me, years of less than stellar conduct on my part, continuing to this very moment."

"My wife would have you confess your love at the earliest opportunity and be done with it. But if you are reluctant to do that—and something tells me you are—then it might not be a bad idea to simply stop antagonizing Helena.

"I know she makes you lose your mind, but at our age, that is no longer a good enough excuse. If you want her admiration, you cannot keep aiming for her abhorrence. Let her ignore you. Give her time. Show her that you are more than merely an assemblage of insults and innuendos in bespoke boots."

Hastings chuckled despite himself. "You are right, of course. And I needed the chastening."

"Patience, my friend," said Fitz. "Rome wasn't built in—"

A knock came.

"Yes?" answered Fitz.

Cobble, Fitz's butler, bowed slightly. "Sir, Mr. Andrew Martin to see you, sir. Are you at home to him?"

*M*y poor girl," said Venetia, Duchess of Lexington, standing at the window of her drawing room and watching Helena's carriage pull away from the curb.

"She did seem quite defeated." Her husband placed his hand on the small of her back. "Not that she wasn't strenuously trying to convince us of the opposite."

"I hope the dinner tonight won't be too taxing for her." She wrapped her arm around his middle. "And thank you, darling, for offering your place in the Highlands for their honeymoon."

"They can have legendary rows there without anyone knowing," said Lexington dryly. "Besides, I'm quite fond of your sister—if it weren't for her shenanigans, you'd never have been at Harvard to hear my lecture. So if there is ever anything I can do for her, *mein Liebling*, you have but to say the word."

"Hmm." Venetia rubbed her cheek against the summer wool of his day coat. "I'm not sure what more we can do for *her* right now, other than to wait and see. But, my goodness, there is much that can be done for *me*, the delicate, expectant mother, thrust into the middle of such demanding circumstances."

"Ah," he said, a smile in his voice. "Do you know, I did receive a letter from the British Museum of Natural History yesterday afternoon. But with our entire evening consumed with your sister's fate, I'd forgotten all about it."

Her heart thumped with excitement. She was very, very fond of the British Museum of Natural History. "Really? What does your letter say?"

"Only that a shipment of tremendous saurian fossils have just arrived and they'd be pleased to let us have a private viewing. Shall I send a note and have them expect us at ten o'clock?"

"Yes. *Yes*," she said. "Nothing pleases and soothes a delicate, expectant mother like crates upon crates of enormous dinosaur remains."

He laughed. "I never thought I'd have a wife who is more excited about going to the British Museum of Natural History than I."

"And aren't you glad of it, darling." She kissed him full on the lips. "Now go write that note, Your Grace. And I will get ready as fast as I can."

*M*artin had come to self-flagellate. He was everything a penitent ought to be, humble, contrite, accepting of all blame. But Hastings was unimpressed. Martin should never have crossed the line in the first place. Then, after giving his word to Fitz, he should never have crossed the line again.

Or perhaps, reflected Hastings grimly, he was only angry because the next time Martin relapsed, he'd be lying with Hastings's wife.

Martin was still talking. "Miss—Lady Hastings was adamant that I not make decisions on her behalf. She asked me to have a care not only for her reputation, but for her happiness. I was terribly conflicted. On the one hand, I'd given my word to you, sir. On the other hand, I'd also given my word to her, earlier, that I'd do everything in my power to make her happy. And here she was, demanding that I honor that promise. When I received a cable that seemed to be from her, I'm afraid her words—rather than yours—were the ones that rang loudest in my ears."

He stopped, biting his lips and seemingly trying to

gauge Fitz's and Hastings's reactions. Hastings said nothing; Martin had not come to see him.

"I cannot approve of your action any more than I can approve of my sister's," said Fitz. "I can only hope that the fact that together you've brought real consequences to her is rebuke enough to you, Mr. Martin."

Fitz's words were not kind, but they were just. Martin's face turned beet red. Hastings looked away. He took no pleasure in Martin's mortification. In fact, he felt almost as uncomfortable as Martin, at being "the real consequences" that had befallen Helena.

"But what is done is done," continued Fitz. "My sister will be Lady Hastings—as salvageable an outcome as could have happened under the circumstances. I trust you will be the soul of discretion on the matter."

"Of course, of course." Martin all but bowed and scraped. "And many congratulations to you, Lord Hastings."

Hastings declined to respond. Martin, ever more red-faced, mumbled a round of good days and showed himself out.

Hastings unclenched his fist. "What a wretch."

Fitz sighed. "A wretch he may be, but remember, David, he is not what stands in your way. You are."

*H*elena had just alighted before Fitz's house when she saw Andrew disappearing around the bend. Her heart prickled with a hot pain. She picked up her skirt and started after him, only to have someone grip her by the arm.

"Let him go," said Hastings. "It's hardly becoming for my wife to chase another man in the streets."

"You've only yourself to blame for that. Mr. Martin and I could have met in a civilized manner, but you had to blackmail me with your daughter. So if you think I won't exploit an accidental meeting, you should be run over by an omnibus for your stupid arrogance."

She yanked her arm free and ran, bittersweet memories flashing before her eyes: Andrew's long-ago shy confession that someday he hoped to author a book worthy of being published by her; a shower of pressed flowers falling out of his letter to land at her feet, one for every day they'd been apart; walking along the Norfolk coast, Andrew telling her that it was his heart's fondest wish to still amble those rough, beautiful cliffs with her when he was an old man, and, when they were too decrepit to walk, to be carried there in chairs to sit hand in hand as they gazed out to the North Sea.

She rounded the street corner but could not see him. Then, as if she'd conjured him, he materialized on the opposite side of the road.

She raced into the street, trying her best not to shout his name aloud. He was walking slowly. She was closing the distance between them. But he'd yet to become aware of her.

And now he was. He turned around. There were shouts. He, too, shouted, his face contorting with horror.

All too late she saw that she was directly in the path of a carriage-and-four. The coachman tried desperately to rein in his horses, but already those in the front reared, their screeches lost in the general din.

The last thing she saw was a hoof the size of a dinner plate coming directly at her face.

CHAPTER 7

*T*he silence choked Hastings.

Compared to the chaos and black fear of the morning—on his knees before Helena's inert body, the scent of her blood pungent in his nostrils, the shouts of the gathering crowd surging like his panic, the screams of the still shying horses piercing his ears—this quiet and order should have seemed a paradise.

And it had for a while. After she'd been brought back to Fitz's house under Miss Redmayne's supervision, after the dining room had been made into an emergency surgery for stitching the wound in her scalp, after Miss Redmayne assured everyone that her life was not in immediate danger, still shaking, but relieved beyond measure, Hastings had sat down to wait for her to wake up.

And waited. And waited. And waited.

He'd waved away offers of elevenses, luncheon, and tea—this last twice. The third time Millie set the tray down on his lap and ordered him in no uncertain terms to eat or be ejected from her house.

Helena, her face bruised and swollen, her head wrapped in white gauze, lay quietly. Much too quietly. From time to time Venetia, her teeth clenched over her lower lip, would lift her wrist and feel her pulse. They'd all tense—and breathe again only when Venetia nodded, signaling that all was still, if not well, then at least no worse.

Someone came to take the tea tray from Hastings. He had no idea whether he'd eaten anything or merely guarded the tray for a while. Fitz sat with his hand gripping his wife's. Venetia, still wearing the mismatched shoes in which she'd arrived in the morning, had one hand on her husband's sleeve, the other around a handkerchief.

There had been a burst of conversation following the first "Shouldn't she be awake by now?" They'd grilled the nurse Miss Redmayne had stationed in the room. The nurse assured them that Miss Redmayne had not used any narcotics, only a surface analgesic. There was no morphia or opium in Lady Hastings's body, holding her consciousness hostage. But yes, she had most certainly suffered a concussion, so perhaps the wait would be slightly more extensive?

For the past hour, no one had spoken a single word.

"Would anyone mind if I read to her?" Hastings broke the silence at last.

There were no responses for a moment; then Venetia dabbed her eyes with her handkerchief and said, "Go ahead."

He was seated next to the small shelf Helena kept in her room. Her clothes had been taken to his house, but the possessions that truly mattered to her, her books, had stayed behind. He pulled out the book nearest him, moved his chair to the side of the bed, and began to read.

he question is often asked, "Shall I go to the expense of having my manuscript typewritten?" Yes, most decidedly. The advantages that writing by machinery possesses over the old method of pen writing are numerous. First, there is increased speed. Ordinary penmanship becomes illegible when twenty to thirty words a minute is exceeded. With the typewriter, fifty to sixty-five words a minute can be accomplished and kept up for several hours without the operator becoming afflicted with "writer's cramp." A clear saving of forty minutes in the hour means money gained.'"

"She wrote the book herself, you said?" Lexington asked.

Hastings nodded. "And published it end of last year, to advise writers concerning the inner workings of publishing."

He'd mocked her for it, as he'd done with every one of her endeavors, telling her that if all she wanted was a publisher for herself, there were easier ways to go about it than forming her own publishing concern.

It boggled the mind that he'd thought it possible for her to fall in love with him, when he'd never been anything but the embodiment of vile smugness.

He glanced at her. She hadn't made so much as a whimper in the nearly ten hours since she'd been brought back into her room. Was she dreaming or was her mind altogether elsewhere?

" 'Secondly, in addition to this great increase of speed is the combined legibility and boldness of typewritten matter as compared with the most copperplate handwriting. Thirdly, by using carbon paper, from two to seven copies can be taken at one operation, twenty by using flimsy, and two to three thousand by a stencil process.' "

"I didn't know that," said Millie. "What else does Helena talk about in this book?"

"Advertising, the entirety of the production process, and all the various means of cost and profit sharing."

Venetia dabbed at her eyes again. "She is very good at her profession, isn't she?"

"Helena has always been good at everything she does," said Fitz, his own eyes glistening with unshed tears.

They were speaking of her in present tense—of course they were. But to Hastings's ears their words seemed to carry every characteristic of a eulogy. He felt like a hollow shell, nothing inside but fear.

"I'm sorry," said Millie. "I didn't mean to disrupt your reading, Hastings. By all means, continue."

He rubbed the heel of his hand across his forehead. "She should have awakened."

"It wasn't just Miss Redmayne who said her life is not in immediate danger," Venetia reminded him, even though anxiety tinged her own voice. "Fitz's physician, Lexington's, and your own—they've all said the same thing."

He knew what they'd said—words that meant nothing to the fear inside.

"There is someone very well spoken of in Paris for this kind of trauma," Lexington said quietly. "Shall I cable him?"

Hastings turned gratefully in Lexington's direction. "I

would be most obliged, sir. I'd like to know that we are doing everything possible for her."

Chances were the Parisian fellow would not be of any more help than the London doctors. But sending for him would give the illusion of action and alleviate the futility of waiting.

"I will compose a telegram," said Lexington. "May I have use of pen and paper, Lord Fitzhugh?"

"Call me Fitz. I'll show you to my study. And, Venetia, why don't you come down with us? You haven't eaten anything all day—that can't be good for the baby. Millie, you, too."

"I'll stay here," said Hastings. "I'm still full from my tea."

Fitz clasped a hand over Hastings's shoulder. "We'll be back soon."

The room emptied, except for the nurse. "Would you care for a bit of supper, Nurse Jennings?" Hastings asked.

"Oh, no, thank you, your lordship, I had a plentiful tea," replied Nurse Jennings. She had a deep, scratchy voice. "But . . . if your lordship don't mind, I could do with a few minutes of fresh air."

"I don't mind at all."

"I won't be but five minutes."

When Nurse Jennings had gone, his gaze returned to Helena. "I think Nurse Jennings was hurting for a cigarette."

She remained as silent and still as Sleeping Beauty, caught in a cursed slumber.

"Wake up, Helena. *Wake up.*"

Not a muscle moved in her face.

He fought back sudden tears and looked down at the

book in his hands. "I've—I've lost my place. What do you want to hear? The section on advertisements to be placed in the books? The use and abuse of reviews? Trade prices and discounts?"

It didn't matter, of course. She already knew everything—they were her words, her expertise. He only thought—idiotic of him—that she would hate the smothering silence as much as he did.

He took hold of her hand. "Come, wake up. Tell me to keep my hand to myself. Tell me to get out of your room. Tell me to—"

This time he could no longer hold back his tears. And with them came words that he'd never been able to say to her his entire life. "I love you, Helena. I have always loved you. Wake up and let me prove it to you."

*T*wenty-four hours later, she was still unconscious. The bruises on her face had turned purple and green. The swelling had gone down, but her cheeks and firmly closed eyes were beginning to look sunken—they'd not been able to feed her much, not even water.

She'd always been slender, but there had been an energetic strength to her—a presence that was greater than her size. Now, for the first time since he'd met her, she looked frail, as if she might float away without the bedcover keeping her in place.

Hastings stood in a corner of the room, his arms crossed, one shoulder against the wall. He'd finished reading her book on publishing. He'd read the entirety of the day's newspaper. He'd grown quite weary of the sound of his own voice.

Venetia was out in the passage, weeping in her husband's arms. Fitz's eyes were red-rimmed, as were Millie's. Hastings hadn't cried again, but he had taken to drinking quantities of strong spirits out of Fitz's view—Fitz had warned Hastings not to bring a bottle near him, as he hadn't been so tempted in years.

More of London's best physicians had been in to see her, as well as the expert from Paris. They all said the same thing: The family must wait and see. Lexington had summoned another expert from Berlin; Hastings doubted the fellow would have a different diagnosis to offer.

From time to time she shivered and mumbled, and they'd all rush to the edges of her bed, calling her name in unison, willing her to awaken. But invariably, as if caught in the sticky grip of a nightmare, she'd sink back into the void that incarcerated her. Ice and heat had both been tried. Venetia and Millie rubbed her hands and forearms. Once, Venetia, feeling desperate, even slapped Helena, only to burst into tears herself.

Miss Redmayne had pulled the family aside and spoken to them of the need to start tube feeding her, should her coma persist. Hastings had listened with what had seemed to him tremendous stoicism. Only later did he realize he had been shaking.

He'd known a few medical students during his time at Oxford. On long-ago nights of drinking and merrymaking, they used to regale him with the more outlandish aspects of their knowledge. Tube feeding involved the insertion of a tube lubricated with glycerin inside the patient's nostril. He'd laughed then at the oddity of such a procedure; now the thought of it terrified him.

Because *she* would be terrified. And she had to know,

somehow. Imprisoned inside her mind, she must be beating at the bars to get out, to be once again mistress of her own fate.

And while they could keep her alive, her muscles would waste away from inactivity. She would become a breathing corpse, someone whose biological functions persisted even though the spirit had fled.

Out in the passage Lexington was gently calming Venetia—persuading her to take a few hours of rest, if only for the sake of the baby. And she was reluctantly agreeing. Inside the room, Fitz and Millie sat shoulder to shoulder on a small chaise, holding on to each other.

Hastings's own fear was riddled with regret. No more. No more lies. No more cowardice. No more hiding his true sentiments behind mockery and derision. If she'd only awaken, he would become a man worthy of her.

If she'd only awaken.

He read her *Alice's Adventures in Wonderland* and gave each character a different voice.

The White Rabbit babbled in a high-pitched squeak. The Cheshire Cat purred languorously. The Queen of Hearts brayed with impetuosity and high passion. Alice herself he made impish, with a touch of both bravado and naïveté.

He didn't know why he bothered. Helena had shown no sign of having heard a single word he'd uttered. But he did it all the same.

At the end of a chapter, Fitz asked, "Are you not tired, David? Your voice must be worn-out."

His voice *was* worn-out, but he shook his head. "I'm

all right. I don't want her to feel as if we are sitting here in a silent vigil."

"We have not been a cheerful bunch, have we?" Fitz sighed. "Thank you, David. None of the rest of us would have read half as well."

"More like none of us can read a quarter as well," Venetia corrected him.

Hastings closed the book. By now Helena must have sickened of his voice—she'd never have consented to listen to him for hours on end if it weren't for her incapacity. He only wished she could have told him to shut up herself.

"Go have your supper, all of you," he said to the gathering. "Especially you, Duchess, you should be eating for two."

There was a round of desultory agreement. "Come with?" said Fitz.

"I had mine two hours ago. You go on without me."

When her family had gone downstairs, he asked Nurse Jennings whether she'd care for some fresh air. Nurse Jennings agreed readily and made haste to rendezvous with her cigarette.

He took Helena's hand in his and brushed his fingers against the uninjured side of her face.

"It will be a gloomy supper downstairs," he told her. "I'm not sure whether you heard the conversation earlier. We've been giving you water and bits of mush, but that's not enough to sustain you. Tomorrow morning they will administer the tube."

He had to take a deep breath before he could continue. "I told them this is not you, Helena. You will not allow yourself to remain in this vegetative state. You will come around. You will speak; you will walk; you will dance.

You will publish a thousand more books. You will live life as it is meant to be lived, on your feet, making your own decisions.

"Wake up, my love. I have loved you for a very long time, and you have never been anything but supremely obstinate. I need you to be more obstinate than you've ever been, Helena. Wake up. Everything depends upon it—my entire life included."

CHAPTER 8

*S*omeone was using a chisel on Helena's skull. She winced and slowly opened her eyes. A plaster medallion greeted her sight—a plaster medallion three feet across in diameter embedded in an unfamiliar ceiling.

Where was she? At a relative's house? Did her Norris cousins have such a ceiling? Or her Carstairs cousins? She tried to sit up, but her body was heavy and unwieldy, and it took a surprising amount of effort to raise herself to her elbows. The strain hurt her shoulders; the movement made her head throb harder.

The source of illumination in the room was a wall sconce that had been covered with dark paper. She stared at this light—there was something odd about it: It didn't flicker, but burned with a disconcerting steadiness. Was she—was she looking at an *electric* light?

Surely not. Electric lights were what inventors demonstrated to curious crowds, not something to be found in an ordinary dwelling.

She forgot about the oddity of the sconce when she realized that she was not alone. A woman in a green dressing gown slept with her head and her folded arms on the edge of Helena's bed. Venetia. But she looked . . . older. Quite a bit older.

Behind Venetia was a man Helena had never seen before, sleeping in a chair, his shoulder leaning against the side of a wardrobe. Helena recoiled in alarm and was just about to shake Venetia's arm when she saw another man dozing with his head tilted back, on a small chaise opposite the bed.

Her mouth opened wide as she recognized *Fitz*. The difference in his appearance was stark. His face, covered with dark stubble—stubble!—had elongated and sharpened from what she recalled. He no longer looked like the boy she remembered, but a man well into his twenties. To compound her shock, a woman was on the chaise with him, sleeping with her arm around his knees, her head on his *thighs*.

Was she still *dreaming*?

She must have made some sound, a whimper perhaps, at the prodigious strangeness of the tableau before her. Her family remained asleep, but a figure in the corner she hadn't noticed before stirred. The person rose and stepped toward the bed. Another man—was there no end to the irregularity of the situation?

His clothes were crumpled, his necktie unknotted. He was unshaven, his hair longish and messy, blond curls that hadn't known the comb for a while. And there were circles under his eyes, as if he hadn't slept for days.

"Helena," he said softly. "You are awake."

His voice was oddly familiar. But as she had no idea who he was, she couldn't possibly have granted him the intimacy of addressing her by her Christian name. She was about to demand his identity—and chastise him for his boldness—when Fitz's voice came, still slow with sleep. "You are already awake, David? What time is it?"

Helena turned toward him. "What is going on, Fitz? Why do you look—"

"My God, Helena!" Fitz sprang up before he remembered the woman on his lap. He shook her. "Millie, Millie, wake up. Helena is awake."

The woman bolted upright, nearly banging into his chin. "What? What did you say?"

Fitz was already pulling her to her feet, dragging her to the edge of the bed. He grabbed hold of Helena's hand. The fine-boned, fine-featured woman he called Millie wrapped her own fingers around their clasped hands.

Her eyes shone with tears. "We were so worried. I cannot tell you how happy I am you've come to."

Helena was shocked to see that Fitz's eyes—at least his eyes still looked the same—were also damp. And he seemed utterly incapable of speech. Her stomach twisted. "What is the mat—"

Before she could finish her question, Venetia squealed. "Helena! My goodness, Helena! Christian, she's awake!"

The man behind Venetia, whom she'd called by his given name, stood up from his seat to help Venetia rise. He smiled at Helena. "Welcome back."

"Welcome back, indeed," echoed Millie.

They all seemed to know her very well. Why didn't she know them in return?

"I would hug you so hard, my love, if I weren't afraid of hurting you," said Venetia, taking Helena's other hand. "Shall we put a few pillows behind your back so you can be more comfortable?"

"That won't be quite necessary." The very thought of having to move made her stomach protest. "Would someone please tell me what is going on?"

Venetia's hand went to her throat. "My goodness, you don't remember?"

"Remember what?"

"Your accident, of course."

Accident? She looked about her and noticed yet another woman in a corner—this one in a nurse's cap and uniform. Were the other men in the room physicians? The one Venetia had called Christian certainly had that air of cool competence about him. She glanced toward the one named David. He stared at her as if she were the Koh-i-Noor itself, a thing of infinite beauty and worth.

She looked away, discomfited and perhaps just a little flattered—for all his dishevelment, he was not an unattractive man. "When was this accident? And what kind of accident are we speaking of?"

"A carriage accident," Fitz answered. "It happened three days ago and you've been unconscious ever since. We were beginning to wonder"—his voice caught—"whether you would ever wake up again."

The accident would explain all her pains and discomforts. A three-day coma was a decent reason for tears and high emotions upon her reawakening. But it still didn't account for the familiarity with which all these strangers treated her; nor was it reason enough for Fitz and Venetia to have aged ten years overnight.

"It's probably a good thing you don't remember," said Millie. "It was a horrible accident. My goodness, when I saw you lying in the middle of the street, blood from your head soaking into the stone dust, I thought—"

Her lips quivered. Fitz handed her his handkerchief. "It's all right. Everything will be all right now."

"Of course." Millie wiped her eyes. "Please excuse me."

Venetia was dabbing at her own eyes. The man named Christian had his hand on her shoulder.

Helena could no longer contain her bewilderment, which was beginning to congeal into a cold, knotted sensation that was not unlike fear. She didn't know whether she ought to demand the reason why her siblings had aged so much before company, so she asked, "Venetia, Fitz, would you please perform the introductions? I'd like to meet our guests."

Her request caused a long moment of communal gaping, followed by dismayed glances among the five people surrounding her bed, which only made her stomach clench with premonition.

"We are not guests," said Millie. "We are your family."

Helena hadn't thought she'd *like* the answer she'd receive, but she had not anticipated that it would turn incipient fear into outright fright. She bolted straight up, ignoring the pain in her head and the roiling in her stomach caused by her abrupt motion, and tried to arrive at a logical explanation. Were they distant cousins? Or perhaps . . . "Did I meet everyone just before my accident? My mind is quite blank concerning that time period."

"No, no." Millie shook her head hard, as if the force of her denial could make a difference in the matter.

"We—you and I—met eight years ago at Lord's, at the Eton and Harrow cricket match."

Helena's father had been a cricket enthusiast. The entire family had attended several Eton and Harrow matches with him, but she had no recollection of ever meeting this Millie. "I'm sorry. I must have forgotten. I imagine we have not seen much of each other since?"

Millie looked aghast. Helena felt her heart sink—she wasn't sure she wanted to hear what Millie might say. Millie, it seemed, shared her reluctance. She looked at Fitz, who looked thunderstruck, before turning her gaze back to Helena.

"We have seen a great deal of each other since, Helena. I am your sister-in-law."

Helena gripped the sheets. But this was preposterous. "You are *married*, Fitz? When did you marry?"

"Eight years ago." Fitz's words were almost ghostly in their feebleness.

"Eight *years* ago? What year is it now?"

"Eighteen ninety-six," said Millie.

Eighteen ninety-six? No wonder Fitz *looked* like a man well into his twenties—he *was* a man well into his twenties. And Helena, born on the same day as he, a woman well into her twenties.

She shook her head, trying to settle her careening, incoherent thoughts. But the movement instead caused a sharp thrust of nausea. She gritted her teeth and turned to Venetia. "Is the gentleman next to you your husband?"

"Yes," said Venetia quietly.

"And have you also been married a long time?"

"No, we married only this Season."

An uneasy silence descended. Helena's agitation began

to scale dizzying new heights as, one by one, her siblings and their spouses looked toward David, who appeared, if possible, even more stunned than they were.

"What about David?" Fitz sounded as if he were pleading. "Surely you remember him—you've known him half your life."

She stared at this David, a tall man with elegant bone structure: etched cheekbones, a sharp jawline, and a nose that would have been almost too perfectly straight if it hadn't been broken a time or two—a face she would not mind looking at had she encountered it at a gathering. But she didn't want him *here*, a stranger granted intimacy, a man who expected her to know him.

"And how are *we* related, sir?"

Her stomach churned as she braced herself for the answer.

He glanced toward Fitz. An unspoken message passed between them. He looked back at Helena, inhaled deeply, and spoke with the sort of care one might use to inform a child that her puppy was no more. "The world knows me as your husband."

Precisely the answer she was hoping not to hear. Her stomach churned even more violently. She clamped down on her lower lip, willing her body to settle down and leave her alone. But the nausea only surged.

She yanked aside her bedcover. "Gentlemen, please clear the room. I'm going to be quite sick."

*W*ith her sister and sister-in-law supporting her, and the nurse trailing behind, Helena made it to the water closet barely in time.

"Sorry," she mumbled, when she'd finished ejecting the contents of her stomach. She hadn't felt so physically miserable since the bout of scarlet fever she'd suffered when she was nine. And she hadn't felt so emotionally miserable since—

She didn't know what to compare her experience to. It had been terrible losing her parents, but at least she had been able to share her grief with her siblings. But this . . . this waking up to find that half of her life had been wiped from her mind and that she was now saddled with a husband she could not remember meeting, let alone choosing— she felt utterly rudderless.

"My poor darling," said Millie as she placed the cover on the blue-enameled commode and pulled the cord to flush.

Venetia was already escorting Helena to the washstand. "Miss Redmayne had said that you might experience nausea and vomiting when you awakened—those are common enough symptoms for people who've suffered a concussion."

"Miss Redmayne is our physician," added Millie helpfully. "She is on her way as we speak."

A woman physician? Helena certainly approved, but she'd had no idea that there were now enough women physicians for the Fitzhugh ladies to have one.

A mirror hung above the washstand. She recoiled at her appearance: Half of her face was bruised, the discoloration almost greenish in color. Still she couldn't help staring: She didn't in the very least *feel* like a child, but how strange—and thrilling, in a way—to suddenly see her own grown-up face.

She covered her mouth. In a gap between the bandaging, she could clearly see her scalp. "What happened to my hair?"

"Miss Redmayne had to shave it in order to stitch the wound on your head," answered Millie.

"All of it?" Her question was a whimper. Fate seemed needlessly cruel.

"Your hair will grow back." Venetia's eyes reddened. "When I think that you could have died on the spot . . ."

Millie patted Venetia's arm. "You mustn't torment yourself with thoughts of what didn't happen. You'll get in a state and it wouldn't be good for the baby."

A *baby*? Helena spun around—and had to grip Millie's shoulder to steady herself. "You are with child?"

"Yes."

She glanced down at Venetia's middle. "You don't look it."

"I still have months and months to go. In fact, we'd just told everyone the good news the night before your accident."

The accident.

Abruptly, everything Helena didn't know about her family closed in around her, a suffocating ignorance. "Do you have any other children, Venetia? Do you, Millie—you don't mind that I call you Millie, do you?"

Before either one of them could give an answer, a fist of panic struck her. "Dear *God*, do *I* have any children?"

"ot the most auspicious of new beginnings, is it?" muttered Hastings.

It was as if some part of her remembered exactly who he was and how much she could not stand him.

He and Fitz were alone in the passage outside her door. Lexington had gone to compose a cable to the *Herr Doktor* from Berlin, informing the latter that his services were no longer required, but that he would be compensated for his time and expenses, should he have already started his journey to London.

"Miss Redmayne told us that she'd be prone to nausea and vomiting upon awakening," Fitz pointed out reasonably. "You know that."

Hastings supposed he did. He sighed. "At least she is awake now. Thank God for that."

If only he could quite comprehend the fact that he was now a complete stranger to her.

Millie came out of the room. "How is she?" Fitz and Hastings asked in unison.

"Back in bed, but already asking the nurse when she will be free of medical supervision."

"She never likes supervision of any sort, does she?" said Fitz. "What about her memory?"

"She was grilling us—she is still grilling Venetia as we speak. She doesn't remember being a publisher. Or attending university. Or Venetia's first two marriages. We've been informing her of the major events of her life and ours."

"What about Andrew Martin?" asked Fitz, saving Hastings the trouble.

"She hasn't brought him up, but I would be quite shocked if she remembered him alone when she has forgotten everything else."

Hastings wanted to know whether Helena had any questions about him, but he couldn't quite bring himself to ask.

Footsteps came up the staircase. Miss Redmayne had arrived. "Lord Fitzhugh, Lady Fitzhugh, Lord Hastings."

"Thank you for coming so quickly," said Hastings.

"Is there anything about Lady Hastings's current condition that I should know?"

It still gave Hastings pause to hear Helena referred to as Lady Hastings. "She vomited a few minutes after she awakened."

Miss Redmayne noted it down. "That is normal and not in itself a cause for concern."

"She has also lost her memory," Hastings added.

Miss Redmayne raised a brow. "You mean she has no recollection of the accident? That is also not uncommon."

Hastings shook his head. "I'm afraid her memory loss is more extensive than that. She has no recollection of ever meeting Lady Fitzhugh or myself—and we've known her many years."

Miss Redmayne tapped the end of her pen on her chin. "That is a more extreme case of amnesia than one usually encounters."

Amnesia. The syllables were ominous. "How soon can we expect her memory to return?"

"There is no fixed schedule of recovery, from what I know of the condition. She could have it back by the end of the day, the end of the month, or the end of the year." Miss Redmayne paused delicately. "Although there is also the possibility that she may not recoup it."

"What?" Fitz exclaimed. "That can't be. We are speaking of years and years of memories here. How can so much recollection vanish into thin air?"

Miss Redmayne's tone was gentle, almost apologetic. "It has been known to happen, and medical science, unfortunately, has yet to fully understand the condition, let alone cure it." She turned to Millie. "Lady Fitzhugh, will you show me in?"

Fitz thrust his hands into his hair. "I can't imagine it, her memory permanently wiped away. At least Venetia and I still share childhood memories with her, but for you and for Millie—"

"For Millie, especially. They were good friends."

"Yes, but even for you . . ."

Hastings shrugged, his own head beginning to throb. There had been no particular friendship between Helena and himself, but to be an absolute stranger to her, after all these years?

"Go get some rest, David," said Fitz. "I know you've slept the least of us all."

"I won't be able to sleep." He was wide-awake, an almost painful alertness, as if he'd consumed several gallons of coffee. "I'll wait here with you."

What was a few more minutes when he'd been waiting days?

Years.

$\mathcal{M}$iss Redmayne was about Helena's age, pretty, smartly dressed, with an air of tremendous competence. "Your brother and your husband tell me you are suffering from a rather dramatic case of memory loss, Lady Hastings."

It took Helena a moment to realize that "Lady Hastings" referred to herself. So her husband was Lord Hastings. Husband—the very word squeezed the air from her lungs. She didn't know *anything* about the man. How could she be married to him?

"When I awakened," she said, striving to sound in charge of herself, "I was surrounded by members of my family. And I recognized fewer than half of them."

"Of those you do not recognize, whom have you known the longest?"

"Lord Hastings"—she could not bring herself to say "my husband"—"according to everyone else."

Miss Redmayne glanced at Venetia. "Can you tell me when they met, Your Grace?"

"The summer Lady Hastings was fourteen. Lord Hastings came to visit at Hampton House, our home in—"

"Oxfordshire," said Helena, grateful to know that much.

"What is the latest in your life you can remember?" asked Miss Redmayne.

She thought hard. "The Christmas after our mother passed away."

Helena had adored her mother and had been quite disconsolate that Christmas. Venetia and Fitz had persisted in telling her joke after joke until she cracked a smile.

"That would have been shortly before you turned fourteen," said Venetia. "You missed remembering meeting Hastings by a few months."

Helena wanted to remember meeting him—and every day of the past thirteen years of her life—but particularly him. She could not be a wife to a stranger. "Please tell me I'll be able to regain my memory."

"I can make no promises," said Miss Redmayne. "Amnesia is an unusual condition, typically accompanying far more severe brain damage than is your case."

She jotted a few things down in her notebook. "If I recall correctly, you studied classics while you were at Lady Margaret Hall?"

Helena nodded, still shocked by the fact that she'd attended university. Not that she hadn't wanted to, but how had Colonel Clements, their guardian, ever agreed to such a thing? She'd have thought that she'd needed to not only come of age, but come into control of her small inheritance before such a feat became possible.

"Were you educated in Latin prior to that?"

"I remember Helena teaching herself some Latin from Fitz's schoolbooks," Venetia answered for her. "But that was when she was a little older. Sixteen, perhaps."

"Qui caput tuum valet?" asked Miss Redmayne. *How does your head feel?*

"Non praecipue iucunde. Quasi equo calcitrata sum, ita aliquis dicat," Helena replied easily. *Not particularly pleasant. As if I've been kicked by a horse, one might say.*

Miss Redmayne nodded. "It's an odd thing. Amnesia strips one of memory of events and people. But it tends not to affect grasp of languages and other acquired skills. If you knew how to ride a bicycle before, for example, you won't need to learn it again."

"You do know how to ride a safety bicycle," Venetia said, looking almost optimistic.

Helena tried to reassure Venetia with a smile, but managed only a partial one—the stretching of her facial muscles caused a sensation in her scalp that was part tearing, part burning. She would give up fluency in Latin and prowess on a bicycle immediately if she could have her memory back instead.

Miss Redmayne unwound Helena's bandaging to check her stitches. Without any hair, Helena's head felt unsettlingly light—and the air in the room unexpectedly cool against her scalp.

"Your head is no longer bleeding," pronounced Miss Redmayne, "but the stitches need to remain another few days."

She asked Helena to get out of bed and walk in a straight line, perform simple computations, and make logical deductions. "Your reasoning is fine, as is your balance—the wobbliness you might experience is caused by weakness of muscles rather than any injury to the brain. The danger now is that there might be some bleeding inside your cranium. I will keep you under watch for the next forty-eight hours."

Helena inhaled—she'd thought the dangers already past.

"But on the other hand," continued Miss Redmayne, "if there is no cranial bleeding, then you may consider yourself to be mending and you may gradually resume your normal activities. In the meanwhile you will likely experience headaches, more episodes of vomiting, perhaps even further temporary losses of consciousness.

"Moreover, in the excitement of waking up you may not be feeling all your pains, but unfortunately your wound extends down to near your temple, and there are quite a few nerves in the face, so certain facial expressions—frowns, for example—might pull at the stitches and be quite uncomfortable."

Helena didn't mind the pain, but the possibility of cranial bleeding was rather frightful. "What should I do now?"

"Take some light nourishment and rest. This is no time to strain yourself," replied Miss Redmayne. "And don't tax your head trying to remember. It will not hasten the recovery of your memory."

"Can I read?"

"In a few days, yes, but for now it will likely exacerbate your headache. You must remember, Lady Hastings, even though you've regained your consciousness, you are still only three days past a major injury."

The mere thought of sitting in bed for days on end with nothing to do already exacerbated her headache. But something in Miss Redmayne's calm authority precluded arguing: Helena would feel too much like a quarrelsome child.

Miss Redmayne allowed Fitz and Hastings to enter the room. Helena's eyes lingered on the latter for a moment—those cheekbones were sharp enough to cut marble. He returned the attention, but instead of the outright adoration from earlier, he gazed upon her with uncertainty, as if he'd been cast upon some distant shore and was encountering the natives for the first time.

"Where is my husband?" asked Venetia.

"He's in the passage outside," answered Fitz. "Now that Helena is better, he doesn't wish to further intrude on her privacy, as he is not a blood relation."

Miss Redmayne repeated much of what she'd told Helena, but added, "Your Grace, my lords, Lady Fitzhugh, I ask you to disperse. You will be of no use sitting here—let the nurse watch over Lady Hastings. She needs to rest and so do you. And if not, at least get some exercise and fresh air. You've been cooped up long enough."

"I'd like Lord Hastings to remain," Helena heard herself say. She'd posed no questions concerning him to Venetia and Millie, partly because she still wished he'd go away, and partly because she believed he should answer her questions himself.

Judging by his flabbergasted reaction, it was as if she'd asked the man to perform a handstand that very instant.

But he was quick to recover. "Yes, of course. There is nothing I'd like more."

That voice of his—she'd heard it earlier, but now she was surprised by its rich, pure timbre.

Venetia, Fitz, and Millie each embraced Helena, taking care not to touch her where she'd been bruised.

"If you'd like a few minutes of privacy, I can have Nurse Jennings leave her shift early," said Miss Redmayne.

"Thank you," replied Helena.

"You have until Nurse Gardner arrives, my lord, my lady. After that Lady Hastings must rest."

Doctor and nurse departed. Helena and Hastings were alone in the room, but he did not approach her bed. Instead he stood near the wall, his hands behind his back. She realized after some time that he was waiting for her to speak first.

"I'm not sure whether I should apologize for not remembering you, or whether I should ask you to apologize for saddling me with a husband out of the blue. What do you recommend?"

He stared at her. Then he shook his head, as if he couldn't quite believe his ears. "So you really don't remember me."

It was less a question to her than a reminder to himself.

"No, I don't remember you at all."

He ran his fingers through his hair. His curls appeared wonderfully springy. "You might be surprised to know that I am usually astonishingly witty and eloquent. But I am currently at a loss for words."

She tilted her head back slightly. "You have a high regard for yourself."

"So do you—a high regard for yourself, that is," he said, smiling slightly. "You believe—believed—that modesty is for those with something to be modest about."

It did sound like something she might agree with.

She felt herself relax a little. The prospect of being married to a man she couldn't remember had wound her tighter than a twisted rope. But speaking with him, so far, was not an unpleasant experience. That voice of his—if a viola could speak, it would probably speak with his voice. And that smile . . .

He was not, perhaps, conventionally handsome, but he was some kind of handsome—perhaps even some kind of gorgeous: beautiful skin, long brows, a dent just beneath his lower lip caused by the slightly forward angle of his chin. His eyes were bloodshot, but they were also of the color of warm oceans, one moment aquamarine, the next turquoise.

"Surprised to be married?" he asked, his tone conspiratorial, as if he understood her reservations. "And I don't mean married to me, but married at all?"

She relaxed a little more. "Shocked. I've . . . I'd always believed I'd prefer to be a spinster."

"Early in your twenties you began to think that perhaps marriage wouldn't be so bad with the right man."

She raised her brow just enough to avoid hurting her stitches. "And you are that right man?"

"I've always thought we'd be a good match," he said. "You want to reign as the queen of all you survey, and I enjoy being the scheming vizier who whispers crafty ideas into your ears."

An unexpected and appealing vision of a marriage, with

a husband who did not need to put himself in the position of a king.

A knock came on the door. The maids delivered their breakfast trays, one with only porridge and tea for her, one with muffins and plain toast for him. He took the seat Venetia's husband had vacated, close but not too close.

"Is that what you eat for breakfast?" she asked. "Rather abstemious."

"It is. But we thought it best not to have bacon or grilled mackerel on my plate, in case the smell upset your stomach."

She gave her porridge a stir, waiting for it to cool. "Tell me something about yourself."

She could have said, "Tell me something about *us*," but she'd decided against the latter. She did not—not yet—want to hear about a wonderful courtship that culminated in a fairy-tale wedding, with herself as the radiant bride. Her current incarnation might be intrigued by him, but she was not in love. And she did not want to be obliged to feel sentiments she did not.

He thought for a moment, chewing meditatively on a bite of muffin. Her eyes were once again drawn to the shape of his jaw—there were probably fjords in the north less impressively carved. As he swallowed, she became aware of his neck. He was a man of strapping build, but there was nothing thick or bulky about his neck. It was quite simply . . . elegant.

"I like *Alice in Wonderland*," he said.

It was with some effort that she looked back up into his eyes. "That's the something you want to tell me?"

"Why not? And eat. We haven't been able to get much

nutrition into you. You woke up just in time, in fact. They were going to tube feed you, starting today."

She'd been wary to break bread so soon after her gastrointestinal tumult. But his words reminded her that her body must be famished from its long sleep. She swallowed a spoonful of her porridge.

"You do know that *Alice in Wonderland* happens to be one of my favorite books, do you not?"

"I do."

His answer was a reminder of the asymmetry of knowledge between the two of them—he probably knew more about her than she did. As engaging as he was to look at—those eyes seemed to shift colors with the smallest movement on his part—and as melodious as he was to listen to, she must not forget that he was most likely a man with a goal.

A goal that resided somewhere below her waist.

She narrowed her eyes slightly. "Are you trying to curry favor with me, Lord Hastings?"

*H*astings could not get enough of being a stranger to her: the courtesy and attentiveness on her part—not to mention the complete absence of scorn and revulsion. Yes, she was wary. But in her shoes, who wouldn't be?

"You are a lover of books; I am one as well," he replied. "Since we can no longer rely on our past history to guide what we say to each other, a book we both enjoy seems a good place to start."

She didn't answer immediately. He was awestruck: She

was considering his answer with care, rather than dismissing it outright as so much rubbish.

"Who is your favorite character in the book?" she asked, lifting another spoonful of porridge toward her lips. There had been a cut on her lower lip; it had largely healed, though a reddish welt still remained.

"The Cheshire Cat," he answered without hesitation.

"Why him?" Her eyes, framed by all that stark white bandaging, were greener than he remembered, the color of a lovingly watered lawn.

"He is mischievous and unpredictable. And he comes and goes as he wishes. When I was a child, I would have loved to be able to disappear at will."

She examined him—she'd been examining him ever since she called for him to stay with her. "And what would you have done with such an ability? Eavesdrop on others?"

It was not, as questions went, particularly probing. Yet if he were to give a proper answer, it would reveal more of himself than he'd ever been willing to let her see.

"Just to get away from where I was," he said.

"And where were you?"

"Under my uncle's control." He bent his face to the plate, almost . . . shy to be speaking so honestly about himself.

"Was he a harsh disciplinarian?"

He raised his head. Her gaze was still fixed upon him, a cautious attention, but one not colored by prior prejudices.

He'd often dreamed that one day she'd suddenly see him as he wished to be seen. This was not the fulfillment of that childish dream, but still, it was beyond anything he could have realistically hoped for: a true new beginning.

"Yes," he said, even though the admission made him feel vulnerable.

She gazed at him a moment longer before looking down to find her teacup. "I'm sorry to hear that. My father was a soldier, but he was no martinet. He loved to laugh. And he was wonderfully kind."

That was the view all the Fitzhugh children took of their father. "Fitz once told me he always called you his beauty."

"Yes, so I could grow up next to Venetia without feeling that I am in her shadow." Her lips curved slightly. "It probably left me with a highly inflated sense of my physical appeal."

"Or perhaps he was simply like me," he said impulsively.

Her expression turned quizzical. "How so?"

"Fitz had warned me about Venetia before my first visit. He said grown men turned into jelly at the mere sight of her. Well, my carriage pulled up to your house, a young girl stuck her head out of an upper-story window, and I turned into jelly right on the seat of the carriage." He broke a piece off the half muffin that remained on his plate, his heart beating rather uncomfortably fast. "But that girl wasn't Venetia. It was you."

He'd never told her of his fierce attraction to her from the very beginning—he couldn't in the face of her indifference and, later, her contempt.

It was hard to tell whether she was pleased by his confession—she lifted the teapot to refill her cup and seemed to have eyes only for her task. "What else do I need to know about you?" Her voice was cool, as was her demeanor.

He'd likely discomfited her, a stranger whom she wished to keep at arm's length going on about how lovely he found her. He broke off another piece of the muffin. "I have a daughter named Beatrice."

His siring of an illegitimate child had never sat well with Helena. But she needed to know about Bea.

His declaration took her aback. "You were married before?"

"No."

She blinked at the implication of his words. Displeasure gathered between her furrowed brows—then further displeasure as she winced from the pressure on her stitches. Her bruises seemed to turn darker, like thunderclouds on her face. "Who is her mother?"

"A London Cyprian by the name of Georgette Chevalier—her real name was Florie Mims. She was my mistress for some time and died of pneumonia when Bea was three months old."

"How old is Bea?"

"Two months short of six."

Suspicion and temper flared in her eyes. "And how long have *we* been married?"

"Not long at all. This Season."

She exhaled. Her face lost some of its severity. "For a moment I thought you'd sired this child during our marriage."

"I would *never* treat our marriage in such a light manner."

Yet he had antagonized her with greater fervor than ever after he gave her no choice but to become his wife.

This Helena, however, did not recall his past idiocy. Her mind was solely focused on the present. "Does she live in your—our household, your daughter?"

His heart thudded at her use of the word *our.* "She lives at Easton Grange, my—our estate in Kent."

She was silent for some time, her eyes boring into his. Then she asked, "Have you ever considered that raising an illegitimate child under the same roof as your future heirs is highly irregular?"

The implied disapproval in her tone disconcerted him, but he met her gaze squarely. "I have. But I am her father and this is how I choose to conduct her upbringing, not from a distance and not diminishing my role to a mere provider of funds."

"I object to that," she declared flatly. "I demand that she be removed from my dwelling."

His heart plummeted. She'd been ready to take Bea in hand only a few days ago. Had she changed so much with her loss of memory? And what could he say that would not alienate her and endanger this fragile new bond of theirs?

"I understand your objections," he heard himself say. "But I will not relegate my daughter to the periphery of my existence simply to please my wife."

Her countenance was unyielding as granite. He could scarcely draw in air. If they should clash on this point . . . if she should prove as obstinate as she was capable of being . . .

Her eyes softened. "Good. Her illegitimacy is not her fault."

He reeled. "But you just—"

"I was testing you." Her small smile was apologetic, almost sheepish. "You are a stranger, yet I must live with you and, well, be your wife. I wanted to know something of your character this instant. Forgive me my impatience."

He breathed hard. "So I passed."

"Beautifully."

That might be the first word of sincere praise he'd ever heard from her.

It wasn't just a new beginning, it was a whole new world.

*H*e turned his face to the side. Helena blinked. His profile was perfect. Beyond perfect—the cameo brooch must have been invented so that someday it could be engraved with the silhouette of his features.

"I'd like to meet Bea at the earliest opportunity," she said, so as not to be wordlessly gawking at him.

He looked back at her. "I'll take you to Easton Grange as soon as you are well enough to travel. And thank you for taking an interest in her."

"You don't need to thank me. I am her stepmother, after all."

He smiled, a warm, lovely smile. "Then I hope you won't mind that I must leave to see Bea today."

This surprised her. "All the way to Kent? Is it her birthday?"

"No, but she expected me on Wednesday. It is already Friday."

"Why not have her brought to London?"

"Eat more," he reminded her. "Unfortunately Bea does not leave Easton Grange."

She dug into her porridge. "Why not?"

"She does not wish to." He gave a barely perceptible

sigh. "And she is not the kind of child who can be bribed with offers of sweets or dolls."

"Not even for the woman who is raising her?"

"She doesn't know you yet—you were going to meet her the day of your accident."

"I see." Helena supposed it made sense that she would leave London only near the end of the Season, but she found it less than impressive that she'd put off meeting the child. She should have introduced herself to Bea as soon as she became engaged to the girl's father, especially given that Bea did not seem to be someone who adjusted easily to changes. "Are you departing now?"

"No, I'm loath to leave your side. I'll probably need to ask Fitz to pull me away. In fact, it will probably take him, Lexington, and a few footmen to shove me into a carriage and then onto the train."

When he'd told his story of turning into jelly at his first sight of her, she'd responded rather severely. There was a contrariness in her that refused to fall too easily in love with him: It would be the expected, expedient thing to do, and she did not want to commit to him simply for the sake of convenience.

But this time she couldn't quite summon the same coolness. She dropped her gaze to her tray and ate the rest of her porridge without speaking.

The day nurse, Nurse Gardner, arrived alongside the maid who came to take away the breakfast trays. "My lord, Miss Redmayne asks that you engage in no further conversation after my lady's breakfast. But you may read to my lady, if you wish, so that she may close her eyes and rest."

"But it is not even midmorning," Helena protested. "And I've been sleeping for three days, haven't I?"

"Nevertheless, doctor's orders," said the nurse.

Hastings rose to examine a small, laden bookshelf by the window.

"You needn't take the trouble. I'm not particularly fond of being read to—too slow."

"Think of it as a therapeutic luxury, then: My voice is generally considered to possess the power to lure unicorns out of their secret forests."

She barely remembered not to raise her brows to her hairline. "Conceited, aren't we?"

"You used to tell me I had enough hot air to power an armada of dirigibles. And when I countered that people thought my voice lovely enough to rival that of a chorus of angels, you said that particular band of angels must have been singing with their rear ends."

It wasn't until she felt the pressure on her stitches that she realized she was smiling. Yes, it hurt, but she did not stop. The sensation of pleasure and mirth was as unexpected as it was wonderful.

"Ready for a few sonnets by Mrs. Browning?" He sat down again and opened the book he'd retrieved. " 'How do I love thee? Let me count the ways.' "

CHAPTER 9

$\mathcal{H}$elena realized, as she began to doze off, that Hastings didn't have a nice voice, but an extraordinary one: dulcet, golden, yet subtly powerful, like a distant rolling of thunder, or the reverberation of a faraway sea.

As she teetered on the edge of sleep, he stood over her and murmured, "If you should remember everything before I come back . . ."

Perhaps sleep overtook her; perhaps he never finished his sentence. The next thing she knew, someone was tapping on her arms. Groggily she opened her eyes—to Venetia's beautiful face.

"Hello, sister dearest," she mumbled.

Venetia smiled. She had a smile as exquisite as Hastings's voice, but it could not altogether hide her concern. "Sorry to disturb you, my love. But we've been instructed to wake you up from time to time, to make sure you haven't again lost consciousness."

She helped Helena sit up. Helena accepted a glass of water and drank thirstily. "How long have I been asleep?"

"Five hours, more or less."

"Is Lord Hastings back yet?"

How odd that this morning his very existence was a shock to her, but now she wanted to know his whereabouts.

"No, sorry. He said not to expect him before dinner. Would you like to eat something? You are in time for a very late lunch, or a very early tea."

"Porridge again?"

"Since you kept down your breakfast, Nurse Gardner has decreed you may have some broth and a bit of a convalescent pudding."

"Hmm, pudding. I am in a state of unspeakable anticipation."

Venetia smiled again and rose to ring for the pudding.

"Did you get any rest yourself, Venetia?"

"I went for a quick drive and a walk in the park with my husband—I'm only with child, not ill. I did, however, lie down for half an hour just now, since he presented me with an irresistible bribe."

With great pomp and circumstance, Venetia revealed the "irresistible bribe." What Helena had imagined to be a piece of pretty bauble turned out to be nothing of the sort, unless during her absence of memory it had become fashionable for ladies to wear sinister-looking talons as accessories to their silk and muslin summer dresses.

"What *is* that?"

"It's a tooth from a prehistoric crocodilian. Those beasts grew to dizzying sizes. They could probably reach up from their swampy dwellings and snap in two most of the smaller saurians coming for a drink of water."

"Good gracious. And your husband gave it to you as a bribe?"

Venetia's face fell a little. "Oh, I forgot you don't remember. I—we—excavated a dinosaur skeleton on the coast of Devon the summer you were fourteen."

"An entire skeleton?"

"Eighty-five percent complete, I'd say."

The impotence of her mind vexed Helena. How could she not remember such a remarkable event as pulling a near-complete dinosaur skeleton out of the ground?

"I have pictures, if you should like to see them," said Venetia tentatively. "You are in the pictures, too."

Helena made herself smile. "Yes, of course. I'd love to see them."

But seeing the pictures would be troubling, wouldn't it, as if she were witnessing someone else live her life?

She changed the topic. "By the way, where am I? I can tell by the smell of the air that we are in London, but is this my house, yours, or—"

"This is Fitz's house; he inherited it along with the title."

"I always thought the title would go to that second cousin of ours, if the earl didn't have any male issue of his own."

"So did we all, but Mr. Randolph Fitzhugh was already quite elderly—he passed away before the earl did."

"Wasn't there still someone else between Fitz and the title?"

"Yes, another cousin—he also didn't outlive the former earl."

"Do we have cousins who survived?" Helena tried for

a joking tone, but she couldn't help a twitch of fear in her heart.

"Our Norris cousins are all doing well. Margaret married a naval officer. Bobby *is* a naval officer. And Sissy is a missionary in Hong Kong."

Sissy who could never sit still in church?

A week ago Helena would have known that Sissy had turned devoutly religious. A week ago she'd have been able to give vivid descriptions of the prehistoric monster Venetia had excavated. A week ago her entire life would have been in a state of perfect order: happy siblings, a thriving firm, and a devoted husband.

She ate some pudding, trying to calm herself. "What about our Carstairs cousins?"

Venetia's expression instantly turned sober. "We don't have any Carstairs cousins left."

"What? There were four of them!"

"Unfortunately they all died within an eighteen-month span. Lydia in childbirth, Crespin from influenza, Jonathan of bad oysters, and Billy"—Venetia grimaced—"Billy died by his own hand—it was whispered he was suffering from an advanced case of syphilis."

The pudding now tasted of mud; Helena set down her spoon. She'd been fond of Billy Carstairs, a moody but kind young man, always saving scraps from the table to give to the village strays. And the rest of the Carstairses had been a noisy, fun-loving bunch, the youngest born on the exact same day as her.

All dead, all gone, leaving behind only a row of headstones in the graveyard of a parish church.

She gripped Venetia's hand. "I'm so glad you are still

here, and Fitz, too. If I should have woken up to find either of you gone . . ."

She couldn't quite continue.

"Now you know how we felt, love." Venetia kissed the back of Helena's hand. "And you can scarcely imagine how thrilled we are to have you back. Don't worry about old memories. We'll make new ones. We are all together now and that's the only thing that counts."

$\mathcal{H}$astings swung between wild euphoria and feral fear.

Helena liked him. She genuinely *liked* him. It was as if he'd looked up from his lonely altar in the Sahara to find it raining. Barely a drizzle, to be sure, but still it was actual precipitation, when there had been nothing but burning sky and parched sand for centuries upon centuries.

Yet by the time he returned to her side . . .

It was one thing to have never been given a drop of rain, quite another to have felt the cool, sweet sprinkling on his face, and then to be denied the experience ever again.

If only he could have stayed with her, soaking up every last ounce of her lovely attention. And if only he could leave this moment to rush back to her side. But he was on one knee before Bea's trunk and likely there to stay for a good long while.

"I know I didn't come when I said I would and I am very sorry for that," he repeated himself for the hundredth time. "But I couldn't, you see. Miss Fitzhugh—Lady Hastings, my wife, your new mother—was injured and I didn't know whether she'd live or die. I couldn't leave her."

No response. Bea hadn't had such a bad case of the trunk for at least six months. But then again, for the longest time he'd been scrupulously careful about his schedule.

"If you were badly hurt, you'd want me to stay with you, wouldn't you, Bea? You wouldn't want me to fly off and visit someone else."

Still no response.

He sighed. He had no idea how long they'd been at it. There were now three telegrams from Fitz in his pocket—he'd asked Fitz to cable him hourly to keep him abreast of Helena's condition. At least she had not succumbed to cranial bleeding. He lowered himself to a sitting position, with his back against the side of the trunk. "Want me to read you a book? One of our stories?"

"I am badly hurt," came her little pip of a voice.

It was the first thing she'd said to him since his arrival. He smiled ruefully, but also in relief. "Where are you hurt, poppet?"

The trunk had a little door at the bottom. It opened and out came her small, thin foot. He took it in hand, turning it one way, then the other.

"Listen," she said.

"Ah, of course. If you will excuse me for a moment." He fetched the stethoscope from his room, returned to the nursery, and rubbed his palm against the chest piece to make it less cold. He put the earpieces into his ears—Bea, who took her medical diagnoses seriously, could see out from the airholes that had been drilled into the sides of the trunk—and listened to her foot.

"Your blood seems to be pumping sluggishly and that is never good for one of the extremities—atrophy might result. In my opinion, dear Bea, you should take a walk. Exercise strengthens muscles and will make your foot better in no time."

She didn't say anything.

"I'll come with you on the walk, of course."

A long silence. "And supper?"

"I will stay for supper. And I will read you a bedtime story, too. Now will you come out? Or at least give me a time for when you'll come out."

Another long silence. "Four."

It was only a few minutes past three, but at least it was something to look forward to. He murmured a silent thanksgiving.

"Sir Hardshell?"

"Of course, poppet."

Sir Hardshell was Bea's pet tortoise and one of Hastings's potential headaches. No one knew exactly how old it was, except that it had been a resident at Easton Grange since the estate was first built sixty years ago, long before the property's acquisition by Hastings's uncle. And before that, Sir Hardshell had served for nearly thirty years as a ship's mascot on various merchant marine vessels.

Hastings could only pray that Sir Hardshell would live to a legendary age. Bea did not deal well with changes, and there was no change more permanent than death. He made a show of listening to the tortoise's heart and various other organs. "He sounds old, poppet, ancient. A hundred twenty, at least. You should brace yourself for the possibility that he might not make it through another winter."

Bea made no reply. He exhaled—at least Sir Hardshell was still alive today. He set the tortoise on the floor to roam the edges of the nursery. "Shall I have some tea and biscuit sent up for you, Bea? And read you a story in the meanwhile?"

"Yes," she said. "Yes, Papa."

His insides invariably turned into a warm puddle when she called him Papa. He rang for her tea, sat down again next to the trunk, and closed his eyes for a moment—awash in both exhaustion and gladness—before opening the storybook he'd hand-made for her. "Shall we start with your favorite, the one about Nanette's birthday?"

*T*he clock struck ten.

Marking at least fifteen minutes of continuous kissing for Fitz and Millie.

Helena hadn't meant to be a Peeping Jane. Around half past nine, after she'd been talking to her brother and sister-in-law for some time, she'd dozed off. When she'd heard the next quarter hour chime on the clock, she'd forced herself to wake up, not wanting to sleep too much too early and then be wide-awake at night.

Also not wanting to miss Hastings. He'd cabled before he left Kent to let them know he was on his way, and she'd experienced a small flutter of anticipation when she'd learned the news.

But when she'd opened her eyes, she'd witnessed Fitz and Millie engaged in a passionate embrace, Fitz's hands in his wife's hair, one of Millie's hands at her husband's nape, the other somewhere too low for Helena to see from her supine position.

The polite thing to do, Helena decided, was to close her eyes and let them finish their kiss before making it known that she was once again conscious. But apparently there was no such thing as finishing a kiss, as far as those two were concerned.

She was mortified—the sounds they made could not be unheard and she'd never be able to look either in the eye again. But at the same time, she was . . .

She would not mind being party to a similarly heated kiss.

How would it feel to grip Hastings's soft curls? To have his lips against hers? And to hear him emit involuntary noises of desire and relish?

A soft knock came on the door. At last Fitz and Millie pulled apart. There came hushed giggles and whispered words as they tried to make Millie's hair look less disheveled.

The knock came again, slightly louder.

Again giggles and whispers, followed by Fitz clearing his throat. "Come in."

The door opened. "I'm sorry," said Hastings. "Were you already asleep?"

That voice of his—it might not lure unicorns out of their secret forests, but it could conceivably make howlingly bad verses sound like a lost Byronic masterpiece. And the question was quite tactful, giving Fitz and Millie an easy excuse for their delay in answering the door.

"We dozed off a bit just now," answered Millie.

Helena was astonished at how guileless Millie sounded. This sister-in-law was more complicated than Helena would have guessed solely by looking at her sweet features and self-effacing demeanor.

"You are late," said Fitz. "Bea was not happy with you, I take it?"

"It took me ages to coax her out of her trunk. How is Helena?"

"Better. She wants to be served a beefsteak tomorrow."

"I thought she doesn't like beefsteaks."

She didn't?

"We'll let her find out for herself whether she still feels the same way," said Fitz. "About beefsteaks . . . and other things."

What other things? Helena decided it was time to join the conversation. She made a soft, sleepy grunt.

"Is she still awake?" asked Hastings.

"She was asleep earlier. Perhaps we are disturbing her by speaking in here."

Helena produced another small grunt and slowly opened her eyes. Hastings took a step toward her. "Did we wake you, Helena?"

His words were soft, but his jaw was tense. In fact, his entire person was tense, as if he were about to meet a battle of impossible odds.

"You are back," she mumbled.

She must have said something comforting, for instantly the strain in his face was replaced by a look of indescribable relief. He smiled. "Yes, I'm back."

"I haven't remembered you," she felt obliged to point out.

He touched his fingertips to the edge of her bed, a startlingly intimate gesture even though he'd done nothing suggestive. "That does not in the least diminish my joy at seeing you again, my dear."

Fitz cleared his throat. If Helena didn't have her stitches to mind, she'd have raised an eyebrow as high as the battlements of the Tower of London. She failed to see why a man who kissed his wife like a starving man devouring a fresh loaf of bread ought to interfere when another man greeted his own wife in a most decorous fashion.

"Did you have supper, David?" Fitz asked.

"I did, thank you." Hastings turned to Fitz. "Where is the night nurse?"

"We told her to get up and stretch her legs. She's been cooped up in that chair for hours," said Millie.

Hastings nodded. "I see."

"Fitz, Millie, why don't you two go take your rest?" said Helena. *Or be up half the night with noisy indecencies, if you so prefer.* "Lord Hastings can stay with me until the night nurse returns."

At her suggestion, a number of looks were exchanged among Fitz, Millie, and Hastings. Helena was vaguely disconcerted. Why did everyone always act surprised whenever she wanted a moment of privacy with her husband?

"Well, then, David, we'll leave her safety and well-being in your capable hands," acceded Fitz.

Fitz and Millie kissed Helena on her good cheek before they murmured their good nights. Hastings closed the door softly behind their departing backs. "How are you, my dear?"

"Much, much better. No more abdominal troubles, only one faint bout of nausea, and . . ." She lost her train of thought for a moment as he came to the foot of the bed. His long fingers traced the tapering segment of the bedpost nearest him—fingers that, given that they were newlyweds, must have freely traced the curves of her body only days ago.

"And what?" he prompted.

"And—the headache is far more tolerable."

143

"Excellent." Now he spread his fingers against the bed-post. She swallowed. "My apologies for waking you up. I wanted to be back sooner, but Bea wouldn't come out of her trunk."

He'd mentioned the trunk earlier, to Fitz and Millie. "What trunk?"

"She has a trunk she climbs into when she is upset."

Belatedly she realized that he looked different: He'd put enough pomade into his hair so that only the very ends still curled. The pomade also made his hair look darker, more brown than blond. "Wouldn't she asphyxiate inside?"

"I had holes drilled in the sides of the trunk. And there is also a small opening near the bottom through which one can hand her a cup of tea and a biscuit."

An odd child. Helena could think of nothing worse than locking herself in a trunk. "She is not like other children, is she?"

"No child is like any other, but she does lack those instincts and skills to even remotely resemble other chil-dren." He sighed softly. "Between you and me, I have no idea whether I am doing the right thing by waiting beside the trunk and coaxing her out. My uncle would have burned the trunk, forcing her to light the match, no less."

She didn't know why she found his uncertainty so attractive. She supposed she must like a man who was both humble enough to question his decisions and brave enough to admit it. "Is she genuinely distressed when she goes into her trunk?"

"Yes."

"Then you are not doing anything wrong by being patient and kind."

He smiled again at her, a smile both tired and happy.

Something tugged at her heart. She slid her fingers along the top of the bedcover. "I never had a trunk—I could not tolerate being inside one even for hide-and-seek. But we did have a very tall tree at Hampton House. When I became particularly upset for any reason, I'd climb to the highest branch and then be stuck there, not knowing how to get back down to the ground.

"My father had a ladder especially built for retrieving me. He married quite late and was forty-five by the time Fitz and I were born. So he was at least fifty when I developed my habit of angry tree scaling. But he always came for me himself instead of sending a servant, and some of my happiest childhood memories consist of being carried on his back while he negotiated his way down that long, long ladder."

He'd gazed at her steadily as she recounted her story, but now that she was silent, she found it more difficult to hold his gaze. "You probably already know the story," she said, for something to say.

"No, it's the first time I've heard it," he answered, sounding thrilled about it. "You think someday Bea will speak of the trunk and her waiting father to someone?"

"She should. I would."

The praise felt too warm—so warm that her cheeks turned hot. The way he watched her, she was sure he sensed this rise in her surface temperature. She cast about for something less warm. "What did you do to your hair? I don't like it as much."

His brow knitted. "How *do* you like it?"

"I prefer the curls."

He looked as if she'd told him she preferred him with three eyes. "You used to make fun of them. You told me that if Bo Peep had a child with one of her sheep it would have hair like mine."

She burst out laughing—and gasped at the pain that shot through her scalp. "You are not making it up, are you? Did I really say that?"

"Sometimes you called me Goldilocks."

She had to remind herself not to laugh again. "And you married me? I sound like a very odious sort of girl."

"I was a very odious sort of boy, so you might say we were evenly matched."

She didn't know enough to comment upon that, but when he was near, she was . . . happier.

Neither of them said anything for some time. The silence was beginning to feel awkward when he glanced at the door and asked, "Fitz and his wife weren't actually dozing, were they?"

That seemed a much safer topic of conversation. She seized upon it. "No, they were kissing as if there were no tomorrow."

He grinned. "And you were peeping as if there were no tomorrow?"

If only she could toss back her head. "I will have you know that once I realized what they were doing, I kept my eyes firmly shut. They should have made sure I was truly asleep before pawing each other."

"It was probably all they could do to dispatch the nurse elsewhere." He looked toward the bedpost, where his fingers probed the depth of its spiral grooves. "When one has kissing on the mind, it becomes difficult to think of many other things."

The man was doing something to her. Despite her

weakness and discomfort from the accident, and despite the fact that only hours ago on this same day she'd had no idea who he was, she felt . . . stirrings. "Did we used to kiss like that?"

Surely she hadn't meant to ask such a question. But there it was, hanging bright and shameless between them.

His fingers stilled. "Occasionally."

She bit the inside of her lower lip. "Only occasionally?"

He glanced at her askance, a half smile about his lips. "How often do you recommend we should have done it?"

She had no choice now but to brazen it out. "As often as I wanted, of course."

Had it not been deep in the night she might not have heard the catch in his breath—or the subsequent unsteadiness as he exhaled. Heat curled in her abdomen.

"In that case, we did it as often as you wanted." His hand was again on the edge of the bed, fingers rubbing against the linen sheets. "And you liked it very, very well, if I may add."

That same heat was now everywhere inside her. "Am I supposed to take your word for it?"

He took a step closer, his eyes the color of a clear sky. "You can have a demonstration if you don't believe me."

A knock came on the door, startling her. "That . . . must be the nurse."

"Drat it," he said, a touch of rue to his smile. "So much prowess, so little chance to prove it."

"Maybe when you have curly hair again."

"Maybe I'll make you kiss me first and prove your sincerity," he said as he walked toward the door, "before I will stop pomading my hair."

After the nurse took her seat, he did not leave, but sat down in the same chair he'd occupied in the morning to read Mrs. Browning's sonnets.

"My lord, my lady needs to rest," the nurse reminded him.

"Yes, of course, good nurse. I will not bother Lady Hastings, but sit here quietly."

Helena was both pleased and surprised. "You don't wish to sleep in a nice bed of your own?"

He shook his head firmly. "I've been away from you long enough this day."

Her heart pitter-pattered. "It will be uncomfortable."

He raised her hand and pressed a kiss into the center of her palm. "What's a little discomfort compared to the joy of being near you? Now sleep, my dear; you've much convalescing left to do."

She did not take much time to go back to sleep. Hastings remained awake for much longer, savoring each moment of her nearness.

It still felt like a dream to be allowed to sit next to her for hours on end. The sweet intimacy of watching her fall asleep was a privilege he'd never hoped for, not even when he wrote fiction about them. And to converse as they did, exchanges that meant something—a whole new world indeed.

He didn't know when he fell asleep, but it was a little past four in the morning when he suddenly awakened with a stark fear in his heart. He immediately looked toward her. In the muted light from the covered electric sconce, she lay flat on her back, her chest rising and falling with a comforting cadence. He let out a sigh of relief—and only then saw that her eyes were open and a trail of tears glistened on her temple.

He touched her hand. "What's the matter?" he whispered, not wanting to wake up the softly snoring night nurse.

"Nothing." Helena wiped away her tears, grimacing a little as her fingers touched still-bruised skin. "I'm just being sentimental."

"May I ask about what or whom?"

She inhaled unsteadily. "My Carstairs cousins. Do you know them?"

"Yes. I went to a great many of their funerals."

Another teardrop rolled down the side of her temple into her hair. "I can't believe they are all gone—especially Billy."

His eyes widened.

She, staring at the ceiling, did not notice his reaction. "He was probably my father's favorite among all my cousins. And mine, too. Such a gentle way he had with animals—they loved him, one and all. And the way he died was so horrible, I can't help feeling heartbroken for him. Which is silly, of course, since I must have already shed buckets of tears earlier."

"You didn't shed any tears for him," he said.

Her lips quivered. "I probably wouldn't have let you see me cry, since we weren't married then."

"You didn't attend his funeral, Helena."

This stopped her tears. "What? Was I ill?"

"No, you were perfectly fine. You didn't go because you loathed Billy."

She scooted higher to rest her back against the head-board. "That's impossible. I adored Billy. You should have seen how sweet he was with my puppy—or even stray dogs."

He recognized her digging in her heels. And he, alas, possessed the questionable talent of making her dig in her heels even harder. But he had no choice but to go on. "Billy was nice to puppies, but he was loathsome to women. He raped five women in his service. Each time it was hushed up, but everyone knew. By the time of his death, there were no women working in the Carstairs house."

She stared at him, her jaw slack.

"You had trouble believing it the first time, too. It wasn't until you were eighteen and walked in on him trying to corner a fourteen-year-old maid that you changed your mind. So if you don't believe me, I understand."

She shook her head much harder than she ought. "No, no, you mistook me. Of course I believe you."

Now it was he who stared at her, incredulous and—ecstatic. She took him at his word. She trusted him. Nothing like this had ever happened before.

"You've no reason to speak ill of the dead," she went on, the fingers of her free hand flexing restlessly. "And it would have been to your advantage, in fact, to say something nice when I was weeping over him. I'm only speechless at how wrong I was. Father died when Billy was twelve, so he can be forgiven for not realizing what a monster Billy would become. But where was I for the next so many years? It should not have taken me that long to see the truth—and here I thought myself so clever in all things."

"You are clever in just about all things," he told her. "Clever, discerning, and wily. But there is also a streak of sentimentality to you. You don't form attachments easily. When you do, you love with a great intensity and you are forgiving of flaws and weaknesses."

She seemed surprised by his defense of her, then grateful, then bashful. "You are not speaking of yourself here, are you? You look like a man full of flaws and weaknesses," she said, her tone half-teasing.

"That I may be, but you've never forgiven a single flaw of mine, much to my disappointment."

She looked away for a moment, her fingers plucking at the sheets. "Well, at least that put an end to my silly weeping."

He reached forward and placed his hand over hers. "Why don't you go back to sleep? You need your rest."

She cast him a sideways glance, but didn't say anything.

"What is it?" he asked.

She only smiled—or perhaps smirked—with her eyes.

His heartbeat accelerated. "You are thinking of something."

"Maybe I am."

"Tell me."

His hand still covered hers. But now she turned her hand so that her thumb grazed a slow line down the center of his palm. His breath caught; heat coursed up his arm.

"That demonstration you offered—I'll take you up on it." Her eyes turned even naughtier. "But not just yet. You must wait more time."

"Really?" he drawled.

He rose from his seat, set his arms on either side of her, and closed the distance between their lips until only a bare inch remained.

She was surprised—and excited. Even in this dingy

light he could see her pupils dilating. She licked her lips; his fingers clawed into the pillows. Their agitated breaths mingled, and all he had to do was lower his head a little farther . . .

He pulled back, sat down again, and smirked as she had. "You are right—not just yet. You must wait more time, my dear."

In the morning light, Helena examined her pate, wondering whether Hastings would have kissed her during the night if she'd had a cloud of soft, wavy hair spread out on the pillow, the visual equivalent of a siren song. "I believe I may declare with great authority that I prefer not being bald," she said ruefully.

She was surrounded by women: the day nurse, waiting to wrap fresh bandaging around her head; Venetia, holding up the mirror; and Millie, one finger on her cheek.

"You are not completely bald," pointed out Millie. "Your hair is already growing back."

"Never mind the hair," said Venetia. "That hoof could have taken out your eye; at least hair grows back."

Helena sighed. That was quite true. "Not to mention I can't remember anything of your dino—"

Into her mind tumbled the recollection of warm summer air brushing against the skin of her nape, alternating with salty, cool breezes from the coast. She'd been sitting under a tree with a book in her hand—*Wuthering Heights*, to be exact—hadn't she? And Venetia had shouted from somewhere behind her, *Fitz, Helena, come look at what I've found.*

"I remember," she said very softly, not wanting to

scatter her newly returned memories. "I *remember.* It was a big brute, your fossil. We knocked about it for an hour before we decided that the three of us were no match for it. Fitz suggested we ask for help from the village, so we did. And every male over the age of five volunteered."

Venetia stared at her for a few seconds. Then she shrieked and hugged Millie hard—the way she couldn't hug Helena. "That's exactly what happened. You do remember! You do, you do!"

She let go of a startled Millie, laughed, and wiped her eyes at the same time. "Well, actually, not exactly what happened. There were no five-year-olds following me. Seven-year-olds, perhaps, but not five-year-olds."

Helena laughed, too, and didn't care at all about the discomfort it caused. "Maybe not *five*-year-olds, but there was that one boy who must have been no more than four, and for the remainder of the excavation he stood six inches from you, staring." She turned to Millie. "You think Venetia is beautiful now, but she can't hold a candle to her sixteen-year-old self. She used to pack the streets with spectators."

Venetia smiled hugely. "Wait till I tell Lexington what a terrible bargain he received, getting my old, ugly self instead of the fresh, pretty one."

She did not need to go find her husband. The door swung open and he was right there. "Are you all right, Duchess? I heard you scream."

Venetia rushed up to him and grabbed his arm. "I'm perfectly fine. Helena remembered our dig."

"The *Cetiosaurus*?" enthused Lexington, placing his hand over his wife's. "Excellent. That's what? Six months later than what she could previously recall?"

"At least seven," Venetia corrected him.

Fitz and Hastings now joined Lexington at the door, which was becoming quite crowded. "What is all the commotion about?" asked Fitz.

"I remember Venetia's dinosaur," Helena announced, feeling as proud as the first time she read a book all by herself.

"Thank *goodness*!" cried Fitz. "That is wonderful news."

Helena's attention turned to Hastings, whose hair was still damp from his bath. He smiled, too, but there was a hollowness to the smile. "Venetia found the dinosaur only weeks before I visited Hampton House for the first time. Do you also remember that?"

Helena's glee deflated some. "No, not that. At least, not yet."

Hastings exhaled. "I suppose it will happen some other time, then."

His reaction puzzled her. Taken together with his relief the night before at her continued state of nonremembrance, and his general nonchalance over their years of shared history wiped clean, one might be tempted to say that he didn't particularly long for the return of her memory.

"My lady," said Nurse Gardner, "we should have your new bandages on."

Helena belatedly remembered her bald head. "Gentlemen, would you mind?"

They murmured their apologies and left. Hastings glanced back at her, his gaze fearful, as if she were not getting better, but worse, and any moment could be their last together.

* * *

*I*t was only a matter of time.

Hastings sat by her bedside, his head in his hands. He knew this. He knew this all along. But he'd hoped for a little more time, a little more of this miracle.

"I see you've wisely decided not to hide your curls from my ravenous sight," she said, startling him.

He straightened in his chair. "You are awake."

"And have been for several minutes."

He helped her sit up higher and rang for her luncheon. "Admiring my cross-between-golden-retriever-and-French-poodle hair?"

One side of her mouth lifted. "I am ravished by the beauty of those curls."

She probably wouldn't speak so flirtatiously had they not been alone. But the day nurse had gone to use the water closet. He retook his seat. "Ravished, eh?"

"Indeed. But I would have been even more ravished if I weren't wondering at the same time why you look so dejected."

Of course she'd notice. Hadn't he himself told her, only hours ago, that she was wily, discerning, and clever? And he hadn't been exactly subtle in his reactions, ricocheting from dread to hope and back again in dizzying succession.

He raked his fingers through his hair. "Sorry. Didn't mean to distract you from the pure joy that is my beauty."

She studied him for a moment. The bruises on her face were fading more rapidly now; in a few more days they would be only faint smudges of discoloration. And her eyes—her gaze was at once intense and sympathetic. He'd seen her look at others this way, but never him.

"Why don't you want me to regain my memory?"

The bluntness of her question made him perspire. But he met her eyes and answered truthfully, "I do want you to regain your memory. You've made many friends and lived an interesting and accomplished life. It would be a crying shame if you can't look back and see this path you've blazed for yourself."

She considered his answer for a moment. "But?"

Was she ready for the whole truth? Was he?

"Do you remember what I told you about melting into a puddle at my first sight of you?"

She smiled just perceptibly. "Yes."

"My sentiments were not reciprocated. You took a look at me and went back to your books. You were not one of those girls who fell in love easily, not to mention I was five inches shorter than you. I, on the other hand . . ."

He'd declared his love again and again when she'd been comatose. But if he uttered those words now, with her perfectly awake and lucid, he'd never be able to repudiate that sentiment. And she would always know.

He played with the edge of her bedding, not quite meeting her eyes. "I, on the other hand, fell madly in love. And when I realized that I was invisible to you, I resorted to gaining your attention by any means possible."

"What did you do?" Her tone was amused, fond even.

"The better question would have been, what didn't I do?" He raised his face. "A week after we first met I tried to pinch your bottom."

She stared at him, halfway between outrage and laughter. "Truly?"

"My only defense is that I knew I wouldn't be able to

156

feel anything—women wore enormous bustles then. All I wanted was for you to notice me."

"Did I hit you?"

"A tremendous, well-deserved punch to my face. I walked around with a black eye for a week—and was a bit sad when it faded away completely."

Her lips trembled with mirth. "My goodness, such a romantic."

"You find it funny now. But imagine if your recently recouped memory had extended a few more weeks to include my first visit to Hampton House. You'd think me quite the despicable snot."

"And all you have to do is prove to me that you are not." Her hand reached up and took a strand of his hair between her fingers. "Simple as that."

She gently pulled on that curl and let it go. "It's so springy."

They'd barely grazed at the truth, but she was satisfied—and distracted. By his hair, of all things.

"I feel like a sheep that has been overlooked during spring shearing," he murmured.

"Yes, adorably fluffy."

Another time he might have protested the use of that adjective. But now he was all too relieved. "Would you like me to pull my chair closer, so you may fondle my hair with greater ease?" he asked.

She beamed at him. "Why, yes, I'd like exactly that."

In the evening she asked him to read *Alice's Adventures in Wonderland*. He gladly obliged, reprising his performance from earlier, with distinct voices and accents for the characters. He did so well that Nurse Jennings, the night nurse, clapped at the end of a chapter.

Helena joined in the applause. "Bravo! Bravo! And you have read the book to me before, have you not? I have a sense that this is not the first time I've heard the Cheshire Cat purr like that."

"No, the only other time I've read the book to you was when you were unconscious."

She appeared mystified. "I don't suppose I can remember anything from those three days, can I? Yet I've a distinct feeling I'd heard you do a similar reading."

Was she about to experience another opening of the floodgate? And how far would she remember this time? His fingers tightened around the pages. "I don't know what to tell you."

She made a resigned pull of her lips. "I must be imagining things, even though I'd swear I'm not."

He looked down at the book. "Would you like me to go on to the next chapter?"

She pondered her choice. "Nurse Jennings, would you care for a bit of fresh air just now?"

Nurse Jennings did not need to be asked twice. "I should dearly love it. Thank you, my lady."

Hastings held his breath. Helena wanted to speak to him in private. Had she remembered something crucial?

The door closed behind Nurse Jennings. Helena turned toward Hastings. "I must have been completely distracted by your ravishing curls earlier. The more I think about it, the more I am puzzled. Why should you dread the return of my memory so much if the worst you ever did was put your hand once on my bum?"

So no further recovery of memory—at least not yet.

"Well, let's see. When I visited your house the next summer, I'd grown two inches, but alas, so had you. You towered over me as much as you ever did and ignored me with vicious cruelty. So I set up a trap to lock the two of us together into a wardrobe in the attic. Unfortunately you were one step ahead of me and locked me in by myself instead."

She grinned toothily. "Well done, me."

"You didn't let me out for six hours—it was only by the grace of God that my bladder held. And when you finally came to release me, you wore such a spectacular smirk—it haunted me for months upon months.

"The summer we were both seventeen I was almost tall enough to look you in the eye, but still frustratingly half an inch short. On the other hand, I was no longer a virgin, having been freshly plucked a fortnight before, so I made sure to corner you at every opportunity and inundate you with all the lurid details.

"You've always been a bit of a beanpole, so I made sure to tell you how enormous the barmaid's bubbies were and how round her arse. Then I told you about her sweet cherry of a mouth—nothing but pout, but which managed to swallow me whole."

Her jaw fell—it was a somewhat shocking conversation, even between spouses. "What did I say to that?"

"You said, 'To fit entirely into a little cherry of a mouth, you must have a tiny endowment.'"

She burst out laughing. "What did you say to *that*?"

"I sputtered something, protesting that hadn't been what I'd meant, but I couldn't exactly pull down my trousers to prove you wrong. You, coldhearted wench, you retorted, 'I'm sure you didn't *mean* to divulge such embarrassing personal details, but don't worry. Pay the barmaids enough and they won't laugh at you.' Then you winked at me. I was utterly humiliated."

She chortled with glee. "My, I was something else."

"So was I, one might say, quite the annoying twit."

And was that conclusion enough to explain his alarm at the possible return of her memory?

She covered her mouth and yawned. "Excuse me. I can't believe how much sleep I need these days."

He felt himself unknotting with relief. "Then sleep. Your health is the most important thing right now."

"Would you mind starting the next chapter of the book?"

"Of course not. I'll read until you fall asleep."

She took one of his curls between her fingers. "Fitz has a room for you. You don't need to sit in a chair all night."

He rubbed a finger on the edge of the book. "I want to."

Now she lay her entire palm against the ends of his hair. "In case I wake up in the middle of the night crying again and need someone to smack some sense into me?"

In case this was the last night he was allowed such a privilege.

"Something like that," he answered. "I might have been a twit and a snot earlier in life, but I've grown up to be the voice of reason and the repository of good sense."

*H*elena's stitches were removed the next morning. She was also declared to be out of danger, no more fears of cranial bleeding. She immediately wanted to be out and about, but acquiesced under the combined weight of Miss Redmayne's advice and her family's insistence that she continued her bed rest for a few more days.

At least she was allowed to read. Hastings introduced her to the book she'd written for writers seeking to understand the inner workings of publishing. He also brought her secretary, Miss Boyle, to her bedside, to furnish the necessary explanations for her to deal with Fitzhugh and Company correspondence that had accumulated during her absence.

It was, interestingly enough, not as dispiriting a process as she'd thought it would be, trying to relearn in scant days everything that had earlier taken her years to master. She was more frustrated by the lack of progress on the part of her memory. Given that she'd regained a not insignificant portion soon after she awakened, she'd expected to make similar progress, if not every day, then at least every other day.

But the recovery of memory, alas, followed no regular schedule. She was beginning to fret that nothing else would come back when, on the fourth day after she awakened, while Hastings was again away in Kent to visit his daughter, she suddenly recalled the weeks surrounding Venetia's first wedding.

Venetia had been seventeen and Helena and Fitz fifteen. Most of Helena's thoughts at the time had revolved around her fear that Venetia might have made a terrible mistake in her choice of a bridegroom. Hastings, alas, did not feature at all in the resurfaced memories, except as an aside from Helena to Fitz, hoping he wouldn't bring his stupid friend to the festivities, and Fitz replying that Hastings couldn't come even if he wanted to, as he had to attend his guardian's funeral on the same day.

When Hastings returned, she eagerly recounted her new recollections and teased him for his unfounded fear: Her opinion of him in the present hadn't been at all affected by the new revelations of the past.

He took a deep breath. "But I wasn't wrong. You didn't like me in the past."

"In the *distant* past," she pointed out. "And I already knew that."

He smiled rather wanly. "Well, congratulations. I know how much you wanted to remember more."

She fluffed his lovely hair. "Don't be so afraid. I'll keep you—if just for your curls."

This second recovery of memory dispelled much of her anxiety: It was only a matter of time before she had everything back. And in the meanwhile, her physical self grew ever stronger and more energetic, her siblings were both well and happy, and she had Hastings, who, when her eyes grew sore and weary from reading correspondence addressed to Fitzhugh and Company, read the letters aloud to her, making even the driest business dispatches sound like love letters from Keats to his beloved Fanny Brawne.

One afternoon, Helena awakened from a short nap to find Fitz, rather than Hastings, sitting by the bed, reading a business report of his own.

"David is at a meeting with his business managers," he informed her before she could ask the question.

"Excellent," she said, "so he does have something else to do. I was beginning to worry that I was his whole life."

"You don't seem worried," Fitz replied wryly. "Indeed you seem greatly pleased that he has devoted so many hours to you."

She grinned and chose not to directly address that comment. "I'm surprised to see you without your wife."

"So am I, as a matter of fact. But she has a charity committee meeting to attend, and I thought I'd profit by calling on another one of my favorite women."

He smiled, the corners of his eyes crinkling very slightly in the sunlight streaming in through the window. Fitz had always been a handsome young man, but she could see now that he was also going to be quite a handsome older man someday.

"I've been such trouble to you," she said impulsively, feeling a rush of love for this dear brother.

"I'm torn between answers." His expression turned mischievous. "Should I say, 'Not at all'? or, 'We are used to it'?"

She chortled. "Either way, you—and everyone else—have been too kind to me."

Fitz set aside his report. "Including David?"

"Yes, including Lord Hastings."

He leaned forward in his seat and regarded her for a moment. "You like him."

She was not yet quite comfortable admitting to an outright attraction to her husband, but she was able to say, "I could do far worse waking up to a stranger as my husband—I am quite grateful to my own good taste."

"Hmm," said Fitz.

She raised a brow—how wonderful to be able to use every muscle of her face without fear of pain. "Now, what does that mean, sir?"

"It means, dear sister, that I'm glad to hear my friend spoken of so highly. He was devastated when you ejected

163

the contents of your stomach upon being introduced to him."

She grimaced. "That was a complete and utter coincidence. My stomach had been feeling unwell from the moment I opened my eyes. The nausea happened to build to a crescendo when Hastings was presented to me—nothing to do with him at all. Besides, I've since formed a favorable opinion of him."

Fitz tented his hands under his chin. "So are you ready to decamp to his house and be his wife?"

"I can't live under my brother's roof forever when I am already a married woman. But as for becoming Hastings's wife in truth—I'll make him court me a little more. Mother always said, bless her memory, that a girl ought not to bestow her favors too easily or too quickly."

She was half jesting, but Fitz's brow furrowed. "You are not planning to flirt, then thwart him, are you, my dear?"

That was not an opinion she'd expected from her own dear brother. "You believe that's what I will do?"

"The truth is, I haven't the least idea what you will do." Fitz sighed. "I only ask that you have a care with my friend, Helena. He is entirely besotted with you, and that puts him utterly in your power. Keep in mind that while he is perfectly capable of making fun of himself, he is far from thick-skinned. If anything, he is more sensitive than most."

This surprised her—Hastings had seemed utterly fearless. "Is he?"

"Yes, very sensitive. And very proud."

She was disconcerted to be reminded that she'd known her husband for only a few days, that her knowledge of him, however intimate to her own mind, was far from complete. "Thank you, Fitz. I will remember that. And . . ." She hesitated a second. "And his heart is safe with me."

Fitz regarded her another long moment before he smiled again. "I'm glad to hear that. Shall I ring for some tea?"

*O*n the last day of Helena's convalescence, Hastings was obliged to travel to Oxford to attend the funeral of a classics professor under whom he'd studied and with whom he'd corresponded regularly in the years since.

He was jittery on the return trip—the last time he'd left her for an appreciable amount of time, she'd recovered a solid block of her memory. Walking into Fitz's house filled him with both anticipation and unease.

The time had probably come to tell her the entire truth. Her life was no longer in danger; her mind was as robust as it had ever been; it would be a discourtesy to continue to keep her in the dark.

She was not in her bed when he entered her room, but sitting before the vanity, frowning at the reflection in the mirror. On her head she wore one of the close-fitting turbans Millie's maid had fashioned for her, this one made from an auburn silk that rather matched the color of her eyebrows.

"I'm back," he said.

She turned her head and regarded him severely. His heart leaped up his throat. What had she remembered now?

"Is it because I am bald that you haven't kissed me?" she demanded.

"What?" He goggled at her, astounded that she could even conceive of such a thing. "Of course not."

"Then why haven't you proceeded to that demonstration yet? It has been almost a week since you offered me one."

"Because—you have been unwell and I don't wish to rush you."

His reply was not dishonest, but he was still reflexively shying away from the greater truth.

"You can't rush me—I won't allow you to rush me," she said, her tone haughty. "But you do owe me that demonstration. A man who dares tell me that I enjoy kissing him had better be ready with the proof."

Her hand reached up and felt around the edge of the turban. The gesture, in sharp contrast to the imperiousness of her words, was quite tentative. It dawned on him that she was genuinely concerned that her lack of hair was somehow responsible for his lack of aggression.

"My dear Helena, I assure you, you are just as pretty without your hair."

She pulled her lips tight. "Liar."

He approached her and, in one quick gesture, yanked the turban from her head.

"Give it back!" she cried. One of her hands covered the top of her head; the other grabbed at the turban.

He took her by the shoulders and turned her toward the mirror. "Look at yourself."

She dropped her hand from her head but kept her gaze firmly averted. "I look like a prisoner."

"I know conventional ideas of femininity demand the presence of hair—a great deal of it, preferably. But set aside your preconceptions. Don't judge your appearance on what it is not, but on what it is."

She glanced at the mirror and grimaced.

"You are beautiful as you are," he murmured. "I don't think I've ever noticed the shape of your cheekbones, the sweep of your eyebrows, or the fullness of your lips as well as I do now."

He cupped her chin, his thumb pressing into the center of her bottom lip. Their gaze met in the mirror. Her lips parted; her breath caressed the top of his hand.

His heart pounded: She *wanted* to kiss him. Not because he'd blackmailed her, not because they had to in order to convince Mrs. Monteth, but because she wanted to feel his lips against hers, his tongue in her mouth.

He meant to do it properly, start slow and soft, and only gradually build toward the wildness that had always characterized their kisses. But the moment he touched his lips to hers, she locked one arm behind his neck, and all thoughts of leisure and gentleness leaped out the window.

He devoured her. And she, her tongue mobile and eager, devoured him in return. He pulled her out of her chair and pushed her against the edge of the vanity. She grabbed his hair and moaned, a sound of stark hunger—and it was all he could do not to push up her nightgown and sink into her then and there.

He pulled back before he could become further aroused. They stared at each other for a moment, panting.

"Is this what always happens when we kiss?" she asked, licking her kiss-swollen lips.

He had to clench his hands so as to not fall upon her again. "Precisely."

She took a few more agitated breaths, then grinned. "You are right. I do like it very, very well."

CHAPTER 10

$\mathscr{I}$t was rather late the next afternoon when Hastings's carriage pulled up to his town house. Venetia had decided to throw a celebratory family picnic. Society had deserted London for the country, and they enjoyed an open-air feast in an uncluttered park on Venetia's best tartan blankets, drinking toasts to Venetia's baby and Helena's return to health.

Hastings and Helena alighted from the carriage. She set her hand on his elbow. "So this is what a great deal of new money buys."

"Among other things." His grandfather had been a mere country lawyer. His uncle, however, had accumulated vast wealth via the manufacture of industrial machinery. "I know you do not mind the fragrance of new money, as you yourself are in a commercial endeavor."

"Indeed not. I like money very well. It is the means to independence and authority."

As she had no recollection of his staff, he assembled them again to welcome her home.

"Thank you," she murmured, once the servants had dispersed to their usual stations.

The closer they grew, the more he dreaded the eventual return of her memory. Yet in the shadow of this very fear, a seed of hope was germinating. "It is my pleasure and privilege to pave the way for you, madam."

"Ah, this is not fair," she teased. "A man with the voice of a siren shouldn't also possess the honeyed tongue of a Casanova."

Compliments—he couldn't get enough of her compliments. "What can I say? God was in a generous mood the day He made me."

She snorted good-naturedly. "But let it be noted He ran out of modesty before it was your turn."

"Let those who have faults be modest, and let me be an unabashed paean to His power and glory."

She laughed. "Blasphemy."

"You like it," he murmured.

She cast him a long, lingering look. "Will we stand about all day or will you eventually show me to my rooms?"

His heart thumped—this time not about the possibly imminent return of her memory. "Let us proceed upstairs, then."

She lowered her voice. "Couldn't you have said that without sounding blatantly suggestive?"

"Couldn't you have heard my innocent words without twisting them into a blatant suggestion?" he whispered back.

She shook her head, grinning. The sight of her, delighted

and companionable, was a dart in his heart. Millie was right: He should have admitted his true sentiments years ago. Then he wouldn't be in such a state, dreading that his happiness would be ripped from him in the next minute.

They climbed the steps arm in arm. Before the door of her apartment, he swung her up into his arms. Almost as if she'd been expecting the gesture, she laced her hands behind his neck and turned her face into his jacket. "Hmm, I like how you smell."

"How do I smell?" he asked, setting her down.

"Of tweed, leather-bound books, and a hint of tobacco. Like someone you aren't—an old-fashioned country squire, perhaps."

Her hands slowly slid down his sleeves, rather obviously feeling the musculature of his arms.

"By the way," he murmured, "in case you haven't noticed, I am also perfectly built."

She tapped his jaw. "Cheeky."

Her eyes brimmed with fondness. His heart stopped: This was how he'd always hoped she'd look upon him someday.

Bibliophile that she was, she headed in the direction of the bookshelves. "Go into the bedroom first," he requested.

She turned around. "Did the good Lord also forget subtlety when He made you?"

"No, He didn't. But He certainly gave you a dirty mind, my dear. I want you to *see* the bedroom, not use it."

"Is it exceptionally pretty?"

He inhaled. "I think so."

She opened the door. "So even if I don't like it, I must shower compliments upon . . ."

Her voice trailed off. Her face lifted and her head swiveled slowly, taking in the panorama that had taken him years to complete, through many a frustrated Season, when reaching her had seemed no more feasible than holding starlight in his hands.

"Did you commission this?" she asked, her voice awed—reverent, almost.

His heart fell back into place. "I painted it myself."

"It's stunning. Breathtaking." She turned around. "For me?"

"Of course."

She approached one of the walls, the one with the view of the distant river, and touched her finger to a line of washing strung between two walls. "My goodness, did you paint these from the etchings I brought back from Tuscany? I recognize so many details."

"Now you remember."

When he'd visited Hampton House, not infrequently would he see her in her room, poring over old photographs, or standing before those prints from Italy, as if she were once again walking under the Tuscan sky, with her mother by her side.

"Did I not remember earlier?"

"No."

"Have the etchings been lost?"

"No, but you haven't visited the house in years. And even when you did, I doubt you took time to study the etchings. One stops paying attention to that which has been around a long, long time."

He, too, had been around a long, long time.

She bent her head for a moment, as if deep in thought. Then she closed the distance between them and traced a finger over one of his brows. "It was utterly inexcusable on my part to not have recognized it earlier. Rest assured it is no reflection on your art, but only a terrible statement of my inattentiveness."

He'd asked himself many times, in pique and in despair, why he loved this one infuriatingly unreceptive woman. He could not remember now why he'd ever doubted. "You like the murals, then?"

"Yes." She broke away to admire them again. "I love them. I have never seen anything so beautiful."

He watched her hand glide gently over the world he'd painstakingly created for her. "Then that's all that matters."

*H*elena could not quite understand the pinched sensation in her chest.

She enjoyed the sight, the sound, the smell, and the feel of her husband. She enjoyed his company. And she enjoyed being the object of his affection. Why then was she not beaming broadly? Why did she feel as close to tears as she did to laughter?

"Would you like to see the books you've published?" asked Hastings.

"You have them here?"

"Of course."

So many of her questions were answered with "of course," as if the alternative were unthinkable. As if this were the only possible path for him to have taken in life. As if *she* were his only possible path.

They walked down the stairs arm in arm, with her glancing at him every other second. The sight of his spectacular profile only caused her feelings to grow more unruly, a chaos of fierce, sweet pain.

His study was everything a study ought to be: bookshelves reaching to the ceiling along every wall, a comfortable corner set up for reading, and a pervasive fragrance of leather binding and book dust.

He took out a key from a large desk before the windows and opened a cabinet, the doors of which had been inset with panes of frosted glass. The cabinet contained some forty, forty-five volumes.

An indescribable joy overtook her—this was her life's work—until she began to examine the spines for the titles.

"The books on the bottom are the vanity projects that you charge to publish," he explained. "The books in the middle are those you publish primarily for their commercial appeal. And those on top are the ones you felt driven to bring out."

"Oh good," she said, relieved. "All these spiritualist manuals in the middle, I was beginning to fear I'd taken a fancy to séances. Do they sell well?"

"According to you, they do."

She inspected the books on the top shelf. The ones having to do with helping women obtain employment and education she certainly endorsed, but some of the other titles baffled her. "Are you sure these haven't been misplaced? I am driven to produce volumes of history on East Anglia? Or did I develop an all-encompassing love of that region at some point during my forgotten years?"

"No, but you did become a great friend to the author of these works."

There was a tightness to his voice. She glanced at him curiously, then pulled out one of the volumes. Few expenses had been spared in the production. The volume was bound in fine leather, the title gilt-embossed, the pages edged in gold.

"A.G.F. Martin." She read the name of the author. "I don't remember him—assuming it is a he."

At the sound of a carriage coming to a stop before the house, he walked to the window and looked out. "Mr. Martin was a classmate of mine at Christ Church. I introduced the two of you—brought him to Henley Park when Fitz and his wife gave their first country house party."

He *did* sound odd. She glanced at him. "You don't like him?"

He recoiled, as if something unspeakably gruesome took place on the street outside.

"What's the matter?"

He breathed heavily, as if he'd been running from a gang of murdering thieves. "We have a caller."

Had the accepted hours for visiting changed so much during her absence of memory? "It's late. We are not obliged to receive this caller, are we?"

His expression was quite wild, but his words rang with certainty. "We are. Or you are, at least. He is your author and your friend."

A footman entered. "Mr. Andrew Martin to see you, Lady Hastings. Are you at home to him?"

She looked at her husband. "The same Mr. A.G.F. Martin?"

He turned to the footman. "You may show Mr. Martin here in five minutes."

"Why make him wait that long?"

His answer was another kiss—this time one that would have made for a proper first kiss. It felt like speaking,

almost, to kiss this way, syllables turned into contact of
lips. The movement of his lips and tongue said that he
adored and cherished her, that he could kiss her like this
forever and never stop.

But he did stop. He rubbed her lips with his thumb and
sucked in a breath when she licked the pad of his thumb.

"Let's tell Mr. Martin to come back tomorrow," she
whispered. "I'm not interested in receiving anyone
except you."

"I wish I could." He set his hands on either side of her
head, careful not to hold her too tight. "Whatever happens,
remember that I love you. That I have always loved you."

*A*nd with that, he turned on his heel and left.
Helena was completely nonplussed—she had
no idea she was meant to receive this Mr. Martin by
herself.

Why?

The man who walked in a minute later was an
agreeable-looking fellow, with an air of scholarship to
him—and an air of timidity. He seemed just as surprised
as she at the absence of her husband.

"H— I mean, Lady Hastings, how do you do?"

"I am very well, thank you. And you, Mr. Martin?
Won't you have a seat?"

He sat down gingerly, stealing glances toward the door
as if expecting Hastings to return any moment. Only after
a minute of awkward silence did he clear his throat and
turn his full attention to her. "Are you well, H—Lady
Hastings?"

She relaxed slightly—this man might not be the most

graceful of conversationalists, but she sensed in him a sincerity and much goodwill—at least toward her. "Yes, I am, thank you very much. Although I am sorry to inform you that I have lost a great deal of memories and therefore do not know who you are, except what my husband has told me—that I am your publisher and that he introduced us to each other years ago at my brother's place in the country."

Tiny beads of perspiration appeared on Mr. Martin's face. "You—you lost your memories?"

"As a result of my accident. Apparently I ran into oncoming traffic and received a hard knock to my head."

He pulled out a neatly folded, snow white handkerchief and dabbed at his upper lip. "You mean to say I am a stranger to you?"

"I'm afraid so."

She thought she'd made herself perfectly clear from the beginning, but he stilled all the same. His handkerchief hovered in midair, like the white flag held up by a surrender party. "I . . . I see."

"Please feel free to tell me anything I need to know. Lord Hastings assured me that I delighted in publishing your books, so I am certain whatever you tell me would be quite welcome."

Mr. Martin swallowed. "There is—there is not much to tell. I'd always wanted to write histories. When you started your publishing firm, you encouraged—compelled me, I might say—to hand over my manuscripts. The books have been very well received and I am exceedingly grateful to you."

"That is wonderful to hear. I am glad I've been able to be of assistance to one of Lord Hastings's friends."

Mr. Martin looked down. He reached for the cup of tea that had been brought for him. She was startled to see that his hand shook.

"I apologize," she said immediately. "My husband did mention that you were also a dear friend to me. How remiss of me to think of you only as his friend."

"No, no, if anyone should apologize, it is I. I believe you were coming after me the day of your accident—probably concerning a matter having to do with my latest manuscript." He laughed a little, not from mirth but from what seemed to be a great and growing uneasiness. "I'm quite despondent to be the cause of so much trouble."

That could explain some of his discomfort, if he thought himself the culprit in her accident. She felt sorry for him, but she also felt as if she'd rehearsed for one play, but had been thrust onstage in the middle of another. "How can I blame you for my own inattention while crossing the street? And you must not blame yourself, either."

He raised his face. "That is perhaps easier said than done."

She realized that he shared her coloring, though his was less intense—reddish brown hair and hazel eyes. "I'm alive and hale—and really not terribly bothered about what I cannot remember."

His face only became more anguished. Why did he and Hastings both exhibit such extreme reactions? Was it possible he was afraid to lose her as a publisher? "Am I contracted to publish further works by you?"

His teeth clamped over his lower lip. "Yes, two more volumes on the history of Anglia."

"Then I shall stand by my commitment. And I will read your works and familiarize—or refamiliarize—myself with them, so as to better prepare for your next manuscript. Our publishing agreement will not be in the least affected by my indisposition."

At her firm reassurance, however, he seemed only to become more dejected. He set down his teacup. "That is most kind of you. I'm glad to see you are doing well, and I really ought not to take up any more of your time."

He rose and bowed slightly.

"Would you not care to speak to me of your books?" she asked, still disoriented by the peculiarity of his demeanor.

But he'd already left.

*H*astings had long considered the addition of the Fitzhugh family to the murals. Their figures would be quite small, their faces too indistinct to be recognizable. But they'd be dressed in English fashion of the previous decade, quite unmistakably a band of tourists.

He traced a finger on the path that wound down the side of a hill. He could put them on the path, and have a breeze lift the ribbons on the ladies' hats. Their attention could very well be drawn to the ruined monastery on the next hill, except for Helena's. Her face he would paint turned directly to the viewer—to him.

"Do all my authors act so strangely in my presence?" Her voice came from the door. "And do you always turn white as a sheet and run when one of them comes to call?"

His heart thudded in thunderous relief—Martin in person had not triggered a collapse of the dam that held back the greater reservoir of her memory.

"Who *is* that man?"

He tensed again. Something in her voice told him that

this time her suspicion had been well and truly aroused, that there would be no distracting her with a head of golden curls, no matter how fluffy and springy.

"Do you have any idea why he thought it acceptable to call on me at such an hour? And why, by the way, did *you* act so strangely?"

He didn't answer immediately.

Her voice became more insistent. "What are you withholding from me, sir? Why haven't you looked once in my direction? Do you know that you are appearing quite guilty, even though I can't fathom what wrongs you might have committed?"

The time for truth, the entire truth, had been thrust upon him.

He slid the pad of his index finger along the top of the wainscoting. "I used to be secretly jealous of Mr. Martin, who was a great favorite of yours," he said, still without looking at her.

Her tone was one of utter bafflement. "Mr. *Martin*?"

"Yes, Mr. Martin."

"But I married you, didn't I? That ought to have settled the debate of who is my greater favorite."

His fingers gripped the edge of the wainscoting, as if so flimsy a hold could anchor him in place when the storm came. "We are not married," he said. "We are only pretending to be married."

*H*elena understood the individual words Hastings spoke, but together they made no sense at all. "How can anyone *pretend* to be married? Did we hold a pretend wedding as well? And why would my family allow such a state of things to stand?" She sucked in a breath. "Or do they even know?"

"They know, but they have no choice but to let the pretense stand, at least to the world at large."

Various muscles in her face contracted and tensed. She had no idea whether she was grimacing or trying to laugh at the ludicrousness of what he was saying. "Explain yourself."

He looked skyward, as if praying for a miraculous intervention. "In the life you no longer remember, it was not me you loved, but Mr. Martin."

Distantly, she marveled that she still remained standing. "I don't believe you," she said. Or perhaps she was shouting, for he seemed startled by the vehemence of her words. "I can't have loved Mr. Martin. I felt nothing—*nothing at all*—when I saw him."

"Nevertheless, you have loved him since you were twenty-two years of age," he said, his eyes melancholy.

Was this a dream from which she couldn't awaken? Five *years* of loving Mr. Martin? "Then why didn't I marry him, if I'd loved him for so long?"

He shrugged. "Circumstances."

She tried to peer through the curtain in her mind, but her past was as impenetrable as a London pea souper. "He is a gentleman and I am a lady. What kind of circumstances would prevent us from marrying if we so chose?"

"He was already slated to marry someone else—not engaged, but under heavy expectations." Hastings slanted his lips to one side. "He did not defy those expectations."

The implication of this last statement thundered in her head. "Mr. Martin is *married*?"

"Very much so."

"When did he marry?"

"February of 'ninety-two, six months after you first met."

She felt as if she'd been shoved to the ground. "And until just before my accident, I was *still* in love with him?"

"You never took to any other suitor. He and his wife had little to do with each other. In time you persuaded him to have an affair with you."

She wasn't just lying on the ground, she was being trampled by a stampede of wildebeests. *"What? When?"*

A shadow of pain crossed Hastings's face. "The two of you would be the only ones to know when it started. All I can tell you is that I discovered you in January of this year. Your sister and sister-in-law immediately took you out of the country."

As well they should—she'd have done the exact same thing.

"Unfortunately the strength of your feelings for him was such that when you returned to London, you side-stepped the surveillance your family put into place, and met him at the Savoy Hotel. That meeting, however, had not been set up by either of you, but by his sister-in-law, intending on exposing wrongdoing on his part."

Her skeleton felt as if it would rattle apart with the force of her shock. She stared at Hastings, wishing his words would stop. But he went on, his tiding of evil news relentless, inexorable.

"I happen to know the sister-in-law's husband, who'd said she was up to something. I also happened to intercept the message she'd sent to Mr. Martin, pretending to be you. I followed Mr. Martin from our club to the hotel. When I realized what was happening, I ran up the stairs to warn you, with his sister-in-law coming up the lift at roughly the same time. There wasn't enough time to get Mr. Martin to safety, so we hid him in the bath and pretended that *we* had eloped and were enjoying our honeymoon."

A part of her still hoped he'd shout, "April Fool!" at any moment. But deep in her heart she recognized the inescapability of truth.

She swallowed. "How much time elapsed between the incident at the Savoy Hotel and my accident?"

"Your accident happened the next morning."

What had Mr. Martin said when he called on her? *If anyone should apologize, it is I. I believe you were coming after me the day of your accident—probably concerning a matter having to do with my latest manuscript.*

Whatever she'd wanted to speak to him about, it would not have concerned his latest manuscript. She flushed. She could not imagine herself chasing him in broad daylight, so intent that she'd very nearly forfeited her life to that carriage.

"You still don't remember, do you?" Hastings asked quietly.

She shook her head. Perhaps it was for the best. She was beyond mortified—a married man, and she pursuing him in the streets as if he'd made off with her reticule.

"What did I see in him?" she asked no one in particular. She could not imagine herself breaking all rules of propriety for someone who inspired as little feeling in her as Mr. Martin.

"He was a sweet, openhearted man. You trusted him utterly."

"My judgment was obviously impaired. I set myself at the risk of ruin, and my family at the risk of utter humiliation and heartache. They would never have been able to acknowledge me again. And my God, Venetia's baby. I'd never have been able to see my nephew or niece."

"This is *your* family we are talking about. They let you become a publisher with little more than a raised brow or two. They would have let you see Venetia's child, but you would have needed to be extremely discreet."

She could scarcely breathe for her searing aversion to this reckless, selfish woman who had been described to her.

"Don't be so hard on yourself," he said gently. "You are judging your action—and Mr. Martin's—without context. He was a winsome young man, very well liked for his bright smiles and good nature. Caving in to his mother's insistence on the matter of his marriage turned him more timid, more doubtful, and, ultimately, less joyful. But you'd fallen in love with someone who had not yet made that terrible mistake, who was full of hopes, dreams, and a sincere idealism.

"You lost him when you loved him the most, a difficult blow that never quite softened with time. When you met Mr. Martin in subsequent years, you saw not the man he became, but only the one he'd been, the one you'd have gladly married if only you'd had the chance. Perhaps you forgave him too much, but who among us would not wish to be so generously loved and generously forgiven?"

She leaned back against the doorjamb. His kindness was a balm to her badly singed soul. She let herself wallow in the magnificence of his compassion, the sweetness of his friendship.

He took a step toward her, his brow furrowed with concern. "Helena, are you all right? I hope you are not angry that we haven't told you sooner. It is a complicated story

184

and not always a happy one, and we didn't quite know how to—"

She held up her hand for him to stop. The only person she was angry at was herself.

"Helena—"

She adjusted the cuff of her right sleeve rather unnecessarily. "Where were you in this doomed, idiotic love affair of mine?"

His surprise at her question was followed by a wistful smile. "On the outside looking in."

"So all this—" She gestured at the glorious mural he'd created for her and didn't quite know how to go on.

"I've always loved you," he said, his eyes a blue that was almost violet. "You know this."

She swallowed a lump in her throat. "I only wonder whether I deserve such devotion."

"Sometimes people fall in love with those who do not return the same strength of feelings. It is as it is," he said with a quiet intensity. "What I give, I give freely. You owe me nothing, not love, not friendship, not even obligation."

CHAPTER 11

$\mathcal{N}$ow everything was out in the open.

Hastings felt at once exhausted and unbearably light, all his secrets unloaded. She, on the other hand, looked as if the weight of a continent had settled on her shoulders.

He closed the distance between them and touched his hand to her sleeve. "It has been a long day. Would you like to take some rest? I can have some refreshments sent up."

She gripped his lapels and yanked him toward her with surprising strength. "How dare you leave me alone in my hour of need."

He had rarely been more startled. "That is not what I—"

"I know." She let go of him and smiled sadly. "And what *I* meant was, 'Stay with me.'"

"Of course. Would you still like to have tea sent up?

There are books you like in the sitting room. I can read to you from—"

She gripped his lapels again. "I thought you were more clever than this."

She looped her free arm about his neck and kissed him, her tongue seeking his with a need that had him all but moaning aloud.

He forced himself to pull back. "Wait!"

"No."

"Helena, you've just been told some shocking news. You are not feeling quite yourself. You should be taking a bath, or having something to eat, not leaping on a fellow you didn't even like ten days ago."

She set her hands to just below his ears, her fingers cool upon his skin. "I want this. And I want this to be our wedding night. Now."

She was looking at his lips. It took a moment for him to remember what he meant to say. "Helena, you can't disown a past you don't even remember by taking me to bed."

"I don't want to disown my past," she whispered. "I just want you. I have never wanted anything as much as I want you at this moment."

His head spun. His ears burned. And his lungs must have collapsed in shock, for he couldn't draw in another breath. It was not only raining in the Sahara Desert; it was pouring like the beginning of the deluge.

In the back of his mind a voice begged him to disengage. This was no time to give in to his yearning, the voice beseeched. She would hate him for it when her memory came back.

But an entire jubilant chorus shouted in objection to the timidity of the lone voice of reason. Why allow all the old memories to have supremacy? Make new ones, memories of such luster and beauty that, should the old ones come back, they would be pallid and impotent in comparison.

"David," she murmured.

His heart thumped. She'd never before called him by his given name.

"David. David. David," she repeated.

Their gaze locked. He tried to find some irrational desperation in her eyes, but he could see only wonder, affinity, and undisguised desire.

Suddenly he was the one yanking her to him, the one kissing her as if this were his final hour on earth, the one lifting his arms heavenward in awe and gratitude as rain came down in torrents in the heart of the Sahara.

*H*elena already knew that her husband was a man of many talents. Now she added supremely deft fingers to that list of gifts. She had no idea he'd opened the bodice of her dress all the way to her waist until he was pushing the sleeves down her arms.

She slapped him lightly on the hand. "This is for dallying with all the other women when you should have been chastely waiting for me."

He kissed her again. "What penance will you order for me? Will you make me fall to my knees and worship you between your beautiful thighs?"

The place between her thighs quivered rather forcefully at his suggestion. She couldn't say a word in return.

"Yes, I believe I shall do just that," he murmured.

"You'd better do it very, very well." She somehow found her voice. "Or I'd consider it not done at all."

189

He spoke directly into her ear. "I love it when you order me to do precisely what I want to do."

The brush of his breath, the nip of his teeth on her earlobe—she trembled with the unexpected rush of pleasure and shoved her fingers into his hair.

He kissed her neck. "I never knew I wanted a woman to tug at my hair—until you."

She pulled him to her by his hair and kissed him hard. "Like this?"

"Dear God, exactly like that."

So she did it again, her throat, on its own, issuing little noises not very different from those Millie had made when she and Fitz had been going at each other in Helena's room.

Distantly she heard a thud and realized it was the sound of her corset hitting the floor. She pushed him back. "You will not remove another article of clothing from me until you remove a few of your own."

He grinned as he yanked out his necktie. "You are such a pushy woman."

"I am." Her hand lifted to play with the curl at her ear, only to remember she had no hair to flirt with. No matter, she tossed aside her turban and batted her eyelashes at him. "But I am only ordering you to do exactly what you want. I'll bet you've been waiting to show off your 'perfectly built' body for years."

His jacket fell to the floor, followed by his waistcoat. He glanced at her sidelong as he extracted his cuff links. "Are you ready? You won't swoon on me, will you?"

She gave her lower lip a long, slow lick. "Make me, darling."

His shirt disappeared. She sucked in a breath—he had

not exaggerated. Everything was shapely: his shoulders, his arms, his flat, well-muscled abdomen.

"Decent enough." She exhaled. "Now the rest."

Which she was suddenly most eager to see.

He tsked and came closer. She might be slim, but she was tremendously tall and not precisely fine-boned. But he lifted her out of her dress as if she weighed no more than a good pair of gentlemen's riding boots. "I've wanted to see you naked for far longer. You'll just have to wait for your turn."

"There had better be sky-high praises waiting for me," she warned him as he divested her of her petticoats. "I do not disrobe for anything less."

"Young lady, you had better earn those sky-high praises." He caught her lips for another kiss. "The youth of today are spoiled with unmerited applause, and I have no intention of giving a single compliment before it is warranted."

He opened all the buttons on her combination and pushed it down to the floor. Then he took two steps back, squinted, and studied her. She grew nervous as the seconds passed. She didn't have the most womanly of figures. When she'd been a child she'd been all sharp knees and sharper elbows. Her breasts were probably the smallest pair God had on hand. And He never did send hips, leaving her with a body about as curvaceous as a plank.

The man before her let out a breath. "I don't know if this constitutes sky-high praise, but I will tell you this: I've spent many, many years imagining what you look like without your clothes. And I have a very fine imagination, one of the best in our generation, I daresay. And you, in person, have put that imagination to shame."

Her heart pounded at the hunger in his eyes. He kept looking at her, his gaze hot, his breath uneven.

"Well, don't just stand there." Her voice, too, had become uneven. "Do something."

Before she'd quite finished speaking he'd already closed the distance between them and placed his palm against her breast. She let out a small whimper.

"Did you know that for years you didn't have any breasts?" he said while kissing her with only his lips. "And I loved to fantasize about your chest, flat as a board, nothing but beautiful, hard nipples."

She swallowed and looked down at his hand. Without moving it, he caught her nipple between two of his fingers and slowly tugged. The sight of it, the sharp pleasure of it—she panted, as if she'd been climbing stairs for hours on end.

"I was almost disappointed when you did sprout those gorgeous breasts—but not anymore," he murmured. "Not anymore."

He rubbed the pad of his thumb on her nipple. Her breath caught. The pleasure shot hard into her abdomen.

He lowered his head and took her nipple into his mouth. She cried aloud—the pressure of his lips, the slow, moist swirl of his tongue, and occasionally, particularly, the unexpected scrape of his teeth.

He did the same to her other nipple while she filled the room with moans and sobs. She gasped when his hand closed on her bottom, his fingers digging into her flesh. He groaned and sank his teeth into her shoulder.

"Might as well put your other hand on it, too," she managed to say, "since you like it so well."

But he didn't. Instead he lifted her and laid her on the

bed, pulling off her shoes as he went. "These must be the most beautiful legs in the entire world," he said, peeling away her stockings.

He climbed into bed himself and kissed his way up her legs. Instincts she didn't even know she possessed made her clench her thighs together. Without any hesitation, he pushed them apart, exposing her to his gaze.

"The doors of the temple, darling, never close to the devout acolyte."

And with that, he began his worship, gentle, almost sweet licks of the tongue just to the outside of her folds, before suddenly dipping his tongue *inside* her. She thrashed, her toes digging into the sheets, her body arching toward him, her hands gripping his hair.

His tongue flicked a most sensitive part of her, but only once, making her moan and order him to do it again. He ignored her until she was so taken with the pleasure he wrought elsewhere that she forgot her own earlier demands. Then he suddenly went back to that spot, lavishing it with attention, making her scream from pleasure and need.

When he put his teeth to use, her pleasure rose to a roaring peak. She buckled and shuddered, crying out incoherently, her thighs shaking as he, not letting her go in the least, took her to another peak, then another, then another.

avid. Oh, David, David, David."

The sound of his name on her lips was heaven's own music. The deluge in the Sahara was flooding his humble temple, drowning him in good fortune and answered prayers.

He kissed his way up her torso. Or perhaps he was pulled up by her hands in his hair.

"Shall I do the same for you?" she asked urgently, her breath ragged.

He almost lost himself right then. "Another time, maybe," he rasped, "when you are not a virgin anymore."

"A what?"

"We all assumed otherwise, but you told us you were still a virgin." He kissed her on her shoulder.

"What kind of an affair was that?" She sounded thunderstruck.

"A prudent one, obviously."

"Well, then, quickly deflower me, so I may take you in my mouth and—"

He kissed her on her eager mouth and pushed himself into her, unable to savor the moment as slowly as he'd always anticipated. Nor could he sink hilt-deep into her as his nearly out-of-control body wanted, for despite being impossibly slick, she was also impossibly tight.

He groaned, maddened by the pleasure.

"Dear God," she murmured.

He was immediately contrite. "I'm sorry. Does it hurt?"

Her hand lowered to grab *his* bottom. "Yes, it does hurt, but I want to hold all of you inside me."

At her incendiary words, he drove deeper—far deeper—into her, unable to help himself.

"So," she said, her fingers on his cheek, "now I've made you mine."

He took her fingers in hand and kissed them one by one. "You made me yours long ago, but now you finally claimed me."

She licked *his* fingers. "I don't know why I waited so long. I love claiming you."

He gritted his teeth. "Stop—everything. Or you will make me ejaculate prematurely."

She sucked on his fingers, her tongue teasing. "What is that?"

He breathed hard. "Spilling my seed without properly pleasuring you first."

Her eyes were infinitely mischievous. "But you've already properly pleasured me. Go ahead, spill your seed. I want you to do it."

He almost did at the sound of those words. "Shut up, Helena. I have my pride to consider."

"Hmm." She kissed him on his neck—she *licked* his neck. Her hand slipped between their bodies to touch the base of his cock.

"Stop." To punctuate his words, he withdrew and propelled into her again.

Her eyes widened. "Oh, my. What's that?"

He did it yet again, deeper, harder. "This?"

She panted. "Yes, that."

"This is what you are *not* getting more of if I come too early," he growled.

"I changed my mind. I want you to keep pounding me like this."

"God!" He swore, nearly undone by another surge of lust. "I am not going to last if you won't be quiet."

She was utterly merciless. "You must—you have your pride to consider. And I *want* to tell you how good you feel inside me, how big and hard and powerful." She wrapped her legs about him. "I might let you have supper later, but

I am not going to let you sleep. You are going to pleasure me all night."

He kissed her to silence her, but there was no stopping her clever hands or her writhing body. Years of nighttime fantasy paled to utter insignificance before the reality of making love to her. For even in his wildest dreams she'd remained just a bit aloof. There was no aloofness here, no reluctance. She was all hot willingness and naughty touches, wanting him so much that she was already shuddering again, moaning deliriously against his lips.

He shook with his own climax, emptying into her more and for longer than he ever thought possible, each convulsion more pleasurable than the previous. She kissed his lips, his nose, the lids of his eyes. He collapsed atop her, his heart bursting with sweetness, utterly drained and utterly undone.

*S*he tugged at his hair.

"I'm awake," he murmured.

"You have been so silent," she said, playing with his earlobe.

He smiled into the crook of her neck. "I was imagining Lake Sahara."

She moved back slightly to look into his eyes. "What is that?"

He lifted one hand to touch her cheek. "I used to think being in love with you was like praying for rain in the middle of the Sahara Desert. Well, rain has come, such a rain that soon half of North Africa will be a lake. There will be new grasslands and forests, an endless supply of fish, abundant wildlife of all sorts. And when the sun rises, birds in flocks of thousands will fly over the lake, their wings white as sails in the morning light."

She gazed at him, her eyes as green and soft as the grasslands of his imagination. "That is beautiful."

He felt like a pilgrim standing on the shores of Lake Sahara, having walked barefoot over hundreds of miles, yet all the hardships forgotten, filled with only wonder and reverence at the marvel of it all.

She kissed him slowly, softly, and then said the loveliest words under the sky. "Let's make it rain some more, David."

CHAPTER 12

$\mathcal{H}$elena was in high spirits. Who wouldn't be, after a night of glorious lovemaking?

Moreover, standing on the platform of the rail station, she was surrounded by her family again—they were all leaving London, she and her David to Kent, Fitz and Millie to Somerset, and Lexington and Venetia to Derbyshire. And on top of that, her recovered memories were making themselves useful.

Two ladies, who were also waiting for their train, had stopped to tender Helena their good wishes for both her health and her wedded bliss. And Helena had not needed to be reintroduced to either, for she'd met them both at Venetia's first wedding and recalled them perfectly.

And miraculously enough, nothing seemed to have changed about either. Miss Tallwood was still bespectacled and slightly stooped, more interested in the history of fabrics than the wearing of them. Her handsome sister Mrs. Damien had persisted in widowhood, preferring the nurture of orchids to the nurture of husbands and children.

Helena enjoyed listening to the sisters talk, though she was also aware that Fitz and David stood a little apart from the cluster, having a discreet conversation of their own.

Miss Tallwood was waxing poetic about a fifteenth-century bolt of brocade she'd recently added to her collection when Mrs. Damien cried, "Oh, look, isn't it that nice Mr. Martin who helped you prove the provenance of your brocade?"

At the mention of that name, Helena's heart thudded unpleasantly. Venetia, Millie, and Lexington all glanced at her—David had written to everyone, informing them that Helena had been told the truth of her past.

"You are right," said Miss Tallwood. "It is him. And you are his publisher, are you not, Lady Hastings?"

Helena kept her voice neutral and her answer short. "Yes."

Mrs. Damien waved at Mr. Martin. "Hullo, Mr. Martin!"

At the sound of his name, Mr. Martin glanced in their direction and immediately turned red. He looked about, as if searching for a place to hide. But Mrs. Damien would countenance no such unsociable urges and called out to him again: "Over here, Mr. Martin."

Now he had no choice but to approach. Helena, with her face carefully set, presented him to Venetia's husband, whom he had yet to meet. Mr. Martin stammered through the introductions. She was embarrassed for him and mortified for herself, feeling ever more incredulous that she'd had anything to do with this man beyond a greeting and a handshake.

She stole a peek at David. He looked tense, but gave her a small lift of the chin as reassurance. The past was the past, said his gesture; no point worrying about what could not be changed.

"Are you going home, Mr. Martin?" asked Miss Tallwood, oblivious to the undercurrents.

Mr. Martin wiped his forehead with a handkerchief. "I—I am going to call on my mother."

"I heard she'd taken ill earlier in the Season," said Millie kindly. "But I understand she has since completely recovered."

"Unfortunately the recovery was not as complete as we would have liked," replied Mr. Martin, looking distraught. "And now this new bout of fever has her physicians worried."

Helena felt an involuntary swell of sympathy for him. He still remembered everything; her coolness to him must be terribly uncomfortable, given how diligently she'd pursued him. And now his mother was so ill he worried for her life. . . .

"I hope Mrs. Martin will make a speedy recovery," she said. "And that you will have her company for many years to come."

Everyone else also offered their good wishes for Mrs. Martin. Mr. Martin mumbled his gratitude, bowed, and left.

Helena exhaled in relief at his retreating back. She did not blame him for anything—it was all too evident that she must have been the one to instigate their affair and to pressure him to agree to her demands. All the same, she was glad that, with the Season ending, she would not run into him again for months upon months.

"Look at the hour," she said brightly. "It's almost time for us to board, Lord Hastings. Shall we say our good-byes?"

$\mathcal{H}$astings's heart was still beating fast when he and Helena settled themselves in his private rail coach. Out of view of those still on the platform, her gloved hand took hold of his.

With her free hand she waved at her family, Miss Tall-wood, and Mrs. Damien. "I am no longer thinking of him and neither should you."

His was a perilous happiness, but moments like this made all the bouts of fearful despair worthwhile. He joined her in the waving. "I wasn't thinking of him, but of us."

A steam whistle blew shrilly, indicating the train's imminent departure. On the platform, a rail guard motioned the crowd to move back. She kept on waving. "You weren't speaking to Fitz about us, were you?"

"Goodness, no, at least not in the manner you are imply-ing. We were talking about Mrs. Englewood, his old sweetheart."

"A sweetheart before he married Millie?"

He looked at her, surprised. "No one has mentioned her to you yet? Fitz had to give her up when he needed to marry an heiress."

She shook her head. "No. Fitz and Millie always speak of their life together as if they'd been in a perfect state of harmony and happiness since the day they first married. I would never have guessed that there was someone else."

"There was. Mrs. Englewood came back from India during the Season—*this* Season—and she and Fitz were ready to set up their own household. He came to his senses only shortly before your accident."

She blinked. "I can't imagine it."

"Neither can I quite believe it now, but that was what happened."

The train began to move, the rumble of its wheels gaining volume and depth. They waved one last time at everyone on the platform. A knot of travelers, recently detrained and in a hurry to leave the rail station, trudged by. One woman turned her head rather sharply to look in Venetia's direction, catching Hastings's attention.

Mrs. Andrew Martin. Martin was somewhere in the same station, catching a train, but his wife had clearly just come back from a different journey. Hastings supposed such must be the norm for a couple leading separate lives.

And the lives of the Martins were so separate, a well-dressed man greeted Mrs. Martin's arrival by taking both her hands in his, however briefly.

"I remember her!" Helena cried.

Startled, and with his heart in his mouth, he turned toward Helena. "You remember *Mrs. Martin*?"

She could not remember Mrs. Martin without first remembering Andrew Martin.

"No, I remember Miss Isabelle Pelham, Fitz's sweetheart." Her eyes were wide, her hand clasped over her throat. "Is *she* the one you called Mrs. Englewood just now?"

"She is."

A great many emotions chased across Helena's features: shock, sadness, wonder. "Fitz loved her so much. And they were so perfect for each other. I remember receiving his cable telling me he'd have to marry a girl he'd met only once—I thought it would destroy him."

"It almost did," Hastings said through suddenly numb lips.

Fitz—and Helena—had been nineteen when Fitz had inherited the earldom. Was that as far as her memory extended, or would she exclaim, any second now, about her first sight of Andrew Martin?

"Do you remember meeting Millie?" he asked, testing her memory obliquely.

She frowned, then shook her head. "No, I still don't remember her."

But before he could exhale in relief, she jerked slightly. Then her eyes narrowed, and she looked at him in a way he remembered all too well, turning his entire person ice cold.

"I still don't remember her," she repeated. "But now I remember *you*."

$\mathcal{H}$is expression would have been laughable, had Helena possessed the least desire to laugh. But she felt only disbelief, dismay, and a deep sense of humiliation, everything made twice as atrocious by the faint but unmistakable churn of nausea.

She *remembered* him.

Not the occasion of their first meeting, but instead a solid four years of his visits: summer, Christmas, and Easter.

He loved visiting Hampton House, and the only thing she loved about those visits was his eventual departure.

She'd received Fitz's cable concerning his impending marriage three weeks after she returned to her school in Switzerland. Before that she'd been at home for Easter holiday, and daily, sometimes hourly, Hastings—she could no longer think of him as David—had pestered her. Sometimes with merely a leer, more often a lewd flick of the tongue when no one else could see him, and the rest of the time a quickly uttered insult as he passed her in a room or a passage. *I see your hair color has not improved over time. Publishing? You are really dying to be a dried-up old maid, aren't you? When God made you, He must have been thinking of the Netherlands—flat and unexciting.*

And it was only the tip of the iceberg.

A fifteen-year-old Hastings outside the parlor window of her old house, using a mirror to reflect sunlight into her eyes. And when she'd thrown a glass of water into his face, he'd waved a white flag—except the white flag had been one of her petticoats that he'd stolen from the laundry.

A sixteen-year-old Hastings telling her that she'd never grow breasts unless she invited him to massage them. *It's the only way to make them bigger, a man's touch.*

And what had he said about Easton Grange? *It has a dungeon, Miss Fitzhugh—my uncle was a good old-fashioned Calvinist, and you know how such men are in the privacy of their own home. I hear there was often a girl in the dungeon, chained to the wall or fastened to a contraption that left her defenseless before a man's baser wishes.*

I'm not saying I take after my uncle. But if I did, you know what I'd love to do? Go down into that dungeon and torment my little slave when I have a houseful of guests, your family included, thinking warm, grateful thoughts of my hospitality.

She couldn't get enough air into her lungs. Her memories stomped over her in a never-ending stampede, Hastings, always smug, always smutty, always determined to reduce her entire existence to a bonfire of unsatisfied spinster desires inside a pair of underwhelming breasts.

Belatedly she realized her fingers still covered his. She yanked back her hand, shot to her feet, and stormed as far away from him as possible without leaping out of the speeding train.

"Helena—"

She glanced back at him. She understood, theoretically, that his expression was sincere and pained, but all she could see was the arrogant, dirty sneer she remembered so well. Her throat burned with revulsion.

She turned her face to a nearby window. "Please leave me alone. You've said quite enough."

CHAPTER 13

*H*astings had feared that Helena's displeasure would spill over into her meeting with Bea. He needed not have worried. Until they came to stand before the nursery door, she'd been coolly aloof. But once the door opened, she was nothing if not warm and smiling.

Bea, however, was more sensitive than most children to tension—perhaps she sensed that Helena's friendly cheer was forced, or that her father was completely distraught. She was never fond of meeting strangers, but today she was twice as frozen. Her motion, as she curtsied to Helena, was badly uncoordinated. Hastings, afraid she'd lose her balance, had his hand held out at the ready.

"I am your stepmother." Helena knelt down on one knee—she had a natural, easy way with children. "May I call you Bea?"

Bea nodded jerkily, as if someone had yanked on a string to move her head.

"I am a publisher of books. Do you like to read?"

Bea nodded again.

"But you don't like to speak?"

Bea looked down and gripped Hastings's hand.

"She is shy," he said.

Shy and afraid, his poor child.

Helena did not acknowledge him. "I am very glad to meet you, Bea. I hope we will become good friends, as we will"—her voice faltered for a moment—"be spending a great deal of time together."

Had she been unable to speak because the thought of marriage to him was a spike through her lungs? His own lungs burned with a futile misery.

Helena straightened. "I've heard it said that children should be seen and not heard. I've never believed it myself. It has been lovely to see you, Bea. I hope someday I will hear your voice."

She smiled again at Bea, but it was a wan smile. It startled Hastings to realize that she was disappointed. Without quite thinking about it, he said, "Remember what Papa told you, poppet? Lady Hastings was badly injured only recently, but she has come all this way to see you. Can you wave at her? Your special wave?"

He realized his mistake as soon as he'd finished speaking. Even normal children often responded unpredictably to sudden demands made upon them. Bea, who was piously devoted to her routine and already nervous at the introduction of a stranger, would be entirely paralyzed by his unexpected request.

And she was. She sucked in her cheeks, pressed her lips together, and stared down at the tips of her small boots. Like a tortoise pulling its head and limbs into its shell when faced with danger and uncertainties, Bea, too, had withdrawn into her shell.

*H*elena bit the inside of her lips. She would have been fine taking her leave of Bea without any special gesture from the child. She did not need Hastings to apply pressure to the girl—or the scene that was likely to result.

Hastings already looked defeated, as if he were about to tell Bea to pay no mind to what he'd just said and go back to what she was doing. But in the next moment, he took a deep breath and lowered himself so that his eyes were level with his daughter's.

"I don't mean to make things difficult for you, poppet, and I apologize if I have. But you see, it is a very special day for Papa to bring Lady Hastings home. And I am so happy and excited."

That voice of his—he could have requested women to remove their corsets in public and some would have agreed. And his profile, that amazingly perfect profile, reminding her of an old-master painting of an archangel at prayer, wholehearted and . . .

Humble.

She was not accustomed to seeing him humble. Her mind could not recognize him as the same nasty boy she'd known in her adolescence, and therefore failed to super-impose the boy's repellent sneers upon his features.

All she could see was the young father of a child who must be handled with delicacy, treating that child with great care and respect.

Bea kept rigidly still, giving no indication she'd heard her father at all. She was not an unlovely child. Her straight, fine hair was an almost icy blond. She had wide, blue eyes, a soft pink mouth, and a rather darling overbite to her teeth. But she lacked entirely the charm and vibrancy that one often encountered in pretty young girls who were much adored by their parents.

"This is Lady Hastings's first visit to the house, poppet. And Papa is thrilled she is here," said Hastings quietly.

Helena felt a hard twist of pain in her heart. Had it been only last evening that she'd thrown herself at him headlong, convinced of their perfect fit and future happiness?

She knew what he'd said to her, that all his misconduct had derived from his inability to declare his love. But she could see no love in his long history of insults and innuendos, only a thorough rottenness.

"I want to make her feel so welcome here that she never wants to leave," he went on. "Will you help Papa, poppet?"

His voice could melt the enmity between heaven and hell. Bea, however, would not be so easily won over. She only continued to stare at her boots, as if the rest of the people in the room no longer existed. Or, as if by ignoring them all long enough, she could conjure them into nonexistence.

Miss McIntyre, Bea's governess, chewed her lips nervously. Helena hadn't meant to grow likewise anxious, hadn't wanted to care about his success or lack thereof. But somehow she was holding her breath.

He spoke no more, but rubbed his thumb gently across

the back of Bea's small, fragile-looking hand, and waited. Helena disliked waiting; it made her restless and cross. But he possessed the patience of a hermit.

A minute passed. Two minutes. Three minutes. Bea's governess was visibly fidgeting. Helena shifted her weight from one foot to the other, then back again. Another man would have banished Bea to her room without supper, but Hastings still waited, lifting his hand from Bea's to smooth a strand of hair that had fallen loose from her braid.

Just as the tension in the nursery was becoming unbearable, Bea lifted her free hand and waved briefly in Helena's general direction, with just her little finger held out. The governess emitted an audible sigh of relief. Helena exhaled almost as forcibly.

"Thank you, Bea," she said. "I can't tell you how touched I am. You have made me feel wonderfully welcome."

Hastings shot her a look unreadable for its intensity. The chaos in her head began to multiply again. "I need to go my room to change and rest," she said to Bea. "I leave your father here with you. Will you look after him?"

Bea nodded immediately, obviously relishing the thought. Her love for him made Helena's heart pinch with a fresh pain.

As she walked past Hastings, he said softly, "Thank you."

She left without answering. But once outside the nursery, she stopped and listened with the door slightly ajar. Contrary to what she'd expected, Bea did not suddenly become loquacious, "Papa" this and "Papa" that.

In fact, father and daughter remained resolutely silent. Helena pushed the door open an inch more and saw Hastings and Bea's clasped hands. They stood before a glass container that held a small tortoise, solemnly watching the creature making its slow but determined round.

*N*o grand murals awaited Helena in the mistress's apartment, but an entire wall of books did, books that she had either already read and enjoyed or would dearly love to read as soon as she had the chance.

Had the previous woman who occupied this room, Hastings's aunt, possessed similar taste to Helena? Or was this another instance of—

She did not let herself complete the thought.

Several maids helped sort her belongings into drawers and wardrobes. She supervised distractedly. After the staff had left, she sat down with a stack of books and tried to read. A knock came at her door half an hour later, when she was still only on page two of the first book. It was a footman, bearing a message from Hastings.

Dear Helena,

If you are not too weary from the journey, Bea and I would like to extend an invitation for you to join us for tea. She has decided, to my delight and surprise, to show you her favorite book. I hope you will enjoy reading it as much as we do.

Your servant,
Hastings

Had the invitation been issued by Hastings alone, Helena would have turned it down: The rail journey had been excruciating with him so near; she needed some more time to herself, away from him. But she did not have the heart to turn down Bea, if indeed it was the girl's own idea to share her favorite book with Helena.

She was guided to a room that the footman referred to as Miss Bea's tearoom. When the door opened before her, she stood for a moment on the threshold, taken aback by the painted vista that greeted her, a pretty pond surrounded by fetching little cottages that sprouted flowers from window boxes, pots affixed to the walls, and, in the case of one particular cottage, the entirety of an earth-covered roof.

But what stopped her in her tracks was not the scenery, but animals dressed in country garb going about their business. Here a squirrel in a large white cap and a brown sack of a dress watered her rosebushes with a dreamy look in her eyes; there stood a group of rabbits in tweeds and short trousers in the midst of a game of cricket; and on the pond, in a small blue rowboat, a pair of ducklings fished, one in a bowler hat with a pipe clamped in his bill, the other, a girl, sporting a straw hat piled high with fresh flowers, much like those Eton rowers wore for the annual Procession of the Boats.

"Thank you for joining us," said Hastings, rising from a table spread with half a dozen small plates of sliced cake and sandwiches.

Helena nodded, not quite looking at him, and took a seat on the other side of Bea, who seemed to be in a much happier frame of mind. She did not smile or speak when Helena greeted her, but she did hold out a thick, clothbound notebook.

When Helena tried to take the notebook into her own hands, however, Bea did not let go. "Ah, I see," said

Hastings sent her a small, grateful smile as he took his seat again. She did not smile back, but bent her attention to the notebook. "So this is your favorite book, Bea?"

After a few seconds, Bea nodded.

"Will you open it for me?"

Bea lifted the blue brocade-bound cover. The first few pages were blank, high-quality paper that appeared heavy yet soft, separated from one another by layers of translucent rice paper—this was not so much a book as an exceptionally well-constructed artist's sketch pad.

The next turning of the page revealed a duckling in country tweed and a deerstalker hat, a jaunty-looking fellow, despite the very staid elbow patches on his jacket and the even more staid tobacco pipe sticking out of one pocket flap.

Helena turned toward the murals and noticed for the first time that they were not yet complete: One wall remained blank; the outlines of a small bridge and a tree with a swing hanging from one branch had been drawn with pencil, but no paint had been applied. The room was a work in progress.

She didn't know why that should cause a twinge in her heart.

"The duckling in the boat on the wall, he is the same one as this?"

Bea nodded again. Helena did not need to ask Hastings to know that he was the artist. Where had he hidden so much talent during their long and unprofitable association?

Next to the duck's feet was written the name Tobias.

"My goodness," said Helena, "I've just noticed he has four feet. Why does Tobias have four feet?"

Bea turned the page. Now Tobias was shown leaning to the side, revealing a girl duckling behind him: the girl duckling from the boat, wearing another flower-laden hat.

"Do you have a hat like this?" Helena asked Bea.

Bea looked toward her father. He gave her an encouraging smile, an expression of infinite kindness and affection. Helena didn't know she was staring at him until Bea tugged at her sleeve. And when Helena pivoted her attention back to the girl, Bea nodded slowly and emphatically, as if she were repeating her answer.

Helena had very nearly forgotten the question. The hat, right, the flowered hat. "Do you like flowers very much?"

Her question was answered with another nod.

"Do you garden yourself?"

This time the answer was more complicated. Bea nodded, frowned, then shook her head, seemingly slightly discouraged.

"She waters a part of the garden on Mondays," Hastings explained.

He hadn't spoken for a few minutes, leaving the conversation to Helena and Bea. At the sound of his voice, she was suddenly back in her sickbed, listening to his reading of the sonnets of Elizabeth Barrett Browning.

She pushed away the memory and bent her head forward a few inches so she could look Bea more directly in the eye. "I have published a book on gardening, a very good one. If you like, Bea, you can ask Papa to read it to you, so that you can learn how to grow the most beautiful flowers. Also, my sister-in-law, Lady Fitzhugh, has one of the finest gardens in England. When you are ready to start your own garden, we will ask her for seeds and cuttings."

What Helena said was not something perfectly suited to either a nod or a shake of the head. Bea appeared disoriented for a moment. After a while she simply looked down and turned the page again.

Now there was a thatch-roofed cottage, its windowsills brimming with asters and geraniums. The cottage was located at the edge of a pond. A flower-lined cobblestone path bisected the lawn and led down to a small pier, where a rowboat was tied.

Helena glanced toward the murals again and found a house exactly like it—except the rowboat, instead of being tethered to the pier, was in use on the pond. "Is this where Tobias and his friend live?"

Bea turned back a page to show the girl duckling's name, written above her shoulders. *Nanette*. She then proceeded to the page after the illustration of the cottage, where the first lines of text appeared, and waited expectantly.

She meant for Helena to read the story aloud.

Helena complied. " 'It has been a while since Tobias and Nanette encountered an Adventure. Two weeks, to be precise. Now, you might say two weeks is hardly any time. But for ducklings, Adventures are like cake. Once you have tasted cake, two weeks becomes a long time to go without.'

"Are you the author, too, Hastings?" she asked without turning her face in his direction.

"Yes."

The Boy Who Leered would grow up to write and illustrate children's stories. Why did that make her feel so . . . cross? Or was she angry because she preferred the simplicity of anger to the staggering complexity of the rest of her emotions?

Bea, who'd already turned the page, tapped on it to gain Helena's attention. Helena smiled apologetically and went on. " 'But on this bright, late-summer morning, they did not need to seek Adventure. Adventure arrived all the way from Egypt on four legs. For you see, it becomes unbearably hot on the Nile this time of the year, and Mr. Crispin Crocodile therefore takes his annual holiday in the north, where the summers are as cool and refreshing as a lemon sorbet.' "

And there was Mr. Crispin Crocodile, in his seersucker summer suit, mopping his brows with a handkerchief. He looked huge and hungry.

" 'Tobias was taking his usual morning walk around the pond. All his neighbors—the squirrels, the beavers, the bunnies, et cetera—seemed to have disappeared. "It must be the time of the year for holidays," he mused to himself. But he was quite happy to remain at the pond with dear Nanette, until he saw Mr. Crispin Crocodile setting down his travel satchel to feel for his keys in his pocket. All of a sudden Tobias understood why his neighbors had fled, and why he was able to purchase his marvelous little cottage the previous autumn at such a bargain.' "

The Boy Who Leered would grow up not only to write and illustrate children's stories, but to do so with exceptional charm and assurance.

Bea tapped at the page again, waiting for Helena to continue.

"I can read for her if you'd prefer not to," Hastings offered.

Still without looking at him, Helena said, "I'm fine. I'll read the rest."

iss McIntyre, Bea's governess, came to retrieve her at the end of tea, leaving Hastings and Helena alone in the room. He expected Helena to depart on Bea's heels, but instead she leveled him a severe gaze and said, "That is a very good story."

His heart almost left his chest at her compliment. "Thank you. I'm glad you like it, since you are publishing that story—and eleven others like it."

Her brow furrowed in fierce concentration, as if she were trying to gather every last detail from all the correspondence and documents she'd recently read. "So you are Miss Evangeline South and this is one of the *Old Toad Pond* tales."

"Correct."

She leaned forward and picked up a cucumber sandwich. He stared at the line of her arm. She had wonderfully long, lissome arms. In a ball gown they were a sight to behold.

"You could have asked for more than one hundred and ten pounds for the copyright," she said.

He shrugged. He didn't need the money and he'd been thrilled she'd offered as much.

"Let me guess: You never told me that you are the author."

"Correct."

Her expression was not revolted, as it had been earlier, but merely, though deeply, irked. "Why not?"

He shrugged again. "I didn't want you to make fun of me."

"I won't deny that I might have made fun of you—at first. But in the end I do not laugh at talent and hard work. And that would have been a far superior way to earn my attention than those loathsome methods of your choosing."

He looked into her eyes, lovely, imperious eyes that had enslaved him from the very beginning. "You are right. I'm sorry."

Her lips parted. For a moment it looked as if she were about to say something in response, but she didn't. She ate the remainder of her sandwich in silence, wiped her hand on a napkin, and left.

*H*elena was about to go to bed when a knock came at the door. "Yes?"

It was Hastings, who could have used the connecting door between their bedrooms, but had chosen to approach via the formal entrance to her apartment.

She'd last seen him at Bea's tea only hours ago, so there was no need for her pulse to accelerate at his proximity. But accelerate it did. Her hands had been all over his hair—and all over the rest of him. She'd licked his beautiful neck. And she'd offered to take his manhood into her mouth and pleasure him until he—

"You need something, Lord Hastings?" At least her voice sounded properly remote.

He had a large envelope in hand. "I have another manuscript for you."

"Another *Old Toad Pond* tale?"

"No, something much less suitable for children."

"What is that?"

"An erotic story."

She blinked, taken aback. "Do children's writers also dabble in pornography these days?"

He hesitated. "It's an erotic story about you and me."

Her heart thudded with both vexation and, unfortunately, further arousal. "You think I'd like a story about how you rogered me and enjoyed it?"

His eyes were on the envelope in his hand, his fingers wrinkling a corner of the flap. "It wasn't written to titillate—or maybe I should say it wasn't written merely to titillate. When your family took you to America at the beginning of the year, they hoped that time and distance would cool your passion for Mr. Martin. I, on the other hand, feared that deprivation would make you reckless, leading you to be caught. Should that be the case I would, of course, step in and offer marriage. And you would accept my hand to spare your family the scandal. But I couldn't help imagining how miserable we'd be in that marriage, which led me to the writing of the story."

His explanation made no sense to her. "And the story would have made us less miserable?"

"It's—" He took a deep breath. "Yes, I thought it would. It's a love letter, you see, full of everything that I could never say to you in person."

A sweet misery engulfed her. So he did try, in however indirect a manner, to court her.

"Regrettably," he went on, "I probably wrote and illustrate the story in such a way as to guarantee that you will never read past the first two pages."

She could strangle him in her disappointment. "You are really your own best enemy, aren't you?"

He raised his face, his eyes a sea grey in the light of the lamps. "Yes, I've known that a long time."

*S*he said nothing in response, but he could almost hear her scream, *You idiot*, in her head. He tapped his fingers against the envelope that contained everything he should have said to her long ago—or a copy of it, since the original was still in her office at Fitzhugh and Company.

"I'll leave this with you, then." He set down the envelope on an end table. "Good night."

At the door, however, her voice stopped him. "When I was still at his house, Fitz told me to remember that you are sensitive and proud. I don't mind people who are sensitive and proud, but you are to sensitive and proud what the Taj Mahal is to an ordinary mausoleum—a white marble monument with gardens, minarets, and a reflecting pool to boot."

She exhaled long and unsteadily, as if trying to calm herself. "Why? Why are you like this?"

He had no idea how to answer such a question.

Her eyes narrowed, then she turned toward the mantel. He realized she was only following the direction of his line of sight, and he had been, without quite intending to, looking toward the photograph of his mother.

She walked to the mantel for a closer look at the photograph, which depicted his mother in costume. The small plaque on the frame read, *Belinda Montagu as Viola*. "Good gracious," she muttered. "Is this your mother?"

He'd inherited the curls and the cheekbones from his mother; the resemblance was undeniable. "Yes."

Helena turned around. "She was an *actress*?"

He could not tell whether Helena assumed the stage was but the venue from which his mother sold her favors, but enough people had done so in his life that he reflexively leaped to the latter's defense. "She was very good at her craft."

"I don't doubt that. I am only shocked that your father's family allowed the marriage to proceed."

"My uncle was sixteen years senior to my father and quite indulgent of his little brother. No doubt my father convinced him that my mother would settle down to become a good little hausfrau, and that in time her past on the stage would be forgotten like last year's news."

It felt strange to speak of his family history—almost as if he were disrobing in public, right down to his underlinen. He'd never had to do it before: Everyone either already knew or soon found out from someone else. And when boys at school had, the only explanations he'd given had been via his fists.

"So did Belinda Montagu ever become the domesticated Mrs. Hillsborough?"

"Her real name was Mary Wensley. And no, after two years she returned to the stage. She and my father were in the middle of an annulment when he died—and I was born eight and a half months later. My uncle was convinced my birth was a shameless ploy on my mother's part to gain a portion of his fortune, since he and his wife were childless."

"But I thought your uncle was your guardian."

"I lived with my mother until I was seven. Then, one

fine day, we came across my uncle. And within weeks he'd assumed guardianship of my person."

Looking back, he realized it was quite possible his mother had engineered the meeting—she'd known she didn't have long to live and she'd wanted him to have everything his uncle could offer. But Hastings had wanted nothing of what his uncle could offer, not when his uncle was determined to repent for his earlier permissiveness with Hastings's father by denying Hastings every freedom and pleasure under the sun.

For as long as his mother lived, he'd run away to visit her every time his governess turned her back. After his mother died, he lived with a band of Gypsies for almost six months until he was caught and brought home. He didn't bother running away from Eton—even with all the bullies it was better than living at home with his uncle. And eventually the bullies had learned to leave him alone, because he was a far nastier fighter than they, and no one came away from a brawl with him unscathed.

Helena frowned, but her eyes had become softer, as if she were beginning to understand something about him that she hadn't before.

"Don't," he said immediately. "Don't excuse me for having been an ass simply because my mother's profession might have caused me difficulties with my uncle and at school. You never did it before and I've always liked that about you—I earned your disfavor not by the grace of my parentage but by dint of my own hard work."

She stared at him, this dunce who would turn down her sympathy. "Well, then, if you say so. You were a complete ass and your lovely mother would have been ashamed of you."

For some reason, the way she handed down her reprimand, with a roll of the eyes that was half wonder, half exasperation, made him smile—the first genuine smile that had come to him since she remembered that, indeed, he had been a complete ass.

The corners of her lips also lifted, but she turned away before he could see whether that seed of mirth became anything more. "Good night," she said. "And you may leave your smutty story here. I may look at it when I've finished with all the other books you own."

As promises went, that was quite good enough for him.

It wasn't until he'd opened the door that he remembered to tell her, "By the way, you spend most of the story tied to a bed. I hope you enjoy."

CHAPTER 14

$\mathcal{H}$elena circled the end table on which the envelope lay, tapping her chin, clearing her throat, regarding Hastings's manuscript askance. It was late; she ought to be resting, and she didn't have much of an appetite for erotica—or at least, she hadn't developed a great appreciation of it by the time she turned nineteen.

But, as it turned out, one did not simply leave unperused a smutty love letter in which one was fastened to the bed for one's husband's pleasure.

The manuscript, titled *The Bride of Larkspear*, had one place where Hastings had left a note saying, *If you read nothing else, read this*. But if she read nothing else, how would she be able to place into context the passage he'd selected?

She opened the manuscript to a random page to see just what it was that she *didn't* absolutely need to read.

"Why are my hands tied?" she murmurs. "Are you afraid of them?"

"Of course," I reply. "A man who stalks a lioness should ever be wary."

"And what does he do when he has caught said lioness and put her in a cage?"

I brush aside a strand of hair that has fallen before her eyes. "He teaches her that captivity can be wonderfully enjoyable—and trains her to become a tame house cat, a sweet, willing little pussy."

Her eyes darken at my not-so-subtle double entendres. "Lionesses do not become house cats."

My hand travels down and grazes her rib cage. "Why belittle your ability to change? It is only your first hour of incarceration."

I have always loved to antagonize her. Little wonder she'd long refused to have me. In the end she'd chose me over absolute ruin—not a choice that greatly flatters me, but now she is mine, for better or for worse.

It really was about them.

"Why?" she asks, her voice tight. "You are a man of wealth and position. You do not lack for feminine attention. I have even heard you described as charming—though I will never understand it. Why then have you chosen to cage me when many would be glad to be your pet, your sweet, willing little pussy?"

I step closer and watch the pulse at her throat accelerate. Her breasts rise and fall in a beautifully agitated cadence. Lust swells like a dark tide in my blood.

"Their eagerness bores me," I whisper, my lips nearly caressing her ear. "It will be more fun to watch you struggle."

A tremor passes through her—my darling is finding me more difficult to ignore.

"You revolt me," she says harshly.

I do not doubt that. But if I revolt her purely and absolutely, we would not be here. Within her cool contempt, there has always been—or so I believe—an element of interest that she refuses to acknowledge.

"Excellent. Nothing spices pleasure like a little revulsion."

Well, so far nothing that was *terribly* smutty.

I palm her breast and rub my thumb along her already hardened nipple.

Helena nearly dropped all the pages. She'd judged too soon; this most certainly *was* an erotic story.

The master of Larkspear brought his reluctant bride to pleasure with his fingers while she was tied to the bedpost. Then he tied her to the headboard and gave her yet another trembling climax—this time with his cock.

It was a few minutes before Helena could stop panting. She dared not read any further, or she'd crash through the connecting door and ravish Hastings—and she was far from sure how she felt about him.

But as she set aside the manuscript, she saw Hastings's note again: *If you read nothing else, read this.*

Oh, why not?

The *petite mort* is powerful, one long, voluptuous convulsion of mutual pleasure. Afterward I untie her wrists and hold her in my arms. She believes it is her body that bewitches me, her smooth skin and tight quaint. She is not wrong; I am beguiled by her smooth skin and tight quaint. But it is this that has me completely in its thrall, this moment of paradise when she is still too suffused with pleasure to use her now-free hands to push me away.

I bury my face in the glory that is her unbound hair. I part her hair and kiss her nape. I stroke her shoulder, her arm, and her sweet soft belly with the greediness of a sot gulping down common gin.

But all too soon, she removes my hands from her person. "I wish to sleep now."

I place my hands underneath my head with a nonchalant air—as if I haven't been rejected again. "Let me tell you a good-night story."

"If it's about what the prince really does to Sleeping Beauty when he finds her, I've heard it before."

"No one sleeps in this story—or at least not when it matters."

She doesn't say anything for a moment. I tense, waiting to be further rejected.

"Well, why not? I might as well hear what other depravities have been rattling around in your head."

She surprises me. I turn toward her, my head propped up on my hand. She gazes at the ceiling, my lovely wife, with no interest to spare for me.

"Once upon a time, there was a country named Pride," I begin. "It was a proud country; everyone from the king and the queen on down to the lowest street sweeper was proud. But no one was prouder than the prince of the realm, a handsome young man by the name of Narcissus."

"And he was so enamored of his beauty that he couldn't stop looking at his own reflection?"

"My love," I admonish, "how little faith you have in me. Would I bother to recount such a hackneyed story to you? Trust me: You have not heard this one."

She shrugs indifferently. "Go on, then."

"The most fashionable mode of travel in the country of Pride was a dirigible powered by none other than its owner's personal pride. The prouder the person, the bigger his or her dirigible, and the higher and faster it flew. No one in all of Pride had a greater and fleeter dirigible than Prince Narcissus's, which was, aptly enough, called *Narcissus's Pride*."

"And which will be thoroughly punctured by the end of your tale?"

I tsk. "Only ignorant foreigners would propose such a repellent deed. In Pride one would no more think of puncturing another's dirigible than one would sell one's mother on the town square."

"And just how common was the practice of mother selling in Pride?"

"Nonexistent, for the people of Pride loved their mothers."

My bride rolled her eyes. "All right. Go on."

"A prince devised his own contest for ladies who wished to win his hand. For seven years running, the prince's contest had been a three-day dirigible race, which he won handily each time. The entire country began to grow anxious for their prince, for he was of an age when he should settle down and beget heirs.

"Unbeknownst to the world at large, Narcissus had long been in love with a young woman of Pride named Fidelia, who owned a bookshop in the capital city. Fidelia knew Narcissus existed, of course; she even had occasional business dealings with him—Narcissus loved books, and Fidelia was the best conveyor of rare and valuable tomes in the land. But Narcissus and his fancy dirigible mattered little to Fidelia. In fact, she made fun of him to her friends, mocking the size of his dirigible, and what one man could possibly do with so much hot air at his disposal.

"Word would get back to Narcissus and he would pace the high ramparts of the palace, unable to sleep. From time to time he turned the telescopes in the astronomy tower to Fidelia's bookshop in the city, to watch the light in her upstairs window, wishing he could be in her room with her, reading together."

"My, for a moment I thought he meant to tie her to her bookshelves," says my bride.

"Please, he is nowhere near as romantic as I am. Now, where am I? Ah, every three months Fidelia went on a book-buying trip to several nearby lands. The prince always watched for her return—when she came back from those trips was when she came to the palace with a crate of her best finds for Narcissus to inspect, and he awaited those meetings with a yearning only those who'd known unrequited love could understand.

"Pride was a country of largely predictable weather. They were in the middle of the dry season. Fidelia's freight of books was loaded on drays normally used for barrels of ale, and not the covered wagons she'd have used in rainier seasons. But as the prince watched her progress on the dusty plains outside the city walls, what should he see but an unseasonable storm on the horizon, fast approaching.

"He immediately called for *Narcissus's Pride*, his dirigible. But by the time he reached her drays, the storm was nearly on top of them. There would be no time to transfer her books for safekeeping inside the gondola of the dirigible.

"The prince did not hesitate. Much to Fidelia's openmouthed shock, he pulled out his dagger and sliced into his dirigible, opening it up into an enormous waterresistant tarp to place over her books. Fidelia, recovering her composure, found large rocks to place all along the edges of the tarp, to keep it from flying away during the storm.

"They finished and ducked inside the gondola just as rain came down in torrents. 'Why have you destroyed your beautiful dirigible?' Fidelia at last asked. 'They are only books.'

"'Maybe,' answered Narcissus. 'But they are your books.'

"To this day people talk about how the prince won the hand of his beloved after first taking a knife to his pride. Narcissus and Fidelia were married the next spring. They lived and ruled happily together for many years."

It was not just a love letter, but a prayer, a devout hope for better things to come. And as Helena closed the manuscript, she found herself hoping for the very same.

CHAPTER 15

*L*ife at Easton Grange revolved around Bea, who hadn't the least idea that such was the arrangement. She was oblivious to many things, but one could count on her to be passionately devoted to her daily routine, going about it with the fastidiousness of a maestro conducting a Beethoven symphony.

She ate breakfast at eight and went for a walk with her father at nine—sticking strictly to three paths, each for two days of the week, plus a special Sunday path. After arriving back at the nursery at ten, she had lessons until luncheon. Another hour of lessons followed in the afternoon, and then came activities particular to each day. Monday she watered the gardens, Tuesday she brushed her dolls' hair and changed their clothes, and so on and so forth. She rode at four, had tea at five, which also served as her supper, took her bath, listened to a story, and went to bed.

If her walk took less time than usual, she would wait outside the nursery until the clock struck the hour. Should a Monday be rainy, she'd still be out in the garden, a watering can in hand, a mackintosh over the rest of her.

These, however, were but quirks. Whenever the integrity of her schedule became threatened, Bea's eyes would grow larger, her face paler. She worried the inside of her cheek, her hands clasping ever more tightly onto each other.

Once at tea, they discovered that the sandwich that had been prepared for her was the wrong kind for Wednesday. Normally a quick word with the kitchen would have fixed the problem. But Wednesday happened to be half day, and the staff enjoyed the afternoon off. By the time Hastings found all the ingredients to assemble the Wednesday sandwich, Bea was in a state of trembling agitation, for fear that she would be late to her bath.

"What would have happened had she been late to her bath?" Helena had asked, as they waited outside the bath while Bea hummed and played with the water in her tub, calm again after the crisis had been averted.

Hastings had tilted his head against the wall. "Disaster. She would have climbed into her trunk and not come out for hours. At least by teatime the day is almost over. God help us if something goes awry in the morning."

"Has she always been like this?"

Hastings sighed. "I can't tell you for certain. When I agreed to take her in, I hired a nanny who came with excellent character letters, set the pair of them in a cottage on the edge of the estate, and thought my duty done. According to the maids who cleaned the cottage—it was they who first alerted me that something was amiss—she'd been a docile enough baby. But about the time she turned two, she became impossibly stubborn. The nanny did not believe children should have any say in their upbringing—and what followed was not pretty."

He stared at the wallpaper on the opposite side of the passage. "I was furious with myself. My earlier excuse for not paying close attention was that I'd spared her a life in the poorhouse. It was not acceptable to be simply better than the worst. I was responsible for this child and I'd allowed her to be mistreated under my very nose, to become this quivering, screaming creature."

Sunlight still poured in from the window at the end of the passage, a bright stream that angled upward and lit him like a halo.

"You've done quite well by her since," said Helena.

He sighed again and raked his fingers through his hair. She envied that hand. She hadn't touched his hair since they came to Easton Grange.

He rested his hand flat on top of his head. "I'm not sure whether we'll ever be able to reverse the damage. You saw how she can be, and that was only at the thought of her schedule being disrupted. I'm not sure what she'd do if her *life* ever became disrupted—between you and me, I live in dread of the day something happens to Sir Hardshell."

Whatever misgivings Helena might hold concerning his suitability as a spouse, she did not doubt his devotion and dependability as a father. One could say his love of Helena still had a hope of a prize in the end: that she would love him back as ardently, and be his private paradise in bed. But his love of Bea sought no gain other than to do the right thing by the girl—and to improve her lot to such a degree that he might someday forgive himself for his earlier negligence.

Every morning Helena walked behind father and daughter, her eyes fastened to the sight of their clasped hands, her ears wallowing in the music of their conversation—mostly a monologue on his part, sometimes regaling Bea with the medicinal properties of a native plant, sometimes recounting a story of the queen as a little girl, sometimes explaining why the housekeeper was miffed at one of the maids.

Explaining the world, detail by detail, to a girl who did not have an instinctive grasp of many of the intricacies of life.

He wasn't content to simply provide for Bea's current comfort; he was thinking of the day she would become a young woman, the challenges she would face. He wanted a normal life for her, or a life as normal as possible, given her various drawbacks.

And it touched Helena—even more than the murals he'd painted for the girl. Both were labors of love, but on this one he would never stop working for as long as he and Bea both drew breath.

*O*ne of Bea's walking routes ended in a pond that must have served as inspiration for Old Toad Pond. It didn't quite possess the whimsical charm of its fictional counterpart, but it did have clear water, abundant fish, a small forest of waving bulrush, and a grassy, sloping bank on which sat a pair of stone benches.

On this day, Bea walked Sir Hardshell on a harness and Hastings sketched, while Helena read letters that Miss Boyle, her secretary, had forwarded. Helena was apparently more ambitious than even she had supposed. Not content to publish only books, at the time of her accident she had also been in the planning stages of a new magazine, aimed at the increasing population of young working women. The editor she'd hired, a Mrs. Edwards, had written Helena about the articles she'd gathered in readiness for the first issue. Helena jotted down her notes in the margins of the letter, including a proposed meeting so she could reacquaint herself with Mrs. Edwards, whom she did not remember in the least.

The next letter, funnily enough, was from Miss Evangeline South, replying to Miss Boyle's inquiry concerning the progress of "her" revisions on some of the later stories of the *Old Toad Pond* collection. Miss South stated that due to an unanticipated emergency in the family, "she" would need an additional fortnight for the revisions.

Helena showed the letter to Hastings, seated at her feet.

"She wrote me," he said, smiling, "so I had to reply."

He had a gorgeous smile. Sometimes she still wanted to shake her head. He could very well have used that smile on her, instead of that leer. "And are you in fact working on the revisions I wanted?"

"Every morning before you get up."

He did seem to be always up before her. "You had better be working on the revisions, and not writing another one of your naughty tales."

He glanced up at her, his eyes as naughty as certain parts of his story. "You never told me how you liked it, my one and only smutty story."

"I haven't finish reading it and therefore cannot render an opinion."

237

He made a face of exaggerated disappointment.

She shook her head. "You authors, so anxious and delicate. Very well, I liked the passages I've read."

Now he bent his face to his sketch and smiled again. And all sorts of hot sensations sizzled along her nerves. She didn't tell him, but she'd been saving the rest of the story for him to read aloud to her.

But she wanted to wait until the remainder of her memory returned—and everything she'd once felt for Mr. Martin was dealt with—before she began developing a collection of silken cords to use on Hastings.

And for him to use on her, too, should the mood strike him, since she was a sharing soul.

"Why are you wearing that smirk?" Hastings demanded. "That is an up-to-no-good smile if I've ever seen one."

She grinned toothily at him. "If *you* were 'married' to a pornographer, wouldn't you smirk to yourself once in a while? Now, enough talk of subjects unfit for genteel ears like mine. What is that you are drawing?"

He glanced back at his sketch. "The design for the last wall of Bea's mural. I am thinking of introducing a new family of characters and adding a new cottage to Old Toad Pond."

The design of this particular little cottage made her exclaim. "My goodness! It looks just like the miniature cottage my father had built for Venetia and me when we were small."

"You are right. I might have been thinking about it—I'd seen that miniature cottage quite a few times when I visited Hampton House."

"We still have it, as far as I know," she said excitedly.

"I can have it shipped to Easton Grange and set down right at the edge of the pond for Bea."

He gazed at her, one long, steady look of longing. She realized that she'd made a commitment, however minor, to Bea—and to him.

"Don't look so overcome," she said, now a little unsure of the wisdom of her gift. "It is an old toy that will need refurbishing, hardly an extravagant gesture."

"Indeed," he said, letting her off the hook, "nothing of the sort. It's probably all maggoty and covered in bird droppings."

She stuck her tongue out at him. "Now you insult me."

He smiled a little and squeezed her hand. "Bea will be very happy, thank you."

He hadn't touched her since they came to Easton Grange. A thrill raced up her arm.

As soon as her memory came back . . .

*T*he miniature cottage from Hampton House arrived a few days later, weathered and worn, but in better condition than Helena had expected. Hastings took charge of the exterior of the structure, painting it himself after the carpenter had done the necessary repairs. Helena arranged for the interior: new wallpaper, new curtains, a small table and chairs with a tea set, and even a little bookshelf to hold, eventually, all the published copies of *Tales from Old Toad Pond*.

To prepare Bea, they showed her a drawing of what the miniature cottage would look like, had her choose the spot where it would be set down, and reviewed with her, almost to the minute, her altered schedule for the day of the grand unveiling.

When the day came, everything went off without a hitch. The weather was lovely: bright sun, fat white clouds, and an endlessly blue sky. The picnic was delicious. The cottage, with its muted pink walls and leaf green trim, almost had Bea drop Sir Hardshell in her rapture.

The perfection of the day did not end there. That afternoon, instead of riding on horseback to accompany Bea on her pony, Hastings and Helena rode safety bicycles—Helena, indeed, remembered how to ride. And Bea did not raise a single complaint.

Helena was delighted. Thrilled, even. But she was still determined to be patient, and to wait for the rest of her memory to come back.

That was, until the stethoscope.

Bea brought Sir Hardshell to tea and presented the tortoise to Hastings without comment. Hastings excused himself, left the tearoom, and came back a few minutes later with the smallest, most adorable stethoscope Helena had ever seen—who knew stethoscopes could be adorable?

He put on the earpieces, then set the chest piece, no larger than a button, on Sir Hardshell's back.

"Very lethargic heartbeat," he said after about fifteen seconds, "but that's normal, considering he is cold-blooded." He turned over the reptile, which had by this point withdrawn both its head and its wrinkly limbs, and listened to its armored stomach. "The same here, more or less. He is still alive, so that is good news."

He held out Sir Hardshell toward Bea. "But he is tremendously old, ninety years we know of, and who knows how many more before there was ever a record on him.

And when a creature is this old, even if it doesn't look sickly, it still might not last much longer."

Bea took her tortoise back, seemingly not having heard a single word of her father's gentle warning. As she tucked enthusiastically into her sandwich, he gave a small sigh.

The chaos and the sweet pain swept back into Helena's heart. She knew then, with absolute certainty, that she not only loved him, but would love him for the rest of her life. And she would stand by his side, holding his hand, as he guided Bea through Sir Hardshell's inevitable demise—and all the other certain-to-come upheavals in any young person's life.

He caught her staring at him and raised a brow. She merely grinned and asked, "Do you, sir, happen to have a music stand in this house?"

*H*astings had just taken off his shirt when the door of his dressing room opened. He turned around to find Helena, a green ribbon in her still quite short hair, leaning against the doorjamb, her fingers casually playing with the sash of her dressing robe. They sometimes opened the connecting door when they needed to speak at bedtime, so it was not an unusual sight to see her dressed so—except tonight there was no nightgown beneath. In fact, the thin green silk did nothing to disguise the shapes of her erect nipples, which pointed directly at his eyes.

His mouth went dry. "I will not further sample your"—she shifted slightly, and now the dressing robe clung slavishly to the outline of her hip and thigh—"admittedly considerable charms until you first remember everything."

She smiled. "I have no intention of letting you touch

my"—she glanced down at her person—"indeed considerable charms. I only need your help moving something."

He was not assured. She looked far too . . . wolfish. "Not my person to your bed, is it?"

"Not in the least."

Her words were uttered without hesitation, but something in her tone made his blood rush south in arousal. "So what then is this something you need moved?"

"My music stand." She walked back toward her room and beckoned him to follow.

She never had told him the purpose for which she needed the music stand: She played no instruments and, as far as he knew, had never learned to read stave notation.

The music stand was in her bedroom, only a little distance from the connecting door, a delicate-looking specimen that was much heavier than it appeared, having been crafted from solid rosewood.

She returned to his bedroom and indicated a spot by the foot of his bed, a monstrous piece of furniture that had served as inspiration for the master of Larkspur's marital bed. "Here, please."

He hefted the music stand across the distance and set it down where she wanted, right by the bedpost, in his mind at least, to which the bride of Larkspur had been tied in the opening scene of his erotic story. "What devilry are you scheming, Helena?"

She did not answer him, but only gave orders. "Stand with your back to the bedpost."

And when he had done so, she considered the stand—which had last been used by a much shorter person, possibly a child—and raised the music rest as high as it would go.

He still wasn't quite sure what use she could wrest from the music stand, but he was beginning to grasp what she had planned for him. The question was, did he want to acquiesce to her wishes?

He must, because as she pulled out the sash from her dressing gown, causing the latter to fall apart and reveal her from sternum to mons pubis, he only stared, his breath coming in gulps. She took his wrists and tied them together behind his back and to the far side of the bedpost. He did nothing to impede her, but only continued to stare, the size of his lust doubling with every glimpse of her pretty, pretty nipples.

"If you will excuse me for a second," she said with excessive politeness, her eyes gleaming.

She disappeared into her room and did *not* come back with the dressing robe. He'd seen her naked in bed, but to see her in motion, her pert breasts bobbing ever so slightly—he panted.

"Read this aloud for me, darling."

He hadn't even noticed that she'd put two sheets of paper on the music stand—two pages from his manuscript. "Read *that*?"

"Yes, that. Or I'm going to put my clothes back on."

He knew that must not happen, but it was nearly impossible to tear his eyes away from her legs and the juncture of her thighs.

She came closer, took his chin, and turned his face toward the music stand. *"Read."*

He cleared his throat and tried to concentrate on the words before him. " 'Now I am the one tied to the bedpost. She inspects me from all angles, smiling as if she has been let in on a marvelous secret.' "

He looked toward Helena; she, too, was smiling, one hand on the bedpost, the other reaching out to trail down his arm. "Keep reading."

Her touch burned. His voice turned unsteady. "'She pulls out her hairpins and shakes her head. Her hair falls free, a glorious cascade, strands of it brushing her taut nipples.'"

"Hmm," said Helena. "Alas, I can't reenact the hair. But at least I still have taut nipples, do I not?"

She touched one nipple, lightly squeezing it between two fingers. Unseemly noises escaped him; his cock swelled to painful dimensions.

"Keep reading if you want anything to happen," she reminded him, licking her lips slowly to emphasize her point.

God help him. He was going to turn illiterate very soon, at the rate he was losing his mind. "'My throat tightens. "You make me mindless with lust," I tell her. She laughs softly. "No, Larkspear, I am *going* to make you mindless with lust. And the first step is the removal of the rest of your clothes."'"

Helena unfastened his trousers and pushed them down. "I like the bride of Larkspear—a woman with a plan."

The next moment Hastings's underlinen, too, had pooled at his feet, exposing his naked desire. She pressed herself into his side and rubbed one nipple along his arm, while her hand wrapped along his shaft; she gave a soft, throaty laugh as it leaped against the prison of her fingers.

"You are deviating from the story," Hastings somehow managed to say.

"I know. But in the story you have her on her knees too soon. I can't do that—I have a reputation to maintain."

She stroked his length; he groaned with the pleasure of it. Now she sucked on the skin of his shoulder, then bent her head to lick his nipple. He bucked against his restraints.

"Don't forget to read."

"I can't anymore."

"I am not getting down on my knees unless the story tells me to."

He growled but acquiesced. " 'In no time at all I was completely naked. She dropped to her knees before me.' "

Helena rounded to his front and knelt, her lips a hair-breadth from his jutting cock, glancing up at him with the tiniest of smirks on her face.

He gave her the next set of instructions. "She extends her tongue and licks the head of my cock."

"Is that what the story says? I seem to remember differently."

"That is exactly what the story says," he lied blatantly.

She smiled, knowing him for the liar he was, and did exactly as he asked, her pink, moist tongue swirling softly where he was most excruciatingly sensitive.

His knees nearly buckled. "Now she opens her mouth wide and takes in as much of my length as she can handle."

And he was inside her mouth, paradise itself. The sensation alone drove him mad, but there was also the sight of it. She was no longer smiling, but stared up at him with a hunger that almost matched his own. Then she moaned, a sound of such stark need that he lost all control over himself.

He shut his eyes, shuddered, and let her milk every last drop.

* * *

*A*s soon as she let him free he pushed her against the bedpost, tied her hands behind her, and returned the favor—several times. Then he untied her, carried her to his bed, and made love to her slowly and properly.

Afterward she giggled against his shoulder. "Ask me again how I like your smutty story."

He turned his face and kissed her forehead. "So . . . how do you like my smutty story, my dear?"

"I must confess, sir"—her tone was mock serious—"I still have not read the entire work. But the parts I have read have been a work of staggering genius. Why, the nuanced characterization, the heightened tension, and the deft use of the silken cords of her restraint to represent the bonds of matrimony . . . I applaud you, sir. I applaud you."

Now she batted her eyelashes, naughty again. "Not to mention it makes me hornier than a camp full of soldiers."

"Hmm. Maybe I'll renege on my word. Maybe instead of working on revisions for you I'll write another smutty story instead."

She poked him in the chest. "That is not allowed. You may, however, write a new smutty story after you are finished with my revisions."

"And will you stage that story, too?"

She turned up her nose. "Only if it is of the highest quality."

He laughed and kissed her on the lips.

"I have an idea," she said, pulling back. "Let us not marry in secret. Let's instead take full advantage of my loss of memory and have a tremendous wedding. After all, what woman can bear to have no recollection of her wedding day?"

He was both startled by her audacity and carried away by her sudden enthusiasm. "I *have* always wanted a grand wedding for us."

She wagged her finger. "And no country wedding, either. We will hold it at Westminster Abbey."

"And we will ransack Millie's gardens to deck the whole place with flowers—up to the rafters."

"Indeed we must. And Venetia's gardens, too. She'd be insulted if we didn't ransack the duke's hothouses as well."

He rubbed her bottom. "We will put you in a virginal white gown, even though you have been more plucked than a guitar."

She flicked his shoulder. "How rude. I was going to deck you out in pearls and diamonds, but now I must reconsider."

"No!" he cried. "Please don't reconsider. I never look as stunning as when I'm in pearls and diamonds."

She chortled and fluffed his hair. "So vain."

"I only want to look good for you."

She sighed, a happy sound that made his heart swell to twice its normal size. "I think for our honeymoon we will go to Lake Sahara, sleep in tents, and hunt like nomads."

It touched him that she remembered Lake Sahara. "And stand on the shores and watch the sunrise together."

"Yes," she said softly, "when birds in flocks of thousands fly over the lake, their wings white as sails."

She fell asleep in his arms. He stayed awake for a long time, wondering whether what they had built together would be enough to withstand the return of her memory in full.

CHAPTER 16

$\mathscr{S}$omeone adjusted Helena's bedcover. She tended to move about a great deal in her sleep and did not always manage to hold on to her blanket. Often in the morning, her feet and ankles would be quite cold—and in this instance, her calves, too, since she'd disrobed thoroughly the night before.

Warm hands rubbed her feet, then her entire lower half was enveloped in a nice, heavy quilt. She sighed in contentment. The same person came nearer and kissed her on her forehead.

"So beautiful," he murmured.

She smiled and sank back into sleep—only to reawaken what seemed but a few seconds later with a violent start.

The room was dim and empty, the shutters still drawn. She closed her eyes again, her head feeling woolly, as if she'd grossly overslept. She lay still for a few more minutes, then slowly pushed to a sitting position, swinging her legs over the side of the bed.

On the nightstand was a photograph of Fitz and her David, standing in the middle of the vast expanse of Tom Quad, the largest college quadrangle at Oxford. Helena had taken the photograph with David's factory-loaded Kodak camera during one of Fitz's visits to the university. Shortly afterward, her friend and classmate Mary Dilhorne had passed by. They'd spent a minute chatting together before Miss Dilhorne went on to her next class and David and Helena saw Fitz off at the rail station.

As soon as Fitz had settled into his compartment, before the train had even started, David was already whispering into her ear, "Was that one of your lesbian friends? When are you going to invite me to watch?"

"After you first invite me to watch you as a catamite," she'd said as she waved at Fitz, "taking it in every orifice."

The present-day Helena smiled. They'd gone at it like Rome and Carthage, hadn't they? And she'd fired off a number of excellent retorts she was proud to recall.

At some point during the night, David had gone to her room, collected her dressing robe, and put it on the back of a chair near the bed. She shrugged into the robe, walked to the window, and threw back the shutters. The sun had risen. Bea's pond reflected brilliantly in the distance. Helena breathed in deeply, filled with a sweet contentment.

Which was disturbed a moment later by a sensation that she'd forgotten something. She chortled to herself. Of course she'd forgotten something—as much as half of her life at one point. But the sensation, as if something had burrowed inside her brain, would not go away.

She shook her head, trying to clear it. Oh, right, the

pages of David's manuscript. She'd better put them away before the servants came through. But when she glanced toward the foot of the bed, the music stand, as well as the manuscript pages, had already been removed—again a demonstration of David's consideration.

Still the strange and increasingly disconcerting sensation remained. Was it something to do with Fitzhugh and Company? Had she forgotten to return a set of corrections to the printer? Or neglected to arrange advertising a particular title?

The sensation receded somewhat when it dawned on Helena that she'd at last remembered Millie. A feeling of tremendous fondness suffused her—dear, dear Millie. How they'd all grown to love her, and how she always kept surprising them. Together she and Fitz had proved to be remarkable hosts, presiding over many a joyful gathering of family and friends.

And, of course, Helena and David were always there at the gatherings, trading barbs and disparagements.

Don't look at him like that.

I shall look at him however I wish to.

He's younger than you.

Doesn't matter.

He has small feet.

Excellent. It will cost less to keep him in shoes.

Don't you know what they say about men with small feet?

Yes: They are less arrogant.

He is too soft for you. You need a man made of steel, Miss Fitzhugh. He is like a bird's nest, built of twigs and fluff.

Why so much interest in how I feel toward another man, Hastings? If you persist in talking about it, I shall have to believe that you are jealous.

Please, Miss Fitzhugh, you'll make me laugh. Surely you know by now that for a woman to interest me she needs a pair of breasts. So my concern for you is entirely humanitarian. Mark my words: You will be yearning for a man with bigger feet and a stiffer . . . spine.

Andrew! They'd been speaking of *Andrew*.

She stumbled backward, her calves hitting the side rail of the bed. She barely felt anything, her horror and dismay obliterating everything else.

Andrew, always happy and eager to talk about all the books under the sun, always gentle and respectful when he didn't agree with her assessment on any particular volume. Andrew, the first person to tell her that she would make a wonderful publisher, when her family still doubted the wisdom of such a course of action. Andrew, who'd left a bouquet of wildflowers outside her door every day, too shy to leave a card alongside the flowers, until she'd caught him in the act. *If you love me, leave another one tomorrow,* she'd told him. The next day he'd left three.

It had been such a magical time in her life.

When he'd broken down and sobbed, apologizing over and over again for misleading her—when he'd been perfectly frank from the very beginning that he was expected to marry someone else—she'd told him, with tears streaming down her face, that she could never be angry with him. That she was grateful to have known him and grateful for the memories.

And all it took was a kick in the head to make her forget everything.

It hurt to breathe. She staggered to the window and pushed it open, gulping. Her poor, sweet Andrew. How he must have felt during their most recent encounters, when she'd treated him as if he were just another bystander in her life.

How would she have felt if she woke up one day and the person she'd loved perennially no longer gave a damn about her?

Someone set his hands on her arms and kissed her on her nape. "Guess what arrived in the morning post? Our special license. Shall we start sending out those scandalous invitations?"

That pain in her heart was black and explosive. She flung aside his hands and stomped away from the window. "Don't touch me."

Behind her came a long silence, then, "I see."

She could not look at him. But it was almost worse to look at the bed and be reminded of her shamelessness the night before. Had it been only lust, she might still have forgiven herself, but she had to talk about weddings and honeymoons, making the commitment of a lifetime.

The only saving grace, perhaps, was the fact that she had not said "I love you" in so many words—but that was only because she'd been saving it for their true wedding night.

Her disloyalty burned like acid upon her skin. She hated the feeling of it. She hated that she didn't know better when she should have. And she hated that each time it had been she who had spread her legs and practically begged him to help himself to her.

"Helena—"

She spun around. "How could you? I'd lost my *mind*. I was barely cognizant, entirely uninformed, and utterly incapable of true consent. Were you any kind of gentleman, you would have restrained yourself and told me to wait. It took only a few weeks—you couldn't have waited that long, you who claim to love me to the moon and the stars?"

"I did tell you to wait, Helena." He looked grieved and hurt, his eyes bright with just the sort of sincerity she did not need to see. "I told you every time that you would be better served by patience."

She couldn't bear the truth of his words. "You knew how I felt about Mr. Martin. You knew how much I loved him. You better than anyone else knew that I would never betray his love and trust. But you saw a horny dimwit and you just had to have your fun, didn't you?"

"Helena!"

His expression began to harden, which only made her wilder. "Why would you think you could ever displace Mr. Martin from my heart? What sort of arrogance and delusion was that? Have you lost your mind, too?"

He did not call her name again—was not even looking at her anymore. She held her breath—she wanted him to keep calling her name. She wanted him to reassure her in that wide-sky-sweet-breezes voice that everything was fine, that she did not need to be buffeted about by this chaotic confusion.

His gaze came back to her. Her heart leaped. But then he leered. "Ah, well, it was good while it lasted—you were the hot little strumpet I'd always suspected you would be. Of course, your breasts remain lacking, but your enthusiasm almost made up for it. My God, the way you swallowed my cock. Real whores couldn't do it better."

Her face burned. Her entire person burned.

"And yes, you were gullible, weren't you?" He went on relentlessly, walking slowly toward her, his eyes harsh, his words harsher. "I've never liked you better than when you were that horny dimwit, your legs spread wider than Siberia, your fingers playing with your own titties, your—"

She slapped him so hard her entire arm hurt. But the pain was nothing compared to the annihilation in her heart.

"Get out!" she bellowed.

He raised a contemptuous brow. "This is my room, my dear Lady Hastings. Or do you not remember that you came here last night famished for cock and wouldn't leave me alone until I'd fucked you well and good?"

Memories of the night before were like grit rubbed into an open wound. The trust she had for him, her utter openness of the heart, and all the hope she nourished for their future.

She walked out without another word.

*T*he connecting door slammed. Hastings stared at it, unable to believe what he'd just become—again.

The man she'd always despised.

Had he not learned anything from the past few weeks? Had he not learned that lying because he couldn't bear to be vulnerable never protected him from pain, but only walled him off from happiness?

He stood in place, breathing hard.

He'd told her that his history of being an ass toward her had been no one's fault but his own, and it was true. But at times like this, so much of him still felt like the boy whose only resort was to hit back hard, because he was never going to make anyone understand anything except how viciously he could strike.

Because sometimes the *appearance* of strength was all that mattered.

But hadn't he already promised himself that there would be no more lies, no more cowardice, and no more hiding his true sentiments behind mockery and derision? Hadn't he promised himself that he would be a man worthy of her?

He pressed two fingers between his brows. He knew what he ought to do, but did he possess courage enough to see it through?

*H*elena sat before the vanity, her head in her hands. The connecting door opened. She leaped up from her chair. "What do you want?"

Hastings closed the door quietly. "I'm here to apologize."

She almost didn't hear his words. How did a man who'd looked so hateful only a minute ago transform into this specimen of humble contrition? "What for?"

His gaze was a blue green of unlimited depth. "For my false and unkind words. They were the absolute opposite of my true feelings. And I'm sorry I reverted to my worst habit when you least needed greater distress."

Until he'd spoken, she'd had no idea how much she longed for him to tell her how sorry he was. But now she had his apology, she could not tell whether it brought relief or only a greater desolation. "So you are remorseful for giving in to my carnal demands?"

He shook his head. "No, I am only apologizing for speaking those words that would have you believe I didn't treasure the privilege of making love to you."

The gentleness of his voice, the infinite sincerity of his words—he was still praying for rain in the Sahara. His persistence moved her and infuriated her at the same time.

"So you *are* glad you slept with me when I didn't know any better?"

"Helena, you lost your memory, not your mind. You were perfectly capable of conducting your business and your life."

She had certainly felt so, hadn't she? Only to wake up from a dream of love torn completely in two. "You say that because the choices I made suited you."

"Think back, Helena. Was there any point during the past few weeks when you weren't the same woman you've always been?"

She was beginning to feel uncomfortably close to tears. He was expressing a level of confidence in her that she could not feel herself, telling her that she should trust the choice she'd made. "That same woman I've always been would never have willingly gone to bed with you."

He inhaled slowly, then exhaled just as carefully. "I suppose the lack of residual feelings for Mr. Martin freed you to fall in love with someone else."

Her nostrils flared. Panic spilled out of her heart into every muscle, every nerve. "Don't be ridiculous. I have *not* fallen in love with you."

She willed him to be nasty to her. She didn't know how much more of his kindness and consideration she could take.

But he only smiled, if a little sadly. "It doesn't matter how we label it—I can recognize depth of feeling when I see it."

She clenched her teeth. "Perhaps it is time for you to purchase a pair of spectacles. I love Mr. Martin, not you."

"I stand by what I said earlier. You loved Mr. Martin as he was five years ago. But that man no longer exists.

Without nostalgia in your heart, he is but an unobjection-able man who holds no particular appeal for you."

If he'd shouted at her, she could have shouted something back. But his almost saintly composure left her defense-less. She returned to her vanity, sat down, and stared into the mirror.

After a while, the connecting door opened and closed, and she was again all alone in the room.

*B*ea tugged on Hastings's sleeve and pointed at a bird.

"It's a . . . it's a . . ." He had to look again at the bird—he'd already forgotten what it was. "It's a chaffinch. You've seen those before, Bea. See those white bars on its wings? Most definitely a chaffinch."

Bea gazed at him solemnly, waiting.

He usually said much more on their walks, didn't he? He'd tell Bea everything he knew about the chaffinch. And if he didn't know enough to fill a teaspoon, which was sometimes the case, he'd veer the topic to something else. Another songbird—the canary, perhaps. Then he'd talk about how one would think the Canary Islands were named after canaries, when in fact the name derived from *Insula Canaria*, which meant "island of the dogs."

Today it was all he could do to put one foot in front of the other.

"This one is a gentleman," he managed. "See its blue cap and reddish chest? A lady chaffinch isn't quite as colorful."

Bea looked behind them, where Helena usually fol-lowed. "Lady?"

"Lady Hastings isn't feeling well—not well at all."

Bea bit her lower lip. "Old?"

On a different day he would have laughed. "No, she isn't old like Sir Hardshell. Sometimes people just need to . . . stay in their rooms."

It wasn't until he was standing in front of the pond that he realized that Bea had altered her route for the day so she could play at the miniature cottage again. Such a sign of greater flexibility on Bea's part should have filled him with joy, but the sight of the cottage, the physical embodiment of how close to happiness he and Helena had come . . .

He did the only thing he could: He sat down and willed the return of Lake Sahara.

*H*elena had just dressed when a footman came to announce a visitor. "Ma'am, there is a Mrs. Andrew Martin to see you. Are you at home to her?"

Helena started. Mrs. Martin? Here? She put on her turban. "I will receive her."

Mrs. Martin wore a gown of deep mourning. Helena's heart seized. Only after a moment did she see that Mrs. Martin's mourning gown was not one for a widow. "How do you do, Mrs. Martin?"

Her sister, Mrs. Monteth, looked like a ferret. Mrs. Martin, however, was a pretty woman of patrician mien. She and Helena spoke of the weather and her journey. But when tea had been brought in and poured, the small talk was put away.

"I can see you have your memories back, Lady Hastings—you look at me with a certain misgiving."

"I am only puzzled by your visit, Mrs. Martin. But you are right: I have regained my full memory."

Enough of it, in any case. She still could not remember

the bum-pinching incident with Hastings—or any part of his first visit to Hampton House. Her heart constricted.

"Excellent, for I'd have come for nothing if you still had no recollection of Mr. Martin. I plan to seek a divorce, you see," said Mrs. Martin, as breezily as if she'd planned to buy a new pair of evening slippers.

Helena stared at her. "A divorce?"

"I have a suitor, an American gentleman who is waiting to marry me—Americans are less fussy about divorces. And five years, wouldn't you agree, is long enough in a marriage that should have never taken place. I married Mr. Martin to please my father, little realizing that if he wasn't pleased with me by the time I turned eighteen, he never would be. Mr. Martin did the same for his mother and she thought no better of him. Well, my father died three years ago and the late Mrs. Martin passed away this week.

"Since my father's passing, I'd made sure that Mr. Martin resided in town and I in the country—since I'd need to claim abandonment as well in order to bring a divorce petition on grounds of adultery."

So that was why Helena hadn't seen the Martins together in years. When Andrew was able to attend so many country parties solo, she had only counted her blessings and not once wondered why Mrs. Martin never accompanied him. "You have been planning this a long time."

"You have no idea, Miss Fitzhugh. Until recently, however, I had a problem: Mr. Martin simply was not an adulterous man. His time and energy went into his manuscripts instead. Then I found a letter among his belongings from a woman who was obviously a paramour and I was overjoyed. It was the last piece that needed to fall into place. I went to my sister, who immediately assured me she would produce firm evidence of this adulterous affair. She had, of course, no idea that I meant to divorce him with that, or she'd never have participated.

"You either know the rest or you can imagine it, Lady Hastings. My sister came back stupefied by having burst in on you and Lord Hastings instead. But I remembered that there had been rumors that Mr. Martin had been in love with you before our marriage. So yesterday, after his mother's passing, I sat him down and we had a frank conversation. He was at first flatly against my plan, but now I would say he is wavering."

Before Helena could object, Mrs. Martin raised a hand. "Don't worry, Lady Hastings: I will not dream of proposing that *you* be caught with him—I can easily pay someone to swear under oath that she and Mr. Martin engaged in an affair. *If* Mr. Martin is willing to go through with the divorce, that is. He is undecided, as he is unsure of what benefits await him.

"Upon further questioning, I discovered that he believes that you are unlikely to have truly married Lord Hastings by the time your accident took place. I thought this was of tremendous importance, but he said no, you'd lost all your memories concerning him and treated him as you would any stranger. He was unwilling to come and see you, as he thought he had no right to interfere in another man's marriage. But I disagreed: He would not be meddling in anyone's marriage if you are not at all married."

The true significance of Mrs. Martin's words was beginning to make itself felt. Helena felt as if she were suspended above a void.

"So this is what I'd like to ask on behalf of Mr. Martin and myself, Lady Hastings: Have you truly married Lord

Hastings? For if you have not, Mr. Martin and I will both be thrilled: I for the inducement it will give him to let the divorce go through uncontested; he for the opportunity to finally marry you, once we are divorced."

This was what Helena had wanted all these years, wasn't it? That somehow, someday, Andrew would again be free to marry her?

She said nothing.

Mrs. Martin leaned forward in her seat. "I know what you are thinking—the scandal will dwarf anything we've seen in a while. It will be punishing for all of us, no doubt. But new scandals will come and old ones will be forgotten. After a while, no one will remember you were ever married to anyone other than Mr. Martin."

But did this mean that someday Hastings would also marry someone else? The thought was a burn mark upon Helena's heart.

"Think about it, will you, Lady Hastings? You have risked everything for the love of Mr. Martin. Now you can have him without any of the risks—love *and* respectability." Mrs. Martin rose. "You needn't give me an answer immediately. If you'd like to speak to Mr. Martin, you can reach him at the house in London. I will show myself out."

*H*elena stopped before Hastings's study. The door was ajar. He was at his desk, an unlit tobacco pipe by his elbow.

"Would you like to come in?" he said without looking up.

Her heart flipped. It was another few seconds before she could cross the threshold.

As she approached the desk, she saw that he was working on the revisions she'd requested in one of the *Old Toad Pond* tales, changing an instance of Mrs. Bunny to Mrs. Porcupine, to avoid having the same character being sunny in one story and sullen in another.

Now he did glance up and smiled faintly. "I am ashamed to admit this, but until you'd pointed it out, I'd had no idea I'd called two different characters by the same name."

She didn't know whether she wanted to throw him out of the window or yank him to her by his hair. She tilted her chin at the tobacco pipe. "Is that Tobias's?"

"I suppose it is. The pipe belonged to my father. I don't much care for pipe smoking, but I like to pack it with fresh tobacco from time to time."

So that was why his clothes sometimes smelled of pipe tobacco. She was suddenly possessed by the desire to roll in a pile of his country tweeds, perhaps naked.

He clasped his hands together on the desk. "I understand Mrs. Martin was here."

The sensation of being suspended above a void returned with a vengeance. "She wants me to marry Mr. Martin."

He came out of his chair. "What?"

He'd been so composed, so serene—it almost comforted her to see a stronger reaction. "She wants a divorce and he hesitates. She hopes the thought of marrying me will make him more cooperative."

He said nothing for a long time; her heart began to beat to the rhythm of his agitated breaths. "You still want to marry him?"

"I only stopped wanting to marry him when I could no longer remember who he was."

He shook his head and went on shaking it. "No. *No.* Stop this madness."

A part of her nodded vigorously in agreement. She tried not to pay any attention. "You can't ask me to change one of my most deeply held wishes simply because we've spent a few weeks together."

He rounded the table and set his hands on her arms. "I can and I do. Don't make this mistake, Helena. Don't confuse what you once wanted with what you now need."

The warmth of his hands through her sleeves—she stepped back. "I'm going to see Mr. Martin."

"Yes," he said slowly. "I suppose you'll need to do that. Would you like me to hold dinner until you return?"

No, what she wanted was . . . histrionics. She wanted him to throw his inkwell across the room, then overturn his entire desk. To not let her go so easily, so gallantly. "If I decide to marry him, then I will not return. The longer I live with you, the bigger the scandal will be."

"You will return to at least say a proper good-bye to Bea. She asked about you just now. Do you know how seldom she asks about people?"

At least his beautiful voice rose a little. She supposed she'd have to satisfy herself with that. "I'd better go now."

He yanked her to him and kissed her, a hard, brief kiss that left her short of breath and light of head.

"Go," he said brusquely. "I'll order your carriage."

She lifted her hand and grazed her lips with her knuckles. He watched her. After a moment, his gaze softened. "Remember Lake Sahara, my dear."

CHAPTER 17

$\mathcal{H}$astings's day only went downhill. One of his grooms broke his arm while exercising a horse. The roof of the mushroom house fell in. And then the coup de grâce: Sir Hardshell gave up the ghost.

By the time Hastings learned the news, Bea was already in her trunk, so upset that when he tried to give her a biscuit and a cup of milk tea, she kept pushing the little tray back out the door at the bottom of the trunk.

After a while he gave up, ate the biscuit himself, and sat down with his back against Bea's trunk, wishing he had a trunk of his own for sanctuary, where he could remain until the world changed.

He didn't know how long he sat there, staring at the wall; he was startled out of his preoccupation only when he heard a small sob. Bea often became tense and distressed, but she rarely cried.

He turned around and tried to peer inside through one of the airholes, seeing nothing but darkness. "Bea, poppet, I know Sir Hardshell isn't coming back, but we can invite his cousin to come and stay with you. I hear his cousin has been looking for a place to stay. Maybe he wouldn't mind inheriting Sir Hardshell's glass tank."

She sniffed but did not answer.

"The cousin's name is Mr. Stoutback. He has a very nice, even temperament. And he is much younger than Sir Hardshell, so he'll be able to live with us for a long, long time."

Bea sobbed again. Hastings wished for fairy godmothers—one for Bea and one for him. "Or we can invite a different one of Sir Hardshell's cousins. What do you think of Miss Carapace? I'll bet she wouldn't mind if you tied a pretty bow around her shell."

"Does lady have cousins?" Bea's question came all of a sudden.

Hastings started. "Lady?"

"Our lady," she said dejectedly.

He was astounded. "You mean Lady Hastings? *She* is the reason you are in there?"

"Does she have cousins?"

If only Helena were as easy to replace as tortoises. "She does have cousins, but none of them can come live with us."

Bea hiccuped. "Is she coming back?"

The all-important question. Hastings sat back down again and resumed his staring at the wall. "I hope so, poppet. I hope so."

As she rang the doorbell of Andrew's town house, Helena came to a disconcerting realization:

Since she left Easton Grange, she had not once thought of Andrew. Half the time she'd been rubbing her lips, as if she were still trying to feel Hastings's kiss. The rest of the time she kept reliving her last glimpse of him, standing before the window of the study, shadowy except for his face and his bright, lovely hair.

He had not waved, but only watched as her carriage pulled away.

Andrew himself opened the door. "Come in, Helena, please come in. I'm so glad you are here."

How different it was to see him when she was firmly in possession of all her memories. When he smiled shyly, she was instantly transported to the small library at Fitz's estate where they'd first run into each other and immediately started discussing the Venerable Bede's works—how his face had glowed with pleasure that afternoon.

She blinked. Was this what Hastings had meant when he said that she saw Andrew not as the man he was, but the one he had been?

Andrew showed her into a parlor and lit a spirit lamp for tea. "It's the servants' half day, so if you don't mind, we will make do with my rusty tea-making skills."

He bustled about, retrieving tea and sugar, then bringing her a plate of toast sandwiches. She was reminded of her first—and only—visit to his house on the beautiful Norfolk coast as part of a group of young people. At her arrival, he'd carried her luggage up the stairs himself. In the course of the high tea later that afternoon, he'd made innumerable trips to bring her everything from lobster salad to cream cake.

Helena frowned: again the throes of nostalgia.

"Is something the matter?" asked Andrew.

"No, everything is fine. Did Mrs. Martin inform you I might be coming?"

Andrew sat down and measured tea leaves into the pot. "Yes, she cabled. I didn't believe her, but I am so glad to be proven wrong."

The stickpin at the center of his necktie—she'd given him one quite like it, with a Roman eagle emblem on the head. It had been the first Christmas party Fitz and Millie had thrown at Henley Park. Mulled wine had flowed freely. She'd pulled him into an alcove to kiss him, and he'd tasted of nutmeg and cloves.

She *was* always thinking of Andrew as he'd been years ago. How, then, would she judge the man he was today? "I'll admit I haven't always been fond of Mrs. Martin," she said. "But after our chat today I've come to quite admire her. I like that she has taken her happiness into her own hands."

"So you will leave Lord Hastings?" Andrew gazed at her. "Assuming, that is, you two have not yet married."

"If I do leave him—"

"Then we can be married," he said breathlessly.

"But what do you plan to do if I can't leave him?"

Andrew fidgeted, rubbing a corner of the tablecloth between his fingers. "I don't know."

"Will you still grant your wife the divorce?"

"I suppose not, then."

This was not the kind of answer she would have liked to hear from him. She kept her face blank and her voice uninflected. "What do you know of her situation?"

"According to her, she has an American chap she fancies. He has promised to marry her if she can obtain a divorce."

"Why not let her go?"

Andrew took the kettle off the spirit lamp and poured hot water into the teapot. "Well, it's a nuisance, isn't it, a divorce?"

She watched him closely. "If you let her go now, she can marry the man of her choice and build a family with him."

He shrugged. "She and I were all right as we were. I know I'm used to it. We'll just carry on as we've always done."

When Helena had awakened from her coma and found herself married to a stranger, she'd administered a test of character. Hastings had refused to put his own happiness above his daughter's welfare and passed the test with flying colors.

Andrew did not. They'd already established that he had no particular objection to a divorce—if Helena would marry him afterward, he was more than willing to go through with it. But without the prospect of personal gain, he would keep his wife in their utterly unprofitable marriage, denying her everything for which she'd striven with such purpose and dedication, simply because he didn't care for the "nuisance" of the process.

"Do one thing for me, Andrew."

"Anything."

"Grant your wife the divorce. Don't keep her tethered to you just because it doesn't matter to you. It matters intensely to her. She is no more at fault in this marriage than you are, and I'd like to see you treat her fairly, the way you yourself would have liked to be treated."

He blinked, confused. "But what will I do then?"

"Anything you like. Your life will hardly change, since you and she haven't been in the same house for years. You will go on writing your histories and I will go on publishing them."

He bit his lower lip. "But you won't marry me?"

"I can't leave Lord Hastings—we are already married."

"Oh," said Andrew.

"Promise me you'll let Mrs. Martin go?"

He nodded dejectedly. She kissed him on the forehead and left the table. "Be sure to send volume three of your history to me as soon as it is finished. And don't dawdle, Andrew—I will not tolerate a manuscript of yours being six months late again."

*H*elena climbed into her train compartment, despondent. She might have known, even before she left Easton Grange, that she would not choose Andrew, but it was still disappointing to have him turn out to be a lesser man than she'd believed.

The train began to move. The last time she'd been on the same train, going toward Kent, the sudden return of four years of memory had completely staggered her. This time it was unlikely anything particularly earth-shattering would happen, since she'd already regained the vast majority of her—

So many different voices. She recognized Venetia's and Fitz's, but none of the rest. They were all talking about her. Why hadn't she woken up yet? Shouldn't she be conscious by now?

What did they mean, she was unconscious? She tried to let them know that she was perfectly aware of what was happening around her. But to her horror, she couldn't

*move her lips, her eyelids, or a single fingertip—she'd
been imprisoned inside her own body.*

*The voices gradually died away. No one spoke any-
more. The silence was excruciating, as if they'd already
forgotten her existence. She shouted. She screamed. She
might as well have been at the bottom of the Atlantic, for
all the notice they took of her.*

Then came his sensationally beautiful voice. Would
anyone mind if I read to her? *At last, someone still remembered her.*

*He read her a fascinating primer on the inner workings
of publishing. Helena loved books: the sight of them, the
feel of them, the smell of them. She adored tracing her
fingers over embossed titles and gilded edges. She cherished the almost inaudible creak a new book's spine made
when it was opened for the first time. And were it at all
possible, she'd like to capture in a vial the scent of a room
full of books antique and new, the redolence of vellum and
parchment commingled with the perfume of fresh ink.*

*He read to her for days on end. She hung onto his
words, his voice, whether he was reading the publishing
primer, the news, or* Alice's Adventures in Wonderland.
*From time to time, when they were alone, he'd ask her to
wake up, and tell her that he loved her, that he'd always,
always loved her.*

*She'd never believed anything in her life as much as she
believed in his love. With all her strength she reached for
him. She* would *leave this invisible prison. She* would *be
part of the world again. And she* would *meet him and tell
him that she loved him every bit as fervently and fiercely.*

Helena gasped. So that was why Hastings's voice had

been familiar to her when she'd awakened. That was why she'd had a vague memory of listening to his impression of the Cheshire Cat. And that was why she'd had a much easier time wrapping her hands around the reins of her business than she'd anticipated, because he'd told her everything she knew.

She had never cried in public, but she did now, tears of joy and gratitude that she could not stop. The man she'd loved earlier had proved himself a lesser man, but the love of her life had proved himself worthy—more than worthy—at every turn.

And how fortunate she was to be going home to him.

$\mathcal{N}$o sounds had come from Bea's trunk for the past twenty minutes. Perhaps she had fallen asleep inside—it had happened before, more than once. Bea, a heavy sleeper, did not mind being carried to bed—if she were actually asleep. If she were still awake and he opened the lid of the trunk, she would become twice as upset.

Hastings rose to his feet, rocking back and forth on his heels, mired in indecision.

"Is Bea all right?"

He turned stock-still with shock. *Helena!*

Slowly, very slowly, he turned around.

She came toward him. "I'm back. And I'm terribly sorry for what I said earlier. Forgive me for being too blind to see the truth right in front of me."

He couldn't speak, but he must have beamed at her. Her face, at first so serious, softened into a smile, her eyes resembling exactly the glimmering waters of Lake Sahara. He was dizzy with happiness.

"Lady!" Bea exclaimed, lifting the lid of the trunk and peering out.

"Yes, I'm back," Helena said again, smiling even wider. "Would you like to come out?"

The trunk closed again. Bea's voice was muffled. "Sir Hardshell died."

"Oh, no, I'm so sorry!"

"Why don't you tell Bea about Sir Hardshell's cousins, Helena?" Hastings finally found his voice. "Mr. Stoutback and Miss Carapace, among others. We can invite one of them to come and live in Sir Hardshell's old glass tank."

"Oh, yes, indeed. I believe that's what Sir Hardshell would have wanted. He wouldn't wish his lovely home to remain empty, all that nice soil, those pretty rocks, and that solid pewter water dish. Why, what a waste."

Silence greeted Helena's enthusiastic enumeration of the virtues of Sir Hardshell's old dwelling. Hastings grabbed her and kissed her hard. She kissed him back with equal force. He could scarcely breathe—but why breathe when he could kiss?

He didn't hear Bea. It was Helena who pulled away and said, "What did you say, sweet girl?"

"Bath?"

Has she had supper? Helena mouthed.

He nodded and imitated the motion of sliding a plate inside the little trunk door—he'd finally succeeded in feeding Bea something. "I'm afraid you'll have to go without your bath tonight, poppet. It's quite late. You'd better be in bed now or you won't be able to get up on time tomorrow."

More silence. He again kissed Helena until he was out of breath. But this time he did not miss it when Bea said, "Papa?"

He lifted her out and had her tucked into bed in no time at all. Then, hand in hand, he and Helena ran for their own rooms, not stopping until they'd slammed the door shut behind them.

*T*wo hours later, Helena punched her David in the solar plexus.

"Oww. What was that for?"

"For being immeasurably stupid all these years. You didn't need to wait until I was almost dead before telling me you loved me." She next punched him in the arm. "And this is for pinching my bottom—I finally remembered it."

"Hmm," he said, putting a hand on her bottom and touching her freely.

She giggled and kissed the places where she'd hit him. "But I shouldn't be too hard on you. You were an ass, but I was a thorough fool myself."

"Thank you for saying it so I don't need to."

"Ha, for that, I will tie you to a bedpost and *not* pleasure you."

"But think of the waste, darling. Why let a perfectly good, hard cock wilt from disuse?"

She burst out laughing. He pulled her on top of him. "Tell me, my very demanding lady, when did you finally realize that you absolutely cannot live without me?"

She glanced at him askance. "Have I ever come to such a maudlin realization?"

"Yes, you have," he answered, cheeky and confident. "Now tell me when."

She rubbed her palm on the beginning of his stubble and thought about it. "Possibly when you told me you'd hold dinner for me before I left. Also possibly when Prince Narcissus took a knife to his pride. Again, possibly, the first time I learned of the existence of Lake Sahara. But definitely when I remembered the days I spent in a coma."

She recounted her memory of those three days, of her frustration and helplessness, and, most important, of his lovely voice keeping her despair at bay.

He cupped her cheek and kissed her tenderly. "All I wanted was for you to not feel alone. And to love you as I'd always meant to."

She returned the kiss. "All *I* wanted was to wake up and tell you I love you."

They kept kissing. His body changed, again ready for love.

She broke the kiss and licked the corner of his lips. "And now that I've told you I love you, we can at last turn our minds to truly important matters."

He raised a brow. "Such as?"

"Such as when you will have your next smutty story ready for me."

He laughed. "That is indeed the pressing question of our time."

"So when will it be ready?" she whispered into his ear.

He rolled her beneath him and kissed her again. "Soon, darling, very soon."

EPILOGUE

$\mathcal{T}$he wedding of Helena Charlotte Fitzhugh and David Hillsborough, Viscount Hastings, was not the wedding of the Season—understandably, since the Season had already ended. But in scope, attendance, and the amount of gossip it generated, taking place long after the couple had been established to have eloped, it rivaled any wedding of the Season in recent memory.

The bride wore a blindingly white wedding gown. The groom dripped with diamonds and pearls—diamond cuff links, diamond stickpin, diamond shirt studs, and a mother-of-pearl pocket watch. The ladies of the bride's family wept openly during the ceremony, and her brother was seen dabbing surreptitiously at his eyes.

To mark this momentous day, the bride and the groom each prepared a gift for the other. Given the grandeur of the occasion, one might be forgiven for guessing those gifts to be comprised of legendary works of art, extraordinary pieces of jewelry, and perhaps exquisite ancient manuscripts. But one would be wrong.

The groom gave the bride a miniature model of a dirigible named *Hastings's Pride*. The bride returned an even less costly present: a wooden sign, the sort to be found everywhere at crossroads and near landmarks.

This particular sign was staked into place by the pond at Easton Grange. One side of the sign read, OLD TOAD POND, the other, LAKE SAHARA.

AUTHOR'S NOTE

The Bride of Larkspear, Hastings's smutty love letter to Helena, is available in its entirety at your preferred vendor of fine e-books.

The text of Helena's book on publishing is borrowed *From Manuscript to Bookstall: The Cost of Printing and Binding Books, with the Various Methods of Publishing Them Explained and Discussed*, a volume published in 1894 by Arthur Dudley Southam, now in the public domain.

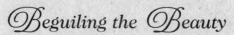

Cambridge, Massachusetts
1896

*T*he ichthyosaur skeleton at Harvard's Museum of Comparative Zoology was incomplete. But the fish lizard was one of the first to be found on American soil, in the state of Wyoming, and the American university was understandably eager to put it on exhibit.

Venetia Fitzhugh Townsend Easterbrook stepped closer to look at its tiny teeth, resembling the blade of a serrated bread knife, which indicated a diet of soft-bodied marine organisms. Squid, perhaps, which had been abundant in the Triassic seas. She examined the minuscule bones of its flappers, fitted together like rows of kernels on the cob. She counted its many rib bones, long and thin like the teeth of a curved comb.

Now that this semblance of scientific scrutiny had been performed, she allowed herself to step back and take in the creature's length, twelve feet from end to end, even with much of its tail missing. She would not lie. It was always the size of these prehistoric beasts that most enthralled her.

"I told you she'd be here," said a familiar voice that belonged to Venetia's younger sister, Helena.

"And right you are," said Millie, the wife of their brother, Fitz.

Venetia turned around. Helena stood five feet eleven inches in her stockings. As if that weren't attention-grabbing enough, she also had red hair, the most magnificent head of it since Good Queen Bess, and malachite green eyes. Millie, at five feet three inches, with brown hair and brown eyes, disappeared easily into a crowd—though that was a mistake on the part of the crowd, as Millie was delicately pretty and much more interesting than she let on.

Venetia smiled. "Did you find interviewing the parents fruitful, my dears?"

"Somewhat," answered Helena.

The upcoming graduating class of Radcliffe, a women's college affiliated with Harvard University, would be the first to have the Harvard president's signature on their diplomas—a privilege roundly denied their English counterparts at Lady Margaret Hall and Girton. Helena was on hand to write about the young ladies of this historic batch for the *Queen* magazine. Venetia and Millie had come along as her chaperones.

On the surface, Helena, an accomplished young woman who had studied at Lady Margaret Hall and currently owned a small but thriving publishing firm, seemed the perfect author for such an article. In reality, she had vehemently resisted the assignment.

But her family had evidence that Helena, an unmarried woman, was conducting a potentially ruinous affair. This presented quite a quandary. Helena, at twenty-seven, had not only come of age long ago, but had also come into her inheritance—in other words, too old and too financially independent to be coerced into more decorous conduct.

Venetia, Fitz, and Millie had agonized over what to do to protect this beloved sister. In the end, they'd decided to remove Helena from the source of temptation without ever mentioning their reasons, in the hope that she'd come to her senses when she'd had some time to reflect upon her choices.

Venetia had all but bribed the editor of the *Queen* to offer the American assignment to Helena, then proceeded to wear down Helena's opposition to leaving England. They'd arrived in the Commonwealth of Massachusetts at the beginning of the spring term. Since then, Venetia and Millie had kept Helena busy with round after round of interviews, class visits, and curriculum studies.

But they wouldn't be able to keep Helena on this side of the Atlantic for much longer. Instead of forgetting, absence seemed to have made Helena's heart yearn ever more strenuously for the one she'd left behind.

As expected, Helena began to mount another protest. "Millie tells me you've even more interviews arranged. *Surely* I've collected more than enough material for an article. Any more and I'll be looking at a whole book on the subject."

Venetia and Millie exchanged a glance.

"It may not be a bad idea to have enough material for a monograph. You can be your own publisher," said Millie, in that quiet, gentle way of hers.

"True, but as outstanding as I find the ladies of Radcliffe College, I do not intend to devote much more of my life to them," answered Helena, an edge to her voice.

Twenty-seven was a difficult age for an unmarried woman. Proposals became scarce, the London Season less a thrill than one long drudgery. Spinsterhood breathed down her neck, yet in spite of it, she must still be accompanied everywhere by either a servant or a chaperone.

Was that why Helena, whom Venetia had thought the most clear-eyed of them all, had rebelled and decided she no longer wished to be sensible? Venetia had yet to ask that question. None of them had. What they all wanted was to pretend that this misstep on Helena's part never happened. To acknowledge it was to acknowledge that Helena was careening toward ruin—and none of them could put a brake to the runaway carriage that was her affair.

Venetia linked arms with Helena. It was better for her to be kept away from England for as long as possible, but they must finesse the point, rather than force it.

"If you are sure you have enough material, then I'll write the rest of the parents we have contacted for interviews and tell them that their participation will no longer be required," she said, as they pushed open the doors of the museum.

A cold gust greeted them. Helena pulled her cloak tighter, looking at once relieved and suspicious. "I'm sure I have enough material."

"Then I will write those letters as soon as we've had our tea. To tell you the truth, I've been feeling a little restless myself. Now that you are finished with your work, we can take the opportunity to do some sightseeing."

"In this weather?" Helena said incredulously.

Spring in New England was gray and harsh. The wind blew like needles against Venetia's cheeks. The redbrick buildings all about them looked as dour and severe as the university's Puritan founders. "Surely you are not going to let a little chill dissuade you. We won't be coming back to America anytime soon. We should see as much of the continent as we can before we leave."

"But my firm—I can't keep neglecting it."

"You are not. You've kept fully abreast of all the developments." Venetia had seen how many letters Helena received from her publishing firm. "In any case, we are not keeping you away indefinitely. You know we must return you to London for the Season."

A huge blast of cold air almost made away with her hat. A man putting up handbills on the sidewalk had trouble holding on to his stack. One escaped his grasp and flew toward Venetia. She barely caught it before it pasted onto her face.

"But—" Helena began again.

"Oh come, Helena," said Venetia, her tone firm. "Are we to think you do not enjoy our company?"

Helena hesitated. Nothing had been said in the open, and perhaps nothing ever would be, but she had to suspect the reason for their precipitous departure from England. And she had to feel at least a little guilty for roundly abusing the trust her family had accorded her.

"Oh all right," she grumbled.

Millie, on Venetia's other side, mouthed, *Well done*. "And what does the handbill say?"

Venetia had entirely forgotten the piece of paper she'd caught. She tried to open it to its full dimensions but the wind kept flapping it back and forth—then ripped it from

287

her hand altogether, leaving only a corner that said *American Society of Nat.*

"Is this the same one?" Millie pointed at a lamppost they'd just passed.

The handbill, glued to the lamppost, read,

American Society of Naturalists and Boston Society
of Natural History jointly present

Lamarck and Darwin: Who was right?

His Grace the Duke of Lexington
Thursday, March 26, 3 PM
Sanders Theatre, Harvard University
Open to the Public

"My goodness, it's Lexington." Venetia gripped Millie's arm. "He's going to speak here next Thursday."

English peerage had suffered from a collective decline in prosperity, brought on by plunging agricultural income. Everywhere one turned, another lordship was brought to his knees by leaking roofs and blocked flues. Venetia's brother, Fitz, for instance, had had to marry for money at nineteen when he had unexpectedly inherited a crumbling earldom.

The Duke of Lexington, however, had no such troubles. He benefitted handsomely from owning nearly half of the best tracts in London, given to the family by the crown when much of the land had been mere grazing grounds.

He was rarely seen in Society—the joke often went that if a young lady wanted a chance at his hand, she had to have a map in one hand and a shovel in the other. He could afford to be elusive: He had no need to jostle before the heiresses du jour, hoping his lordliness would harpoon him a whale of a fortune. Instead, he traveled to remote places, excavated fossil sites, and published articles in scientific journals.

Which was too bad. In fact, when Venetia and Millie commiserated between themselves over yet another failed Season for Helena, they invariably dragged Lexington into the conversation.

She said Belfort wasn't serious enough.

I'll bet Lexington is made of solemnity and high-mindedness.

She thought Linwood smirked too much.

A quid says Lexington never experienced a lecherous thought in his life.

Widmore is too much of a fuddy-duddy. Helena is convinced he'd complain about her endeavors.

Lexington is modern and eccentric—a man who digs fossils wouldn't object to a woman who publishes books.

They were not quite serious. Lexington in reality was probably arrogant and awkward, as reclusive eccentrics often were. But as long as he remained beyond introduction, they could look to him as a faint beam of hope in their increasingly demoralized endeavor.

That it had been so difficult to find Helena a husband mystified everyone. Helena was lovely, intelligent, and personable. She'd never struck Venetia as unreasonable or particularly hard to please. And yet since her first Season, she'd dismissed perfectly likable, eligible gentlemen out of hand as if they were a passel of murdering outlaws who also defecated on the lawn.

"You've always wanted to meet Lexington, haven't you, Venetia?" asked Millie.

Interesting how Millie, with her quiet, trustworthy demeanor, made the most convincing liar of them all. Venetia took her cue. "He likes fossils. That's quite enough to endear a man to me."

They were cutting across the grounds of the law school. The bare trees shivered in the wind. The lawns were invisible beneath the previous day's blanket of snow. The main lecture hall, rotund and Romanesque, had probably been a revolt against the rest of the university's severely rectangular architectural uniformity.

A group of students coming toward them slowed to a halt, gaping at Venetia. She nodded absently in their direction.

"So you plan to attend the lecture?" asked Helena, looking over the flyer. "It's more than a week away."

"True, but he has been impossible to meet at home. Do you know, I hear he has his own private natural history museum at Algernon House? I should be like a cat in cream, were I the mistress of that manor."

Helena frowned slightly. "I've never heard you mention a particular interest in him."

Because she had none. But what kind of a sister would she be if she didn't make sure that the most eligible—and possibly the most suitable—bachelor in all of England was introduced to Helena? "Well, he *is* a good prospect. It would be a shame to not meet him when I can. And while we wait for him, we can begin our sightseeing. There are some lovely islands off Cape Cod, I hear. Connecticut is said to be very pretty, and Montreal is just a quick rail journey away."

"How exciting," seconded Millie.

"A little rest and relaxation before the Season begins in earnest," said Venetia.

Helena pressed li^{ng the Beauty}

be worth the trouble." ...ether. "The duke had better

"A man rich in both poun... ...g and fossils?" Venetia

pretended to fan herself. "He sh...

You'll see." ...orth every trouble.

O have a letter from Fitz," said Millie.

Helena was in the bath, and Venetia and Mi...e
were alone in the parlor of the cottage they'd leased for
their time at Radcliffe College.

Venetia moved closer to Millie and lowered her voice.
"What does he say?"

In January Helena had gone to Huntington, Lord Wrenworth's country seat, chaperoned by her friend Mrs. Denbigh. Fitz's best friend, Viscount Hastings, had also been
in attendance. Hastings left the house party early and
called on Fitz and Millie at their seat, where Venetia also
happened to be visiting. He told them that while at Huntington, for three consecutive nights he'd seen Helena
walking back to her room at four o'clock in the morning.

Venetia had immediately set out for Huntington, show-
ing up brimming with smiling apologies for missing her
sister too much. There were still rooms at Huntington, but
she'd insisted on sharing one with Helena and made sure
never to let Helena out of her sight.

Then they'd squirreled Helena out of the country as
quickly as they could, and left Fitz to ascertain the identity
of Helena's partner in sin.

"Including Huntington, she'd attended four house parties since the end of the Season—five, if you count the one
at Henley Park that Fitz and I hosted. Hastings was at four

...our suspect. Lady Avery
of them—but he is obvic...four of them, including the
and Lady Somersby...
one at Huntington...read. "I can't believe she'd carry on
Venetia shoo...under the same roof."
with those g...down the list. "The Rowleys were at three
Millie...es. So were the Jack Dormers."
of the F... Mr. Rowley was fifty-five. And the Jack Dormers
...re newlyweds devoted to each other. Venetia drew a
deep breath. "What about the Andrew Martins?"

A number of years ago, Helena had developed a
tendresse for Mr. Martin. All evidence pointed to her sentiments being fervently reciprocated. But in time Mr. Martin had proposed to and married a young lady who had
been intended for him since birth.

Millie smoothed the folds of Fitz's letter, her eyes worried. "Come to think of it, I have not seen the Andrew
Martins together in a while. Mr. Martin came by himself
to three parties. And at each house, he requested an out-
of-the-way room, citing his need for peace and quiet in
order to work on his next book."

All the more convenient for conducting an illicit affair.
"Does Fitz suspect anyone else?" Venetia asked without
much hope.

"Not among those at Huntington."

If Helena's lover was indeed Mr. Martin, this would not
end well. Were they to be discovered, the Fitzhugh family
wouldn't even be able to pressure him to do the honorable
thing by Helena—for Mr. Martin remained very much
married, his wife as robust as a vintage claret.

Venetia rubbed her temples. "What does Fitz think we
should do?"

"Fitz is going to exercise restraint—for now. He is worried that he might do Helena more harm than good by confronting Mr. Martin. What if Mr. Martin is not the one? Then word might leak that Helena was out and about when she ought not to be."

A woman's reputation was as fragile as a dragonfly's wings. "Thank goodness Fitz is levelheaded."

"Yes, he is very good in a crisis," said Millie, slipping the letter into her pocket. "Do you think it will help to introduce the duke to Helena?"

"No, but we still must try."

"Let us hope the duke does not fall for the wrong sister," said Millie with a small smile.

"Pah," said Venetia. "I am nearly middle-aged and almost certainly older than he is."

"I'm sure His Grace will be more than willing to overlook a very minor age difference."

"I've had more than my share of husbands and plan to be happily unmarried for the rest of my—"

Footsteps. Helena's.

"Of course I shan't bestow my hand freely," Venetia said, raising her voice. "But if the duke woos me with a monster of a fossil, who knows how I might reward him."

*H*elena listened carefully. Venetia was in her bath. Millie had gone to change out of her walking gown. She should be safe enough.

She pulled aside the curtain and opened the window of the parlor. The boy she'd employed to take her letters to Andrew directly to the post office was there, waiting. The boy had his hand extended. She set a letter and two shining copper pennies in his palm and quickly closed the window again.

Now on to the letters that had arrived for her in the afternoon. She looked for any that had come in Fitzhugh & Company's own envelopes. Before she'd left England, she'd given a supply of those to Andrew with the instruction to have her American address typed on the front once he had it. Then he was to draw a small asterisk under the postage stamp, so that she might know it was from him and not her secretary.

Except on this particular letter, he did not put an asterisk, but a tiny heart beneath the queen's likeness. She shook her head fondly. Oh, her sweet Andrew.

My Dearest,

What joy! What bliss! When I called at the poste res-tante office in St. Martin's le Grand this morning, there were not one, not two, but three letters from you. My pleasure is all the greater for the disappointment of the past two days, when my trips into London bore no fruits at the post office.

And as for your question, the work on volume three of A History of East Anglia *comes along slowly. King Æthelberht is about to be killed and Offa of Mercia soon to subjugate the kingdom. For some reason I rather dread this part of the history, but I believe my pace should pick up again when I reach the rebellion thirty years later that would restore independence to the Kingdom of the East Angles.*

I'd like to write more. But I must be on my way home—I am due to call on my mother at Lawton Pri-

ory and you know how much she deplores unpunctuality, especially mine.

So I will end with a fervent wish for your early return.

Your servant

Helena shook her head. She'd instructed Andrew never to sign his name on his letters. That precaution became moot when he referred to both his book and his mother's house by name. But this was not his fault. If he were capable of subterfuge, he wouldn't be the man she loved.

She was tucking the letter into the inside pocket of her jacket when Venetia returned to the room, smiling. "What do you say we make a foray to Boston tomorrow, my love, and see what their milliners have to offer? Those hats you've brought are perfectly serviceable for speaking to professors and lady students. But we must do better for meeting dukes."

"He will have eyes only for you."

"Balderdash," said Venetia firmly. "You are one of the loveliest women I know. Besides, if he has any sense, he will know that the best way to judge a woman is to observe how she treats other women. And when he sees you with your plain hat from two Seasons ago, he will immediately conclude that I am a selfish cow who ornaments myself like a Christmas tree and leaves you dressed in rags."

If Venetia wanted Helena to believe that she was interested in the duke, then she shouldn't have spent the four years since she became a widow for the second time cordially turning down every proposal that had come her way. In fact, Helena was convinced Venetia would swim the English Channel before she took another husband.

But Helena would play along, as she'd played along since Venetia unexpectedly turned up at Huntington. "All right, then, but only for you, and only because you are getting on in years and soon will only have gentlemen callers when they mistake your door for their grandmother's."

Venetia laughed, spectacularly beautiful. "Piffle. Twenty-nine isn't that old—yet. But it's true I might not have another chance of becoming a duchess if this one goes by. So you'd better have a proper hat."

"I will allow you to select one for me that looks like a carnival."

Venetia placed her arm around Helena. "Wouldn't it be marvelous if you met the perfect man this Season and accepted his proposal? Then we could have a double wedding."

I've already met *man. I won't marry anyone else.*

Helena smiled. "Yes, wouldn't it?"